I0710353

# Taming the Night

## The Nightshade Series Book 2

### By J. F. Posthumus

Three Ravens Publishing
Chickamauga, GA USA

Taming The Night The Nightshade Series Book 2 By J. F. Posthumus
Published by Three Ravens Publishing
threeravenspublishing@gmail.com
P O Box 851, Chickamauga, Ga 30707
https://www.threeravenspublishing.com
Copyright © 2023 by J. F. Posthumus

All rights reserved. No part of this publication may be reproduced, distributed, or transmitted in any form or by any means, including photocopying, recording, or other electronic or mechanical methods, without the prior written permission of the publisher, except in the case of brief quotations embodied in critical reviews and certain other noncommercial uses permitted by copyright law.

For permission requests, contact the publisher listed above, addressed "Attention: Permissions".

Publishers Note: This is a work of fiction. Names, characters, places, and incidents are a product of the author's imagination. Locales and public names are sometimes used for atmospheric purposes. Any resemblance to actual people, living or dead, or to businesses, companies, events, institutions, or locales is completely coincidental.

Credits:
Taming The Night The Nightshade Series Book 2 was written by J. F. Posthumus
Cover art by J. F. Posthumus
TAMING THE NIGHT THE NIGHTSHADE SERIES BOOK 2
by: J F. POSTHUMUS /Three Ravens Publishing – 1st edition, 2023

Ebook ISBN: 978-1-962791-32-8
Trade Paperback ISBN: 978-1-962791-33-5
Audiobook ISBN: 978-1-962791-34-2

Table of Contents

# Chapter One

Crime was increasing in the city once more. The peace between the two largest Families held, but that seemed to have inflamed the smaller ones, the gangs, and the independents. The wide-spread rise in drug-related crimes, assaults, and theft could not be pinned to one faction. It was unlikely answers would be forthcoming in the near future.

The Sandman knew many of the career criminals and rising leaders, as well as most of their underlings. It was getting more difficult to keep track as dealers, pushers, hitters and the like were being put down; for each one gone, two new recruits would be on the streets in days. Someone, or perhaps several someones, looked to be expanding their territory. No one had pushed hard enough to truly gain the attention and wrath of either the Vaschetti or the Lascari syndicates, but that situation remained in flux. By the time they did, who knew what damage would have been caused to the city and its citizens.

While all of those things mattered to the Sandman, he had less time to ponder them. He had been going out nightly, often staying out until just before dawn. He patrolled, working against the new faces and old adversaries. He had worked without Nightshade and managed well. But the hotter things became, the more he needed someone at his back and on his side.

Selia, fully attired in her Nightshade persona, reflected on those things as she cleared another roof. She wore her dark brown hair pinned up beneath a shoulder-length wavy blonde wig with green tips. A black V-neck Kevlar vest and pants worn over a thin black blouse, and water-proof boots. Her hands were protected by neoprene gloves, and she even wore a fully-stocked utility belt. The black trench she wore had sheathes built into it for her beloved two-body sharp Kodachi blades and hid her shoulder holsters that held twin M&P .45s. A scarf wrapped snugly around her lower face and neck concealed any identifying features. Her normally brown eyes were a startling green, the same color as the wig's tips, thanks to cosmetic contacts.

The spell that drew her to her mate was steady, and she was eager to join her beloved in battle. He did not know she was joining him. Selia had entered the lair with her own pass card, checked the video records and journal entries, then suited up. Once those tasks had been done, she cast the spell that would lead her to the Sandman.

He was now below her, in another alleyway. It seemed the two of them spent more time in alleyways than any other place when they went out as Nightshade and the Sandman. She hoped they could raid another warehouse, darken out a regular street... or even bust into a party sometime.

Instead, here she was, looking at a pair of buildings that were nearly identical. Amongst a city full of buildings that had the view she now witnessed, or nearly identical to it. Even most of the rooftops in this section of the city were almost uniform, like block buildings in a video game.

*A change of scenery would be nice*, she reflected. Selia did not look at the scene below. She mounted the fire escape and began her descent.

Tonight it was the smallest Family, the Scarlatiis, fighting over territory that usually belonged to the second-largest gang in New Campania, the Dreddz. Named after a fictional judge more than the hairstyle, the Dreddz claimed they owned their streets, and everyone had to obey their style of justice. They carried large caliber weapons and preferred clothing consisting mostly of black, deep reds, and stark blues.

They would have had a distinct advantage over most rivals, were it not for the fact that they, as many before them, believed that larger calibers made up for indiscriminate destruction and poor marksmanship. It was even possible they thought their strict law of killing no women or children made them the lesser of evils.

For this evening, at least, it seemed the Sandman agreed with that theory. He danced among the members of the Scarlatti clan. He struck them down with the baton in his right hand. Crippling them with shots from the Kimber Raptor .45 handgun in his left.

He made no aggressive actions toward the Dreddz at the other end of the alleyway. They were firing with little regard for anything towards the end where the Scarlatti and the Sandman fought.

Nightshade drew both of her .45 caliber semi-automatics. From two stories up she decided to teach the Dreddz a thing or two about proper shot placement.

Ten rounds later, nine Dreddz were dead. The remaining one would never shoot right-handed again. It would be months of physical therapy and surgery before walking unassisted would be possible. With ten more rounds left between the two guns, Nightshade put off reloading in favor of checking in on the Sandman. She pivoted on the tiny steel mesh landing of the fire escape and surveyed the other end of the alleyway.

A smile formed beneath her scarf as she watched him.

The black balaclava he wore beneath his ever-present Australian Fedora hid every feature possible. Even his eyes were hidden by a pair of infra-red sunglasses that he rarely removed. Like her, he favored a black trench coat, neoprene gloves, and a suit of Kevlar. Even his boots, waterproof and as black as pitch, were more protective than the average pair bought at a local store. Unlike her, however, his utility belt was filled with more non-lethal goodies.

Despite the few months they'd been fighting together, the Sandman still favored disarming and disabling adversaries over killing. This time it was costing him. Scarlatti members that the Sandman had shot in the chest, hip, or legs were getting up and attacking again.

Perhaps, Nightshade mused, there were some that had studied the actual technique of the Sandman's attacks and were wearing Kevlar to avoid being taken down by his usual methods. The ones that had been struck in the head or had bones broken, were not getting up.

There were nine people against the Sandman at that moment. Five of them had been previously lying on the ground in the alleyway. The Sandman attacked more viciously, likely reasoning out the same conclusion Nightshade had reached.

The metal of the Raptor .45's barrel caught the light of the overhead lamp and gleamed just before smashing into one man's cheekbone. The man standing just behind, who had a bullet hole in the chest of his shirt, had a moment to see the gun's barrel being brought back from the now-unconscious person in front of him. Then the gun roared, and a new hole formed just above his Adam's apple.

Turning as the second man fell to the ground, the Sandman brought up his baton in a defensive position. The man to his right could not stop his swinging fist. Something he no doubt regretted, since it sounded like three of four knuckles in his oversized fist broke against the steel of the baton.

Ignoring the screeching howl of the third man, the Sandman dropped and spun on one heel. His left arm extended, he fired twice at goons four and five. Both men convulsed at the waist, threw up, and fell to the ground, cradling their groins.

Nightshade felt a strong and intense desire for her man. She always loved watching him move. Only one kind of movement turned her buttons to "on" more than seeing him move like a warrior. She wanted to get to that, now, and those remaining goons were in the way of it. She fired four more rounds, dropping the remaining henchmen where they stood, poised to attack the Sandman. Holstering her guns, Nightshade leaped off the landing and landed in front of the Sandman.

His greeting was not what she expected. He immediately raised the .45 in his left hand towards her. When she knew he had recognized her but not lowered his weapon, she realized two things at once.

She drew her right-hand gun, pointing it towards him.

Both guns went off.

The sound of thudding bodies was barely audible over the fading report of the firearms. Even with the protective ear-wear that they both wore to protect their hearing from gunfire and explosions, Nightshade barely heard the man with the broken hand fall lifelessly to the street, or the skull of the surviving Dreddz member strike the pavement. She looked behind her, noticing that the Sandman was looking over his shoulder as well.

The man Nightshade had shot, the one with the broken hand, was face down. That concealed, at least partially, the unnatural reshaping of his head caused by her .45 bullet entering the back of his skull and bouncing against the front. As she looked to the one gang member that she had allowed to live, she took note of the monstrous .50 AE caliber semiautomatic handgun now held limply in his left hand, and the entry of the Sandman's bullet, which had passed through the man's left eye before carving into the brain.

She and the Sandman looked back at each other.

"Thanks," the duo said at the same time.

The Sandman stepped past her and went to the fallen Dreddz. After a few moments, he looked up at her.

"All head-shots," he observed. "Are you practicing for the zombie apocalypse?"

She laughed. "Love you, too. Come on, let's get to it."

As they listened for the police, both of them searched the bodies for clues and cash.

They found extra ammo, cell phones, other weapons, drugs, hastily written notes, wallets filled with ID's and all manner of plastic cards, and a great deal of money. The money, notes, and a few cell phones were taken, and the rest was left for the police. As the sound of sirens came within a block of the alleyway, Nightshade covered the Sandman and her own body with a spell that rendered them invisible to others. They made their way to the nearest rooftop.

Two blocks away, the duo stopped and took inventory of what had been confiscated. The Sandman was downloading the phone calls, texts, and contact information from the cells onto a portable storage device. Later, he would go over the data to see what useful information could be found. She sorted the notes and put them into a plastic bag. Since her task ended faster, Nightshade counted the money.

"Five thousand. Various denominations, non-sequential, no dye packs or counterfeit bills," she reported.

The Sandman nodded. He put the bag into his utility belt and programmed the cell phones to their original factory settings.

"I'm thinking a donation to the women's rape recovery center," he said.

"The one that's a block and a half down from the lair?" she asked. "The cash and the cell phones?" He nodded again. She smiled under her scarf and nodded back. "Sounds good to me."

The next morning, Selia snuggled up next to the warmth of Wil, giving a contented sigh as she felt him pull her closer. Nuzzling against his chest, she heard the steady beat of his heart as he kissed the top of her head.

"Rise and shine, beautiful," he said.

She shook her head slightly before snuggling even closer. A rumble of laughter was her reply before he slid away from her.

"Don't wanna," she mumbled, rolling over and pulling the blankets tighter against her chest.

Wil chuckled. "If you don't get up and get dressed, Soren is going to either call or send someone for you."

That got Selia's attention. Her eyes popped open, and she rolled over and sat up. She took a few minutes to enjoy the sight of her lover standing next to the bed in the nude. His dark brown hair was trimmed short, and he had a physique that made her swoon. The man had a fit, lean body that was all muscle. His brown eyes twinkled with mischief and desire as they met her gaze. His lips pulled up into a slow smile.

"If you keep looking at me like that, you're going to miss your ship," he teased.

"Oh, crap! I forgot about that!" Rolling out of bed, Selia glanced at the clock on her nightstand and groaned. "Papa is going to *kill* me!"

Wil followed her gaze to the clock and grinned. "It's only nine-thirty, Selia. You still have five minutes to get dressed."

Hopping out of the bed, she swatted at his hip as she grabbed the first thing she came to, which also happened to be what she wore to Wil's place the night before. Wiggling into the skin-tight leather pants before donning a lacy bra and sleeveless red blouse, she searched around the room for her shoes that had been kicked off somewhere. She ran a brush through her dark brown hair and smiled as she remembered how the clothes had been tossed everywhere as they'd stripped each other before falling onto the bed. She'd not yet been able to keep the upper hand in their lovemaking, but it was so much fun trying.

Finally finding her shoes, kicked to the other side of the room, she stepped into the black stiletto heels and turned to face Wil. The outfit emphasized her narrow waist, long lean legs, and Amazonian physique.

"Under five minutes," she said with a grin. "Now, we just have to get everything into the car."

Forty minutes later, Selia and Wil were trudging up the plank onto the deck of the ship that she and Soren were taking to Temeria. She still wasn't entirely certain about the trip, but Soren had assured her she wouldn't be killed on sight. The queen had agreed to allow her back onto the island due to Moreisa.

A necromancer from Temeria, Moreisa had helped a traitor to the Lascari syndicate attempt to sell out Temeria only a couple months earlier. Selia and Wil, as Nightshade and the Sandman, had thwarted her plot and killed Alfi, the Lascari syndicate's traitor.

Soren, Selia noticed, was watching them with his usual calm façade as they boarded the ship. Soren cut a dashing form in the tailored three-piece suit, brown eyes, and salt-and-pepper hair. He was fit and handsome, and someone she had admired from the first time she met him, when she was sixteen and fleeing from certain death.

She smiled sheepishly as she and Wil handed over her luggage to one of the crew. Soren raised a single brow at Wil's current disguise and his lips twitched as though he were trying not to laugh. Glancing at Wil, she gave an all-too-innocent smile.

Wil was wearing a shaggy red wig, giving him an almost beatnik appearance, a red beard, and contacts that made his eyes gray. He wore a knit pullover and jeans that gave him a very rugged appearance.

The man was a wiz when it came to disguises, she thought in admiration.

"Hi, Papa," Selia said before yawning.

"Good morning, dear. Cutting it close, aren't you?" Soren asked, not taking his eyes off Wil.

Selia shrugged, not bothering to hide her sheepish grin. "We, um, had a late night."

"No doubt, and how are you doing this morning… I forget your name again?" Soren replied, amused.

"Liam Noel," Wil replied with a thick British accent, as he lazily offered Soren his left hand. "A pleasure to meet you, mate."

"Ah, yes. I'm surprised you didn't bring your guitar this time," Soren said, barely shaking the offered limp hand.

"Nah, mate," Wil drawled. "I'm more into the lute these days. It's such a *pure* instrument, ya know."

Soren narrowed his eyes, looking between Wil and Selia. Sarcastically, he observed, "It's such a shame you won't be with us on the voyage."

Selia giggled quietly as Wil replied, "I know… right, man? We could have become one with the music of the ocean."

"Is he always going to use this disguise when in public," Soren whispered through gritted teeth.

"Nah, man, you'll get to meet the other five members of the band. Just be patient. I might even bring the brass section someday. They're lovely cats, ya know," Wil replied, laughter dancing in his eyes.

"Behave," Selia scolded Wil in a low voice, trying to not laugh at his antics. She wasn't sure if he was doing it to tease her or annoy Soren.

"Yeah, behave, daddy-o! Chill out, relax. You're going on a cruise," Wil invited.

Soren looked closely at Selia. "Are you sure you didn't miscast that 'mate' spell?"

Selia stared at Soren in dumbfounded embarrassment.

"I keep asking her that, man," Wil drawled out. "But she never answers. We just keep mating, and mating, and mating…"

"He just wants to see what it'll take to shoot him, doesn't he?" Soren asked pleasantly.

Nudging Wil sharply with her elbow, she shot him a glower. "You, *dear*, need to behave." She turned to Soren and shrugged. "I'm pretty sure I didn't, since it took me to him." She nodded towards Wil. "It's not like I've ever used it before, Papa."

Wil kissed her on the head. "Just a bit of fun, love." He sighed. "I thought you Italians were a fun-loving people."

"We are!" Soren exclaimed cheerily. "Do you know when we have the most fun?"

Wil tilted his head. "Weddings?"

Selia felt her face burn in embarrassment yet again. She leapt forward and grabbed Soren and turned him towards the cabins.

"Love you, dear! See you soon!" She hastily called over her shoulder.

"What? Dad isn't going to give me a hug? Wow!" Wil called to her. "Talk about a letdown."

"Forget the cabins, lead me to the bar." Soren groaned and Selia burst out laughing.

# Chapter Two

"We need to have a talk," Soren said.

Stretched out in a lounge chair, wearing a pair of micro-shorts and tank-top, Selia looked up from her favorite Earl Stanley Gardner novel to find Soren standing above her. They were a day's travel away from New Campania's shore, and she was surprised at Soren's flat tone.

"About what, Papa?" she asked, without thinking. She added hastily as she stood, "Sorry. I know I'm not… that is, I shouldn't question you. Where do you want to talk?"

"My cabin," Soren replied, before turning and walking away.

Selia dropped her book on the lounge and followed behind him. She wondered if the affection was mostly on her part and if it was, where that truly left her. Odd that she'd think of this now. Perhaps it was the fact she was on the same ship that had brought her to New Campania, and it was bringing back memories and feelings that had remained dormant for just over a decade.

Soren's cabin hadn't changed in the last eleven years. Or rather, the outer room hadn't changed. A desk sat tucked against a wall, with a chair in front of it and a large sofa curved around a television set. Cabinets, tables, and bookshelves lined the walls and reminded her more of a living room in a comfy little house than the cabin of a ship. A marble bar sat tucked into the far right corner, complete with barstools. Behind it was a cabinet lined with shelves of liquor secured safely inside Plexiglass doors. Not even the roughest seas would break anything inside that cabinet.

A pair of doors sat on each side of the television set. One led to the bedroom and bathroom, while the other led to a small closet. It had been that closet Soren had tucked her into all those years ago.

Selia turned to Soren, her face carefully schooled to keep any unwanted emotion from showing.

"Where do you see yourself in ten years?" Soren asked, walking to the bar.

Watching him carefully, Selia turned as he crossed the room. That definitely wasn't the question she expected.

"I hadn't really thought of it," she answered truthfully. "I certainly wouldn't object to being with, um… being a wife, maybe a mother, by that time."

She bit her cheek and flinched at the fact she'd nearly said Wil's name. The last thing she needed to do was tell Soren the real name of the guy she was dating.

"I expected that to be your answer," Soren countered. "Do you want to be in the same position you are now? Tied to the Family as you are? Do you want to be more involved with the illegal aspects of our operations?"

Selia shifted her weight from one foot to the other. "Should I marry my mate, I certainly don't want to be more involved with *those* aspects of the Family. As for the Family… the more distance I can put between Al and my mate, and subsequently me… the better I'll feel."

Soren thought about that before saying, "Al won't be around forever."

Narrowing her eyes, Selia studied Soren. "Planning on taking over the Family, Papa?"

"It's one possibility," he admitted. "Here's another: Whether it's me or one of the other underbosses, most of us want to decrease the amount of illegal business we do.

It's not necessary anymore. We can generate enough business to keep our financial status without the shadier aspects." He paused, poured some amber liquid from a decanter into a tumbler and smiled. "At least no shadier than all the other 'legitimate' empires."

"What does that have to do with me? Short of a coup, Al isn't going to die anytime soon, let alone retire." Selia countered. "The only skills I have are the ones I learned under you. It's not like I learned to be an actual secretary and I'm not selling my magical skills to anyone ever again."

"Let's say you do remain with your *'mate'*," Soren said with only mild sarcasm. "Are you planning to be barefoot and pregnant all the time? Or just stalk the night and live off of the royalties from your action figures?"

"How do you-? Shit." She glanced briefly away from him before meeting his gaze once more. "Unless you plan on firing me, I thought I'd remain under your employ until I figured something out. It's not as though I have a lot of choice in the matter, *sir*."

Soren winced. "Okay, maybe I came on a little heavy." He shrugged, tossing back half the glass's contents. "I worry about you, more than ever before. Sooner or later, one or more of your secrets is going to come out. If nothing else has changed, that's going to cause problems. More overwhelming than the three of us can handle."

The fact Soren was including Wil, made her feel better, but it still left a question hanging.

Of course, it could also be the doubts and fears of returning to Temeria overwhelming her.

"You worry about me?" she asked softly, veiling her eyes as she spoke. "I've obeyed you. I became a docile little rabbit who let almost everyone run over me. When the time came to take a stand, and stop running, you chided me and threatened the one person who believed in me and helped me remember who and what I am." Challenge rang in her voice and darkened her eyes as she finally looked at him. "Do you worry about me because I'm your adopted kin, or because you're afraid of losing the investment you took under your wing?"

"If you were an investment, I'd have traded you, sold you, or shot you for the danger you've put me in. If you were my son, I'd have shot you in the foot by now, to show you the consequences of rash and ill-conceived actions." His words roared through the cabin, against her ears. His fists clenched and his voice softened as he added, "But you're my daughter, so I worry about you."

Tears filled Selia's eyes, and she wiped them away quickly.

"I'm sorry," she whispered.

She dropped her head, feeling foolish, upset, and angry for allowing her self-doubts to shadow her judgment of him. She should have known he'd meant every word he'd spoken after she'd healed him. She had, after all, lived with him long enough to know his every tell.

He crossed the room and took her into his arms. "You've opened one hell of a potential mess for us, my dear, but no one close has been killed yet. Well, no one who didn't deserve it." Selia chuckled a little and leaned his embrace, hugging him. Soren stroked her hair as he continued. "But we can make it work, I think, if we plan ahead and are cautious."

Sniffling, Selia sighed. "I'm sorry, Papa. I'm sorry for the mess I've gotten all of us into. But I couldn't keep running.

Now it seems I'm the only one who can solve the problem of the necromancer."

Soren laughed. "If that were the only problem in this mess, I'd have more confidence."

"It's not my fault I fell for the adversary," she grumbled, a smile tugging at her lips.

"I'm not going to comment on that, aside from wondering why you haven't tried to bring him over to our side," Soren said with a smile.

She looked up, raising her brows. "Do you honestly think he'd turn to the dark side of the law? I'm pretty damned sure even I don't have the talents to do that, Papa."

He patted her on the shoulder and said, "I'm just kidding, sweetheart. If anything, he represents more of what I thought I would be at that age."

Selia thought about that and smiled. It wasn't too hard to imagine Soren kicking ass and taking names.

"So what do we do?" she finally asked, resting her head against his shoulder once more.

"We get through this," Soren replied. "And I have a plan."

"I'm glad one of us does," Selia teased.

"I'm betting you're man has some plans. Hopefully they will dovetail with mine, at least somewhat." Soren observed. He took a deep breath and explained. "I think if we can keep you on good terms with Temeria and Al for a while longer, my plan will come to fruition. It will also improve my influence. You must have noticed that I try to eliminate the need for illegal or violent business dealings. The Sandman certainly has."

"I thought that was why you wanted me to use my magic on certain people," Selia mused thoughtfully. "It prevented you from strong-arming them, or worse. I thought it was the least of the evils."

Soren nodded, approving. "I don't just do that with people who come into my office. Companies all over the world make money, expand, and overpower other businesses without the use of a gun or baseball bat. I try to do the same. Many of the Family members are coming around to the same kind of mindset or already had it. Al, unfortunately, is not one of those, but he's not immortal."

"Very true," she replied.

In fact, all of that was true. In the last couple months, she'd really started paying attention to the conversations around her and realized there was only a handful that still really enjoyed the strong-arm tactics of 'the good old days'.

Tilting her head back, she asked the one question that had plagued her ever since she had heard the rumor. In an almost childish voice, she asked, "Do you… do you have Temerian blood in you?"

"My great-grandfather came from Temeria," Soren reminisced. "He was sold to a childless widower from the Lascari family. The widower was preparing to start business in the New World. When they arrived, he called my great-grandfather his natural-born son and they lived the rest of their lives that way. Only my parents and I know that, and now, you."

"The past repeats itself, in some ways, doesn't it?" Selia asked softly.

"It usually does," Soren replied.

Not wanting to end the embrace or their bonding, she asked, "So, what can you tell me about this plan?"

"I intend to make you my replacement as the Master Trader of the Lascari family with Temeria." Soren announced. "If the mark of death is no longer upon you and I can gain enough support in the Family, there is no reason you cannot take my position. I've held it longer than I've been an underboss. Hell, longer than anyone else before me, in fact."

"I wouldn't object to taking over trade with my people," Selia replied softly. "I may not desire to live on the island, but that doesn't mean I don't want to ever visit there again." She tilted her head to the side. "How did you get the position? Gods, how did the families even *learn* of Temeria in the first place?"

"I inherited the position from my father. As for how we learned, that's a tale for another time," Soren replied. "Get your sea legs and relax. If you need anything, the staff will take care of you."

"Okay, Papa," Selia replied, as she gave him a hug and kissed his cheek. "I think I'll go take a nap before my beloved calls me." Pausing for a heartbeat, she added mischievously, "We got home by midnight, but I didn't fall asleep until a couple hours later. Good thing you don't 'wait up' for me anymore!"

Soren groaned. "I need another drink.

# Chapter Three

The tune 'Mr. Sandman' started playing and Selia reached towards her nightstand. The nightstand wasn't in its usual place, though. She sleepily blinked her eyes, before remembering she was on her father's ship heading to Temeria.

Rolling over to the other side of her bed, she grabbed the phone and swiped her finger across it before it went to voicemail.

"Hello?" she asked, yawning.

"Did I wake you?" Wil asked, his voice dropping into what was normally reserved for the Sandman.

"Mmmm," Selia murmured, snuggling under the Egyptian silk sheets. "I like being woken by you."

"Pity I'm not there to wake you in person," he countered.

"Indeed," she replied, smiling. "I'd like that the best."

Wil chuckled softly. "Enjoying the voyage?"

"It's been rather interesting. Papa and I had a rather long chat already about the mess I've gotten us into."

"Oh?" Wil asked, and she could imagine him leaning forward on the sofa, intrigued and wary.

"Yeah, we had our first father-daughter fight. Followed by some much-needed bonding time. And realizing I really need to start distancing myself from the Family before someone figures out my… our… secrets." Selia snuggled into the feather-down pillows, wishing she were curled up next to Wil, instead.

"Yeah, that's a good idea. Glad to hear the voyage is going well, too," Wil replied, sounding relaxed.

"Thanks. He's hoping to put me in charge of the trade with Temeria," she said, almost cautiously.

"Really?" Wil replied, sounding very interested. "Any ideas on how he plans on making that happen?"

"Well, he said he inherited the position from his father. I'm thinking that he hopes by removing my death mark and smoothing things over with my people? It will place me in a more favorable position as a trader."

"That makes perfect sense," Wil replied. "Does he have any intentions toward getting you out of the Family?"

"You're asking if he's wanting to move me into the more legit side of things," Selia clarified. "Obviously, he is, love. I'm a daughter to him, and that's not just speculation. He means it. I'm certain if it weren't for Al, and some of the others, there would be little to no illegal activity in the Lascari syndicate."

"Not that I've observed," Will agreed. "The majority of that syndicate are happier with mostly legitimate business. Less legal headaches, no reason for vigilantes to come busting heads."

She sighed heavily. "There's no possible way I can break completely away from the Family. For one, I love my father. For another, I've endeared myself to many members of the Lascari Family. They wouldn't be happy letting me walk away from them. To be honest, I don't think I could do that. It isn't as though I hate everyone and everything about the family I've been adopted into. Okay, well, I wouldn't mind walking away from Al and a couple others, but…"

She trailed off hoping Wil understood. She'd lived with Soren for ten years and had grown to love, even adore, some of those her care had been entrusted to. The only way she could completely 'break free' would be to move to the other side of the states, like California, but she wasn't going to do that. New Campania was her home, and she wasn't going to leave, nor did she think Wil would move away.

"Oh, I get it. I knew you were a complicated woman when I met you. Haven't changed so far," he said with humor in his voice. "It seems like Soren's interests and my interests aren't so far off."

"Oh, what are your interests?" Selia asked, intrigued.

"Reducing crime," Wil began. "Making the streets safer for everyone, and of course, making you happy."

Damn it, why did he have to stay home? She wondered, feeling giddy. "Did you have any suggestions on how to distance myself from the Family?"

There was a long pause before he said, almost shyly, "Just run away with me and send Soren emails letting him know you're happy and alive?"

Selia giggled. "So very tempting, my love. But knowing you, you'd still want to return to your home."

"Well, I never said we were running that far," he countered.

Laughing, she shook her head. "I love you."

Chuckling, he answered, "I love you, too, and I had more of a plan than that, but-"

"Now's not the time?" She interjected. "That seems to be a running theme today."

"Um, okay," Wil replied. "What else is on your mind, beautiful?"

"How are you? How are things in the city?"

"Busy and busier than usual," Wil said with a sigh. "It seems like something bigger is coming as well."

"The bitch with the nine lives?" Selia asked, laughter ebbing from her voice as she thought of the necromancer, Moreisa. "Or something else?"

"I doubt we're done with old dimpled-and-wrinkled." Wil observed. "But unless she's going around and getting all the second-class criminals hot and bothered, I don't think we can blame her for the increase in attacks and pushes on territories."

"Ships are a delightful method of transport, but the time it takes sucks," Selia grumbled. "Maybe I can ask Papa if he has any ideas on what could be going on."

"Couldn't hurt," was Wil's short reply.

"You don't approve or agree with involving him?"

"I'm just at a loss and he might not want to help his adversary. I think Soren has an eye on the bigger picture. But you never know where a person's pettiness might lie," Wil said.

"You remind him of what he could have been." She wasn't certain if she should have told Wil, but it wasn't like Wil would tell Soren on her. "He knows about us. If nothing else, he'd help because I'm involved. In his own fatherly way, he does approve of you and what we do." More or less, but she wasn't going to say *that* aloud.

"He said that?" Wil sounded incredulous.

"Yeah," Selia replied, amused. "I'm not going to tell lies against you or him, silly."

"I'm not silly. I'm complicated," he said, repeating a joke that had now become commonplace between them.

Laughing, Selia stretched and stifled another yawn. "You're silly, but I love you."

"Me silly!" he cheered in a child-like voice. "Pretty lady love me! Me win!"

"I would smack you if I were there," she teased, laughter in her voice.

"All the more reason to take advantage of you not being here," he replied.

"I have one question for you, my beloved, before I'm called for whatever mealtime it is," Selia said with a laugh.

"I await the melodious tones of your question."

"How in all the hells did Papa find out about my royalties for the action figures?" Selia questioned in curious disbelief.

Wil cleared his throat. "He probably saw the figures in a store and went fishing for answers from you."

"Damn. He really is my father, isn't he?" she asked with not a little amusement.

"Did he ask you about all the lawsuits the criminals' surviving family members keep trying to throw at us?" Wil asked.

"No, he didn't," she replied, thoughtfully. "If he knew about one, why wouldn't he learn about the other?"

"He's really being a dad and not trying to think about them," Wil agreed.

"Well, I won't mention them if he doesn't," she reassured Wil. "I already learned the hard way, just how much he does care for me. Really don't want to repeat that scene anytime soon." A knock on the door sounded and she groaned. "Guess that's my cue to bid you a fond farewell for now, my beloved. Have any messages for my dearest daddy?"

"I hope he's doing well. Sorry about the obnoxious behavior before, I had to stay in character and make it believable."

"I'll let him know," Selia said with a smile. "Might want to consider picking one and sticking with it." She added with a laugh, "Something that isn't going to annoy him, either."

He sighed. "Unfortunately, it can't be a lot like my real personality. Nor can it be someone people want to get too close to."

"Fine, just don't go with something that will annoy me or make me laugh at every other sentence."

"I'm open to suggestions," Wil invited.

"I'll think on that, lover," Selia said with a sigh. It was tempting to ask Papa for advice, but she wasn't certain how helpful he would be. "Call me again at the same time tomorrow?"

"Be safe. I love you," Wil said.

"I will be. Love you, too."

There was a pause then silence as he ended the call. Reluctantly, she got out of bed, and headed towards Soren's cabin for dinner. It was going to be a long, if not enjoyable, voyage.

# Chapter Four

One of the best benefits of being the daughter to a powerful, wealthy man was when you went on extended vacations, you had access not only to the best food and a luxurious cabin, but also didn't have to worry about phone charges. That meant she was able to talk to Wil anytime she wanted without worry about extravagant fees. Especially since her beloved adopted father approved of her suitor. They spoke at least twice a day and video-chatted on their phones during the voyage.

Standing on the deck, leaning against the railing, she watched as the beaches of Temeria came into view. Over ten years had passed since she'd seen her homeland and now, she was nervous about stepping foot on the island. Despite the assurance from her father she wouldn't be killed.

"I don't know about this," Selia said into the phone as the ship moved closer to the wooden docks.

"You'll be fine, sweetheart," Wil assured her, and the low murmur of his voice sent warm tingles down her spine. "Soren wouldn't let you go back just to have them kill you."

"Speaking of my father," Selia said with a sigh. "He's giving me that look again."

Wil laughed and it eased her nerves. Soren had become the epitome of a loving, doting, protective father since their little argument on board. Often under the same roof.

"I'll keep the phone close," Wil assured her. "Enjoy your homecoming while you can, though."

"Yes, dear," she replied, her voice demure, which elicited another laugh from Wil. "I'll bring you a souvenir."

"You do that," he replied before hanging up.

Selia slid her phone into a pocket and turned towards Soren. "You're sure about this, Papa?"

"The queen agreed to give you a reprieve. Albeit it's currently a temporary one, due to the necromancer back home," Soren assured her. His voice, as always, was confident, easing her tension and uncertainty. "Once we dock, there will be an escort awaiting us. They'll take us both to the queen, and as long as you don't break any laws while here, they'll allow you to remain the length of my visit."

"If you're sure," Selia replied, trying to curb the twisting of her stomach.

It had been one thing to run away and not look back. It was something else entirely to return to a land where your fellow people had wanted to see you dead. She tugged at her tunic, hoping she'd chosen wisely. The garment was light-weight, almost sheer, and emphasized her athletic figure. Thigh-length, she didn't bother wearing anything other than her usual lingerie and a pair of snug, thin leggings. A pair of thick-soled ankle boots with a wide heel, gave her good traction while still being comfortable.

She had been tempted to wear her old mage robes that still fit, but she knew better than to even attempt to appear as though she were a Temerian. Dressing as a foreigner, yet with just enough attention to her heritage, she hoped to give the appearance that she honored her land and people, yet knew her place in the society.

She glanced at Soren and smiled slightly. He had chosen a short-sleeved dress shirt and light-weight khakis. He didn't dress as a Clansman or in the typical island trader robes. He even wore a shoulder-holster with his favored semi-automatic tucked into it, despite the law against firearms being used on the island.

Everyone played power games, she supposed, and Soren had been doing them longer than she'd been alive. A memory flickered to life: Soren hadn't been wearing a gun when she had quite literally run to him nearly a dozen years ago.

Perhaps the weapon was for more than just show.

The ship pulled into the dock and Selia walked down the plank to the pier below. Mounted sentries waited for them alongside a horse-drawn carriage. Soren gave her a slight smile and together they walked to their armed escort. The sentries' clothing hadn't changed in the time Selia had been gone. They still carried spears and wore the hard leather bodices and shorts made from the larger lizards that lived on the opposite side of the island. Even their boots were made from the almost-armor-like dimiethra hide. Lances were nestled on the sides of their saddles and bows with filled quivers sat against their backs.

Every one of the sentries stared at Selia with schooled expressions, though she recognized intense interest in their eyes. Apparently, never before had any of their people returned to the island after leaving it. Or, maybe it was Soren's shining black weapon.

Selia didn't count on it being the latter.

The plush seats of the carriage sank beneath her and Soren. Once they were settled, the driver of the carriage called out to her horses, and they began the long ride to the castle. Or rather, what passed for a castle on Temeria. It didn't have turrets, a moat, or even sprawl out over acres upon acres of land. Instead, it was fashioned like the ancient Greek temples with pillars, curving windows, and arched doorways. The castle was nestled amongst the trees and plants. Several other large buildings were sprinkled around the center one, which the carriage now approached.

Brightly colored birds perched amongst the more drab colored ones. Lizards sunned themselves on rocks while monkeys called from the trees. Two large tigers lay comfortably in the sun near the foot of the stairs leading into the Grand Hall where the royal family held their Court. Sentries stood to each side, holding spears.

A servant, a young boy about twelve, appeared from seemingly nowhere and quickly opened the door to the carriage and bowed low. His eyes never moved away from the ground. Selia felt odd by the boy's passiveness after being away for so long. But this was how males were raised and treated. They were less than servants and barely a step above pets.

It no longer felt right or normal to Selia. Not after living in New Campania for so long. Still, she ignored it all and stepped down with Soren behind her. No, she decided, as yet another young boy opened the door to the Grand Hall, there was no possible way she could ever make a life for herself again here on the island.

# Chapter Five

Walking side-by-side, a sentry escorted Selia and Soren into the Throne Room. Another warrior followed behind them and Selia couldn't help the wry smile that pulled at her lips. At one time, she had walked these halls unhindered and unescorted. Probably would be today had she not made a decision that changed her life.

Was it for the worse? She no longer believed so. How could she when she had found a family and love?

The sentry stepped into the throne hall between a pair of royal guards, who crossed their lances in front of Selia and Soren. Selia took the opportunity to reacquaint herself with the room.

About the size of a high school football field, the roof towered above them. The walls were laden with shields and tapestries. Today, only the queen, her consort, the eldest princess, and Mistress Anore held court.

No courtiers or other traders filled the room. Nor was there the usual plethora of guards or servants offering beverages and trays of food. Selia kept her face neutral as she gazed at the etchings on the walls, depicting bountiful feasts and battles against opposing clans.

She turned her gaze away from the life-like art and to the queen. The beautiful woman, who appeared to be in her mid-fifties, was actually several centuries old. Her silvery hair was pulled back in braids away from her face and tied by a piece of leather, before falling down her back in gorgeous curls. A tiara sparkled in the light allowed in by the windows in the roof. Her hazel eyes were sharp, and her full lips held no smile.

She sat atop a cushioned marble throne. Beside and slightly behind the queen sat her consort on an equally elaborate, cushioned throne made from teak wood. To the right stood the princess, her raven-black hair tucked behind her ears. Held in place by a gold band.

The woman to the queen's left held Selia's attention the longest. Mistress Anore, slender and petite, reminded Selia of the gymnasts of Soren's world. Her petite stature was unusual, but she certainly wasn't a weak woman. Anore was the single most powerful mage in Clan Breisleyn. Today, she wore the robes of her status: deep burgundy silk trimmed in silver and gold. The symbol of the Head Mistress and top mage advisor, a cat's eye held at the corners by a bird's talons, was embroidered in gold above Anore's heart.

The sentry returned from talking to the queen and tapped the bottom of her spear against the floor. The guards lifted the lances, allowing Selia and Soren to move forward to the base of the queen's diadem.

"Welcome again to Temeria, and the Clan Breisleyn, Master Tradesman Soren Lascari," the queen said from the throne. Soren stepped forward and gave a short bow.

"Greetings, once again, Queen Zarasina," Soren replied. He didn't kneel or lower his gaze from the queen, a fact that wasn't missed by Selia. "It's always a pleasure to visit and enjoy your gracious hospitality. I extend my thanks, once again, for allowing the return of Selia."

"Yes," the princess said. Selia searched her memories and realized it wasn't the eldest, but the third born, Analise.

"Selia Laios. We were surprised you gave her safe passage even after you were told she was a wanted fugitive."

Soren gave the princess a contemplative gaze. His tone remained cool and businesslike. "Selia made a bargain, and I am not one who would turn away a child. She explained the situation and I decided to grant her a reprieve. Believing she would be more beneficial alive than dead." He paused before turning his gaze back to the queen. "It appears my instincts were proven true. Were it not for Selia, a traitor would have lived, and your island would no longer be a secret."

The queen glared at her daughter and Analise ducked her head. Zarasina settled back in her chair, obviously not pleased with the circumstances.

"Your choice was yours to make and since she was slated for death, the method didn't matter." There was a pause before the queen continued. "We granted her a reprieve to return and declare her intentions."

Selia stepped forward, knowing exactly what was required. "Your Majesty," she said, tendering a perfect bow. Rising, she kept her gaze even with the queen's as she spoke. "My intentions are solely to learn the information needed to defeat the necromancer, Moreisa, and be allowed use of the clan's library. I have no desire to see the destruction of my homeland, even though I have made a home for myself on other shores."

From the corner of her eyes, Selia could see Mistress Anore's lips curve into a smile as she gave Selia a slight nod. Princess Analise appeared a bit surprised, and the queen's glower only darkened.

"You aren't begging to return and make a life in your homeland?" Zarasina demanded. Behind her, the consort smirked and leaned back in his throne.

Selia gave a polite smile. "No, Majesty; I am not. I have a life with Soren, one I enjoy greatly. I can help Temeria from the city of New Campania far more than I could possibly help you here." She noticed Soren bit back a laugh as the queen's face burned with anger. Selia explained. "I am but one mage amongst many in this land, Your Majesty. In New Campania, I am a mage amongst mortals. It was those skills that allowed me to protect Temeria only a few months ago. As such, I am the only one capable of removing the threat that is Moreisa."

"That is, unfortunately, very true," Mistress Anore said, finally speaking up. "I fear none of the warriors or mages here could move about Master Tradesman Soren's city with the ease and confidence that you can, Selia." The queen glanced sharply at Anore but remained silent. Anore continued, her calm voice never wavering in tone. "However, you have been banished and were condemned to death prior to the banishment. If you desire to see our libraries and learn the answers you seek, you will have to accept a Challenge."

"That wasn't part of the agreement," Soren interrupted.

The queen finally smiled, and it was one filled with venom and malice. "It is the choice she is given, Master Tradesman. It isn't an offer we give lightly: She is, so far, the only one to receive such a reprieve and we do this solely because of… Moreisa."

Selia realized, as the queen spat the name out as though it were something far too nasty to keep in her mouth, that Zarasina, the entire royal family, and probably every advisor and powerful mage knew of the necromancer before recent events. It was that hatred that had allowed this so-called second-chance.

Selia didn't have to like it, but she'd take it.

"What is the Challenge?" Selia asked.

"You know of the Caves of Aeress," Anore said. Selia nodded and the elder mage continued. "The Challenge, should you accept it, is to go to the Caves of Aeress, collect a crystal, and return."

It sounded so simple. Go to some caves, harvest a crystal or two, and return to the village. Selia, however, knew it was far from simple. The caves were nestled at the foot of the Meseringue Mountains. That meant going through the jungle and then into the territory of the aberlin. Twice the size of a normal jungle cat, such as the tigers they'd passed to enter the castle, the aberlin crept through the mountainous region with the stealth of a leopard. The population was small, mostly because they were slow to breed, and their terrain was limited.

Anyone who managed to kill one typically skinned the animal to prove their accomplishment. Those survivors were considered the best warriors of a clan. Of course, more often than not, anyone who went after one didn't come back alive. Aberlin were vicious, silent killers.

"Selia, you can't possibly be thinking of accepting this foolish task," Soren hissed in Italian; a language most in the clans didn't understand. Only those who dealt with outsiders were taught the various languages used by traders. Which included the nobles and the mage within the room.

The guards tensed at the unknown words. Selia knew, even if it hadn't been for the growing tension in the room and her knowledge of the lands, Soren had broken tradition and rules to talk in relative privacy.

The royals and Anore watched in silence, understanding his words perfectly. The glower had returned to the queen's features, showing her obvious dislike of Soren breaking tradition.

In perfect Temerian, he added, "You've been gone for over a decade. The island has changed since you've been away."

"Do you have such little faith in your ward, Master Tradesman, that you would suggest she not attempt this Trial?" the queen asked, tapping her fingers against the arm of her throne. "Every mage and warrior must take a Rite of Passage before being declared adult, surely even you know this."

Selia turned away from the royals and Anore, giving Soren her undivided attention. She, too, broke tradition by giving Soren the position of an advisor. Not only did it reveal she didn't fear the royals or the guards, but also that she gave Soren the highly treasured position of advisor. A position no male would ever have been granted by another Temerian.

Soren glowered at the queen, who had a remarkably smug expression on her face. Selia knew what he was thinking by the way his fingers twitched: her father wanted to blow a hole through the smug bitch's head. However, Selia was equally certain it wouldn't do anything good towards trade negotiations or her current dilemma. Nor could she say that she didn't want to do the same.

"It's the only way I have to learn the answers I need. To finish what you started," Selia told Soren, hoping he understood what she meant by the latter statement. She turned back to the queen. "I accept this Challenge."

The princess had a sour expression, the queen remained smug, and Anore looked concerned. The consort, a brown-haired man with handsomely chiseled features, was nodding at Selia with open approval in his deep blue eyes.

It was odd, she thought, that he would approve, but then, perhaps he was enjoying the idea of the queen being proven wrong about something.

The queen rose suddenly and stormed off, followed by the princess and the queen's consort. Anore remained where she was until the other three departed, then approached them.

"Follow me," she instructed, before turning and striding out a door to Selia's left. With a shrug, she followed Anore with Soren at her side. In an antechamber, Anore turned to the pair. "You may speak here without fear of being overheard or spied upon. I cannot influence the Trial, but I can tell you this: the aberlin sleeps during the hottest part of the day and is susceptible to a poison made from black orchids. You should remember how to turn the orchid bloom into a sticky liquid. One capable of being brushed on a spear or arrow head." She paused as Selia nodded. "Take only what the land provides and go with the gods' protections."

Anore left the room, giving Selia and Soren much needed privacy. Selia turned to Soren. In Italian, she said, "I won't die, I promise. Don't mention this to the Sandman?" She paused before adding, "You can find me if anything should happen, right?"

Soren laughed. He replied in Italian, "I won't tell. That will be your job. And yes, I'll be able to find you." He pulled a charm from beneath his shirt and Selia laughed. He asked teasingly, "How do you think I always found you so easily all these years? Mistress Anore gave it to me before we left when I saved your skin. She thought I might need a way to keep up with my little warrior princess."

Selia shook her head, laughing softly and gave him a hug. She might have to leave in the morning to complete a deed that could very well lead to her death. But she was eternally thankful she had Soren in her life. At least Wil wasn't there. He'd probably follow along behind her, which wouldn't be very beneficial to her completing a task that was supposed to be done alone.

# Chapter Six

Selia set out the following morning after breakfast with Soren. He hadn't been thrilled with the turn of events, not that either of them had a real choice in the matter. She either survived the excursion and returned with a crystal or be banished all over again.

She didn't have a choice. She had to accept the Challenge and return victorious. Not that survival allowed much margin for error or second chances. But at that moment Selia realized how much easier things were back in the States, in what had become her city, her home.

Although, she admitted to herself, the simple beauty surrounding the village was unparalleled anywhere else she had been. As her footsteps took her away from the village, she drank in the beauty of the flora that she remembered from her earlier life.

She closed her eyes and strained for the familiar sounds of her past home to fully immerse her mind in those past times. Selia indulged herself for moment before continuing to the edge of the forest.

The forest itself hadn't changed. The sights and sounds brought back fond memories of Selia's childhood. She had hunted deer, rabbit, quail, squirrel, and just about everything edible in the forest. Looking up at the majestic trees, she smiled at the memory of climbing every type that covered the landscape. Taught what was edible, what was poison, and what could be used to heal the sick, Selia's youth had been a mixture of games and lessons.

There were no footpaths to follow, only game trails made by the wildlife. The farther she walked, the more she remembered. She felt as though she were a young teenager once again out hunting for meats, spice, or other needed resources.

Standing, she took a sip of her canteen and continued on. Old lessons returning with each step she took, her senses growing more in tune with the forest and the life it contained.

The mountains loomed in the distance as the sun was setting. Selia knew she'd be at the foot of those mountains by noon the next day. If she were lucky, she'd be able to sneak in, mine some crystals, and leave without coming across a single aberlin.

Considering the journey so far had been completely uneventful, she doubted her luck would hold out. Climbing one of the large oaks, Selia settled in the crook of a pair of branches for a long night. Unlike when she'd been a child and found it fun to sleep in trees, she knew she wouldn't fall into a deep slumber this time. She was more cautious and respectful of danger now than as a child.

The nightlife of Temeria was considerably different from the day. There were the usual nocturnal forest creatures and such, but then there were the more deadly animals indigenous only to Temeria.

Large canines with rhino-like hides and jutting teeth trotted by in packs, their barks shrill and loud. Furred lizards with lion-like manes the size of house cats jumped from tree to tree, looking for bugs and smaller mammals to munch.

In the distance an aberlin roared.

By the time the sun rose, Selia was awake and feeding a parrot part of the apple she was eating for breakfast. Cutting off the last slice, she dropped the core to the ground. Nature would take its normal course, returning it to compost or be scavenged by an animal. Climbing down, Selia shouldered her backpack and trudged on towards the caves. She hoped the ones she remembered hadn't been closed due to a rock slide or cave-in.

By noon, the sun was beating down on her and she was approaching the rocky walls of the mountains. Several caves, a good twenty to thirty feet above her, were black against the orange, tan, and off-white stones.

Following the rock wall along the bottom, she peered behind boulders and brush, looking for an entrance lower to the ground. Just when she was ready to tackle climbing the rock wall, she found a cave entrance behind some laurel and moss-covered boulders.

Smiling slyly, Selia pulled out the one accessory she'd snuck into her backpack. Maybe it was cheating a little, but she'd learned years ago, her people were anything but fair. Everyone had their own 'honor code'.

Sliding the infrared sunglasses on, her smile widened as everything changed to hues of green. Everything was going too easy, and she wouldn't put it past the queen or one of the princesses to set up an ambush in the caves.

This way, she had an added advantage of knowing if there was anything else living within the caverns. Rules be damned. She'd obeyed enough of them without questions and so far, they had only gotten her into trouble. Breaking them had ended up saving her life and the lives of those around her. Drawing a deep breath, she entered the dark cavern and followed the narrow dirt path into the recesses of the mountain.

Selia ignored the cobwebs and the skittering sounds of what were probably scorpions. She continued walking along the walled-in path until it opened into a large cavern some fifty yards under ground. Stalactites dropped from the ceiling as stalagmites rose to eventually meet them.

The cavern was cool. The air, though deep underground, was fresh and smelled slightly damp and musty. Selia looked up to find a large colony of bats clinging to the stalactites. Turning to the rest of the cavern, she didn't see anything else other than the formations and bats.

Shrugging, she searched her memory for details on where the crystals would be found, and decided her best bet would be to continue downward. Searching the ground for tracks, she found the path straight ahead had nothing going in or out and decided to try that way.

Twenty minutes and a dozen twisting, turning tunnels later, Selia stared in amazement. She'd found a room filled with crystals. Clusters stuck out from the walls, the ground, and even from the ceiling.

The crystals ranged from the length of a decent hunting knife or short dagger, to barely a few inches long. Not exactly certain what she'd do with the crystal once she returned, Selia set about searching for the perfect specimens to return with to the village, as well as New Campania.

Settling on a pair of unblemished sections about twelve inches long, she collected them as well as a dozen smaller crystals, either completely unblemished or with only a few imperfections. Wrapping them in supple leather and soft cloth, she tucked them into her backpack.

Selia took a little longer to return to the surface. Not because of losing her way, but because she was enjoying the caverns. The formations the calcium and dripping water had created over the decades, even centuries, were an incredible view.

She enjoyed the sights a little too much. Not focusing on her footing, Selia twisted her ankle on wet rock, barely able to keep herself upright when it happened. Cursing, she checked her ankle. Nothing was broken, but she'd be limping for a while.

Removing the sunglasses, she tucked them back into her backpack, Selia studied her surroundings before completely exiting the cavern entrance. It was quiet, but not in a foreboding, evil-was-ready-to-pounce way. It was the normal quiet of an afternoon far away from civilization.

There were no other Temerians in the vicinity, so she wasn't concerned about anyone discovering her ability to use magic. Healers were rare, especially those who were strong in magic. If the queen discovered her ability, she might change her mind and insist Selia remain as a healer. Something Selia had absolutely no desire to do.

There was no need to hobble, when the magic used would be small. Plus, it was better to not be hindered by an injury should she encounter something dangerous. May it be animal or human.

Taking a few moments to heal her ankle, Selia began the long trek back to the castle, the queen, and her father.

# Chapter Seven

The trek passed without incident. Unless one included the bugs that decided she was a tasty snack and a snake that also believed she would make a suitable meal.

A little more than two hours left in her trip, Selia heard a distinct coughing sound that sent chills down her spine. Instinctively, she started scanning the thick underbrush and trees in search of the predator that sent many grown warriors running in fear.

The aberlin could throw its voice, much like a mountain lion. It could be right above you, ready to drop down without a warning while sounding like it was yards or miles away. Even the direction could change, making a person wonder if she were being hunted by one or more aberlins.

Selia looked around and found a climbable tree. She hurried up the branches until she was twenty feet off the ground with a fair view of her surroundings. The spear remained at the base of the tree. It would do her little good in the tree. If she went to ground to fight, better she knew its location. She perched on a thick branch, searching for the aberlin.

Not locating the creature, unslung her bow and knocked an arrow. She scanned the area hoping the infrared lenses would give her an advantage. Then she unslung her bow and knocked an arrow. The cat was huge and should have a heat signature that would practically scream against the rest of the green foliage. It wasn't anywhere in front of her, nor to either side. She shifted carefully, trying to get a good view of the area behind her.

Nothing.

Which made Selia more than a little nervous. She wondered if perhaps the cat was too far away. Maybe she could put more distance between her and it. The closer she was to the village, the better.

Selia decided to wait the creature out.

. After over thirty minutes, nothing had crossed into her field of vision from any direction. The sun waned in the sky, dropping behind the mountains. If the beast was coming, she wished it would make an appearance.

The wind shifted and the smell of the aberlin was strong on the breeze.

Where could it be? Selia wondered.

A single leaf fell on her shoulder from a branch above her. That small leaf concerned her. It was not cold enough for leaves to turn, and the tree she was on was healthy. There was no reason for leaves to fall, unless...

Selia looked up.

The aberlin was only eight feet above her, perched lazily on another limb. The creature looked at her and almost seemed to smile. Selia reared back and loosed the arrow from the bow. It bounced off the limb holding the aberlin and struck the massive cat in the shoulder. Selia had been aiming for its eye. She wasn't happy with the shot's results. The aberlin hissed as it brought its body up. Selia wished she had brought her M&P handguns instead while she whipped another arrow out of her quiver.

The aberlin leapt. Selia pivoted to track it with the arrow and lost her balance.

As she fell, Selia twisted, trying to keep her bearings. Managing to catch a small limb with her bow, She interrupted her fall for a brief second. The bow and branch found their breaking points and snapped.

The delaydid work in one way: It delayed her fall enough that she landed on the aberlin instead of the ground. Selia bounced off the cat's back, and her backpack tore loose, landing a few feet away. Luckily, she'd landed near to her spear.

Grabbing for her spear, Selia scrambled to her feet.

The aberlin was not happy. It let out a low growling rumble. The arrows jutting from its body, blood oozed in small streams.

Selia cursed herself for not poisoning the tips of the arrows beforehand.

She stood stolidly, the tree's massive trunk at her back. The spear held firmly in both hands.

Her adversary paced before Selia, eyes sizing her up. Selia remained still. When the beast attacked, she was ready.

The aberlin swiped a massive claw at her. Selia angled the broad, razor-sharp tip so the animal's paws and forelimbs were cut before the strike came close to her body.

The cat hissed and spat at her, drawing its paws back from the injuries. Its face contorted in pain and rage. The aberlin lunged, attempting to bite her. Selia shifted her body, avoiding the cat's open maw. She thrust, succeeding in getting the spear past its toothy maw, then with a short sweep and stab of the spear, she penetrated the beasts furry flesh and severed the artery along the left side of its neck.

Blood sprayed from the wound and the cat jerked away. Selia dropped to the ground. The pain from the fall and exhaustion had caught up. The aberlin was all but chasing its tail, seeming to be trying to attack the blood jettisoning from its body. Selia got to one knee and held up the spear at ready, prepared for another attack. The cat whirled around, claws and teeth lashing at nothing and everything.

Its pelt and the ground beneath it were soaked through with blood. Selia had no idea how long it might take for the beast to bleed out. The cat had come too close for comfort before.

Again it charged forward. Selia clubbed its head with the blunt end of the spear, breaking away the lower half of the spear, which left her with just over three feet of shaft intact and the spear's bladed tip. The cat had tensed from the impact and only brushed against Selia. The glancing blow was enough to send her sprawling once more to the ground. She hit the ground and rolled, keeping a firm grip on the broken spear shaft.

The aberlin rolled and thrashed, fighting its death. Selia glanced around and groaned.

Her backpack, along with most of the medical supplies that had fallen out from the impact, was covered in the aberlin's blood.

She turned back to the aberlin. The arterial spray had slowed considerably but was still flowing. Selia waited and watched it bleed out. Even when it collapsed, she did not move for a long while. She watched the flow of blood until it stopped. When there was no doubt to be had, Selia clutched the spear in her right hand, and hobbled over to the aberlin's corpse.

# Chapter Eight

Selia finally understood without a doubt, how Wil and Soren had felt after she had healed them. Despite having an unusually high threshold for pain, she didn't want to feel anything against her skin. Not even air. She didn't want to move after the Master Healer had finished healing and patching her up. Soren had remained at her bedside and watched over her like a hawk.

No, she thought in amusement, more like the ferociousness of an angry mother aberlin whose cub had been threatened.

He had extended the stay on the island by a couple days, giving her time to heal and speak with both the queen and Mistress Anore. Citizenship had been granted to Selia once more. She had completed the quest without question and returned with proof she had fought and defeated possibly the most feared creature on the island.

The look on Soren's face when she returned, draped in the bloody hide of slain aberlin had been priceless. The queen had, albeit grudgingly, allowed Selia to be granted the title of 'master sorceress'. With the title came the gift of several thick and exceedingly heavy tomes.

The crystals were also hers to keep. She now had a gorgeous crystal dagger from one of the larger specimens and several charms from the smaller crystals. Selia had gifted the queen with one of the smaller perfect crystals as a sort of peace offering. The greedy bitch *she* was, the queen readily accepted it and welcomed Selia back into the Clan. Perhaps not with open arms, but at least with less obvious venom.

By the last day on the island, Selia still moved with the stiffness of a warrior recuperating from grievous injuries.

Once she boarded the ship, she'd have to continue doing calisthenics in order to keep her body from stiffening up. It was amazing the kind of workout she received while fighting crime in her city, but she had to admit she hadn't been getting near the amount of exercise during the voyage.

Standing on the docks talking with a childhood friend, Selia couldn't keep from smiling. Being able to talk with old friends again was heartwarming for her. But knowing she'd be able to return filled her with joy.

"I know you're enjoying all the sentiment of being here," Soren said, "but we need to finish boarding."

She gave her friend then hurried towards her father.

"It's been fun," Selia replied, walking over to him. "But I'm ready to go home. I miss my mate." For maybe the millionth time, Selia wished she could use Wil's name, but she understood his reluctance. "You've really got to have a talk with him, sometime soon. Not using his name is getting annoying."

"Well, any time he wants to retire his nightlife, I would be happy to know him, personally," Soren observed.

Scowling, she glared at her beloved father. "You men can be so damned stubborn and difficult. You know that, right?"

"We're aware. We learn it from our mothers," he countered.

"That's not fair," Selia said, laughing as she gave him a hug. "We both know he's not going to retire from his night job, any more than I am. If for no other reason than me,

Papa, will you please try to come to some agreement with him?"

"I have been considering it for a while." Soren admitted, returning the embrace. "But I can only go so far without him."

Selia sighed and dropped her head against his shoulder. "He's afraid you'll... harm him. He doesn't trust you. He thinks you'll use it against him... or something." She shrugged helplessly. "You know my secrets and you wouldn't betray me, but you also call me your daughter. I don't think you'd betray him, but he doesn't know or trust you like I do."

"I can't fault him for having that mentality. It's healthy paranoia." Soren stated. "After all, a great deal of damage could be had by revealing his real identity." He smiled. "I'm betting a lot of lawyers would love to know where to find the Sandman so they could have court summons issued."

"Gods, Papa," Selia moaned. "How much do you know about him and me?"

"Would you like me to email you the file I've composed?" he asked with a childish glee.

"Um, I'm almost tempted to say 'yes'," she admitted. "But I'm terrified of learning what you know!" She paused, her brows furrowing as she asked, "How can you know so much, but not know who he is or where he lives? How long have you been researching him?"

"Since he showed up on the scene, I have been compiling data," admitted Soren. "How much I know about him is actually very minor. I know where he patrols, what his methods are, and how many deaths and injuries he is probably responsible for. It's a much smaller number than the press and the public believe. Or the Families believe, for that matter."

Breathing a sigh of relief, Selia allowed herself to relax. "Okay, that makes sense. I figured Nightshade had taken more lives and created more havoc than he had." She grinned sheepishly. Looking up at him, she asked, "You wouldn't really move against him or turn over anything about him to anyone, would you?"

"Not unless he's threatening my livelihood or life, I wouldn't." Soren looked at her sternly. "But I am not like most people he has to deal with."

"I know that," Selia said sharply. "The problem is convincing him that you aren't going to betray him to the highest bidder. He's been doing this for so long on his own, I can understand his reluctance to part with his secrets; especially when the person involved is part of the opposition."

"It isn't just me, Selia." Sighing, Soren continued. "I don't think you understand how monumental a trust he's put in you. If anyone, from any aspect of my family or businesses, were to discover his secrets, or yours, it could be disastrous, dangerous, and yes, the end of everything for his life. Possibly yours as well. You have, after all, committed to the same activities."

Leaning against Soren, Selia sighed heavily. "I just couldn't fall in love with a normal, handsome man. Oh, no. I had to fall in love with the city's only vigilante and adversary to the Mafia syndicates. There's no way he can be around me without a disguise." She paused and sighed again. "I am so screwed, aren't I?"

"Change always comes. We'll just have to do our best and see where it goes. As for this adventure, we accomplished your return to the island's graces and what you'll be doing for the Family in the foreseeable future." He kissed her, and then gave her a mild nudge. "Come on. We need to board."

# Chapter Nine

The return voyage was quiet and serene. Selia kept mainly to herself, engrossed in the pages of the massive tomes. Every spell, core belief, even the structure of Tamarian society was detailed within. Bound in covers made from ancient skins, written on papyrus with the blood of long dead animals. In her childhood she had only witnessed the existence of most of these works.

The day before they were to dock, Soren threatened to lock the tomes in his personal vault if she didn't take a break from them and come out of her cabin.

By the time the dock came into view, Selia stood at the railing. She bounced on the balls of her feet, barely able to contain herself. She was eager to see Wil and sneak away with him for some alone time. A part of her wanted to continue studying the books on spells and magic, but the idea of being in her lover's arms was far more enticing at the moment. A hand squeezed her shoulder, and she looked up to find Soren. Soren smiled, then chuckled before he kissed the top of her head.

"Eager to be back on land?" he asked, a sly twinkle in his brown eyes.

She rolled her eyes. "What gave it away?"

"I wonder what he'll be wearing this time," Soren mused quietly.

Selia shrugged, fingering the crystal she wore as a necklace. Pale pink with blue and purple veins, it caught the sunlight and reflected it. Warm to the touch, she couldn't help but smile.

"I don't know. Probably the same as when he dropped me off," she murmured. "I didn't ask him during our last phone call."

They could clearly make out the shaggy ginger hair and beard of Wil's "musician" disguise as they neared the dock. Today, however, he wore a deep blue suit with a white silk polo shirt open at the throat. There were no skin tight leather pants, or blue jeans, or one of the seemingly endless t-shirts that "Liam" wore on every other outing. He stood patiently near one of the moors, puffing on his electric blue cigarette. He seemed to be in a conversation with one of the dock workers.

"Well, at least he almost looks respectable today," grumbled Soren as the large vessel ebbed into its place at the dock. Crewmen began securing the lines. Orders were yelled. Selia waited at the end of the ship, silently urging the worker with the portable stairway to hurry the hell up so she could run down it and jump into Wil's arms.

Wil glanced up at her and smiled between words spoken to the dock worker in front of him. He finally shook the man's hand and moved towards the stairs. While she had been focused on him, she'd missed that the stairs had been secured.

Selia all but flew down the stairs and jumped into Wil's arms. He laughed, caught her, and carried her away. She kissed him passionately, and he responded in kind. She did not want to pull away when she heard a man clearing his throat near them, but Wil pulled back and looked to the source of the interruption. Selia looked over and saw the dock worker Wil had been speaking to. He was smiling, rocking back and forth on his heels. Wil took his right hand off Selia's hip and fished into his coat jacket for something.

"I told ya she'd do it." The dock worker declared. He was in his late thirties, with blond hair that was cut short to help hide the receding hairline and empty spots on his scalp. He had a cherub-like face and twinkling blue eyes.

"That you did! Brilliant, mate," Wil replied with the British accent reserved for the character he was playing today. He held out a folded fifty dollar bill and said cheerfully, "There you go. You earned it. Pleasure doing business with you."

The dock worker took the bill, stuffing into the breast pocket of his coveralls.

"You treat her good, now," the worker advised. "Don't let a stranger figure her out better than you."

"Proper advice," acknowledged Wil. He kissed Selia and asked her, "Shall we fetch your bags, love?"

"Only because we can't sneak into my cabin," she murmured, kissing him again. "Come on, let's get my bags and I'll tell Papa I'll see him later."

They stepped over to where crewmen were dropping off hers and Soren's luggage. Soren came down from the ship and made his way over to them.

"Looks like you had a proper trip. Twice as many bags upon your return." Wil observed. He looked to Soren. "Trip went well, then? Did you get what you were looking for?"

"Better than expected," replied Soren. "Nice of you to meet her at the docks, Liam."

Wil shrugged. "Wish I could have gone on the voyage, instead." He seemed to ponder something. "Next trip, I might send along my PR man. Nice bloke, American. Quiet fellow named Wil. You might like him. He can do his job from anywhere. Even on a ship in the middle of the ocean." Squeezing Selia's waist, he added, "Gotta be careful, though. He might just steal our lovely Selia here away from me."

"Perish the thought." Soren muttered, then grabbed his duffel bag and briefcase before turning back to the two of them. "I will see you both later."

"I'll see you later, Papa," Selia said as she hugged him.

"Cheers," Wil said, bidding him a farewell as he shook Soren's hand.

Soren looked past them with an odd expression on his face for a moment, and then walked away.

"Get me to my place, your place, or a dark parking lot as fast as possible," Selia demanded, her voice dropping to a seductive whisper.

"Never say no to a pretty lady. That's my motto," Wil replied cheerily. They gathered her luggage and continued off the docks.

"Soren tried to tell me how it went," boomed the voice of Angelo 'Big Al' Lascari, the head of the Mafioso family that employed both Soren and Selia. "But I want to hear it from you, Selia."

The duo turned around and faced the man. He was of average height, broad of shoulder, and deeply tanned. His black hair glistened in the light. The Lascari godfather wore an impeccable suit of fine gray material and shoes that shone brighter than his beady dark eyes. He smiled at Selia but nodded towards Wil.

"But first, aren't you going to introduce me to your gentleman friend?" he invited.

*Damn it all to hell,* Selia thought, forcing a pleasant, cheerful smile on her face. It was better than scowling at the man. Doing so would undoubtedly cause Angelo to question everything twice as much. She had hoped to avoid this kind of meeting until Wil settled on what "persona" was going to marry her.

*Damn it.*

"This is Liam," Selia said, glancing at Wil and trying to not worry overly much about screwing up and saying the wrong thing. Couldn't Al have waited until later? "He's a musician." A genuine smile bloomed across her features as she glanced at Wil. "He's very talented... in many things."

"Liam Noel, sir." Wil said in his happiest 'Liam' voice. He smiled brightly and put out his hand. "Pleasure to meet you. Your niece-" he nodded at Selia "-has told me lovely things about you. And I must say, your resemblance to that actor is rather striking. I almost thought he had come for a visit."

"Oh? Well, thank you. I've always thought I looked like him, too. That's why he's my favorite!" Al replied jovially and shook Wil's hand with a crushing grip. Wil laughed with Al, and Selia wondered what actor Wil was referring to. She also noticed a brief look of concern on Al's face and how he suddenly broke the handshake.

"A musician, eh?" Al invited.

"Yes, sir. The guitar," Wil offered, holding up his hands. "Nearly my whole life and worked in the fish market before hitting the big time. Gave me strong mitts. Sorry, did I squeeze too hard?"

"No, no, not at all," Al replied a bit too quickly.

Selia glanced quickly at Al's hands: He was flexing his right hand as if trying to get circulation back into it. She bit back a laugh and gave Wil a demure smile.

"Ah, good," Wil said, keeping his joviality on high. "I meet so many people who just put a limp paw out for a shake. Drives me nutters."

"Yes, I have the same problem." Al tried to counter. "It's rather annoying."

"It is, isn't it? Makes you want to grab those weak hands and mash the owners faces in, doesn't it?"

Soren, who'd returned and was now standing behind Al, came forward quickly.

"Al, these young ones would like to get underway," he interjected. "I would prefer to get our debriefing done so I can grab a real shower and a drink that doesn't have rum in it."

"Of course," Al said, although he didn't sound pleased. He looked at Selia. "Go ahead then, make your report."

"Um, everything went smoothly," Selia offered. "I'm welcomed back home again, appeased everyone and ended up with admiration from a great many. I also have a new-found respect for a few aspects of my heritage that I hadn't before." She glanced pointedly at Soren, giving him a knowing smile. "I'll be welcomed back, and it could prove to be beneficial in trade. Though, is the dock really the proper place for this conversation?" She paused, smiling sweetly as she added, "Perhaps after I've regained my land-legs and have had time to organize my thoughts?"

"Oh, the larger portion of details can be conveyed at the office." Al assured her. "I just wanted to hear that it was a success from you. You never could lie to me."

Selia smiled to cover the laugh that wanted to erupt from her lungs. She'd been successfully lying to him since she was seventeen.

"Nope, you always sniffed me out." Selia said, trying to look as if caught. "But this voyage was a success. At least as far as I know and can give first-hand knowledge on."

"Good enough for now," Al responded. "All right. I will see you in the office in two days. Get your land legs back and get the sea out of your hair."

Selia smiled and squeezed Wil's hand. "I plan to do a great deal more than that."

62 | P a g e

# Chapter Ten

A knock on the door woke Selia the next morning. Curled up in Wil's arms, snuggled next to his bare body, she groaned. Her clock flashed just past eight and she sighed. It was too damned early to be getting up to someone intruding on her first day back in the city. Untangling herself from Wil, who asked sleepily what was happening, she kissed his cheek and rolled from the bed. Wrapping a silk robe around her, she padded to her front door and opened it.

A large bouquet of flowers greeted her.

"What?" Selia asked, still trying to wake up. "Um, bring them in. Put them on the coffee table." Who in the hells would deliver flowers this damned early in the morning?

A teenager, eighteen or nineteen years old with short brown hair and wearing jeans and a polo shirt with the florist's logo on the back, set the flowers down on the table. He held a package out to her.

"This goes with it, ma'am," he said in a pleasant voice. "Sorry to have woken you."

Selia took the package as she walked to a desk and opened a drawer. Pulling out a twenty from an envelope, she shoved the drawer shut, the soft click of it locking muffled by her hip.

"That's okay, ma'am! The person who placed the order already tipped us generously." The boy shuffled his feet nervously and Selia suspected he hadn't been placed in such a predicament before.

"Please, I insist," Selia told him as she pressed the cash into his right hand. "I tip like I mean it."

The boy took it, his bright blue eyes widening. "Uh, thank you!"

"Most welcome," Selia replied, smiling.

Nodding to her, the young man departed, and she suspected he was going to be a bit stunned for a while longer, if the way he was clutching the money was any indication. Turning back to the package, she frowned. Flowers she could understand, but a small package? Flipping it in her hand, she walked slowly back to the bedroom.

"What was that all about?" Wil asked, propped up in the bed.

She tossed him the package, which he caught deftly. "That and a large bouquet of rather beautiful flowers were just delivered. I'm tempted to give the flowers a good shower to make sure there's nothing 'extra' included in them." Shutting the door behind her, she dropped the robe to the floor and crawled back into the bed,

"Might not be a bad idea," Wil agreed. "I'll give it a good look over shortly." He turned the package over a few times before shaking it. "You want to open it, or should I?"

"Go ahead," Selia said, smiling.

Wil unwrapped the simple white wrapping paper to reveal a long, black box that resembled a jewelry box. He raised his brows. "Something you want to tell me about, love?"

"I've got a lot to tell you about in regard to the trip, but if you're asking who in the hells is sending me jewelry, I don't know," Selia replied, frowning at the box.

The box chose that moment to ring.

Wil and Selia stared at the container. Wil lifted the lid off gingerly and they stared at a tiny smartphone that was nestled in the center of the velvet-lined container.

Picking it up, Selia swiped her finger across the phone then tapped the speaker icon. "Hello?"

"Good morning, Selia. Your return home was, I trust, successful?" The voice of Lucien Vaschetti, head of the Vaschetti crime syndicate, came through the phone's speaker. She'd known him almost as long as she had Soren. While in different families, and therefore, syndicates, the two men had a comfortable working relationship. If he was asking about her trip, Lucien must have been informed of it by Soren.

"Good morning, Lucien. This is a bit of a surprise," Selia said, giving Wil a confused expression and slight shrug. "The trip was successful, but I'm glad to be home."

"Ah... even after you return, you continue to regard our city as your home," observed Lucien. "Excellent. This coincides well with what I have in mind."

"I'm almost afraid to ask," Selia said, frowning at the phone.

"Well, we certainly aren't going to discuss it over the phone. You may choose the location of our meeting," he said, the tone of his voice conveying that he was allowing her a big favor. Then, he added, "Also, you should bring a member of your Family to be witness to my proposal."

Brows still furrowed, Selia said, "How about Soren's office? I believe he is currently your, ah, contact and unofficial liaison with my Family."

"For now, yes. I shall be at his office at eleven this morning. Until then, belladonna."

"Until then, Lucien," Selia said. Her response was 'call ended' popping up on the phone. She turned to Wil. "Looks like I have a meeting in three hours."

"Any idea what this one is about?" Wil inquired,

"I have no clue," Selia replied. "Pretty sure Al isn't going to be too happy if he catches wind of either that phone call or the meeting."

"Perhaps you should tell him about both." Her mate suggested. "Make a preemptive strike?"

She pondered his suggestion and grabbed her cell from the nightstand. Punching in Soren's direct number to his office, she waited for him to answer.

Three rings later, she said, "Morning, Papa! Have you heard anything from Lucien?"

"I have a note from his office that suggested I might be seeing him tomorrow." Soren replied. "Good morning to you, too."

"Um, he just called me, saying to meet him at your office at eleven," Selia said hesitantly. "Should I call Al and tell him I've spoken to Lucien or hope and pray that it stays beneath his radar?"

There was a long, ponderous silence.

"Best to tell him," Soren sighed. "If he finds out any other way, it could inflame his paranoia. You, me, or both of us could be the next basis for the conspiracy theory of the month."

"I'll give him a call," Selia grumbled. "So much for enjoying a quiet morning in bed."

"Better to have to wait on that, than risk everything by waiting on the other."

"Too true, Papa." Selia snuggled next to Wil and stifled a yawn. "I'll see you in a couple hours. Keep your fingers crossed that Al doesn't go berserk when he finds out about Lucien."

She ended the call and then pulled up Al's number. Hoping to avoid talking to him, she used the general office number and got one of the secretaries.

"Hey, Sandy," Selia said upon hearing the woman's soft, dulcet tones. "It's Selia. Is Angelo available?"

"Oh, Selia," Sandy said, her pleasant, yet almost-flat tone was warm and becoming more lively. "Did you have a good trip?"

"It was fun," Selia replied honestly. "I got a nice tan and brought back a few souvenirs."

"Glad to hear you had a good time," the secretary replied. "Let me transfer you to Al. He should be available for his niece."

"Thanks, Sandy." The phone went silent before elevator music began playing.

Less than eight bars of music later, Al came on the line.

"What's gotten you out of bed?" he practically demanded, even though there was a general jovial quality in his voice.

"Good morning to you, too," Selia responded. "I actually have a question for you and I'm hoping you don't get mad at me for it."

"Go ahead." Al promptly answered. "It's been an interesting morning already."

"Um, okay," Selia said, slightly curious. "Do you know why Lucien Vaschetti would be calling me?"

The line was silent for so long, she wondered if he had hung up or had a stroke.

"What did he say to you?" he finally asked.

"He said he wanted to meet me, with one of my Family as a witness to the event," she replied carefully. She held the phone so Wil could hear easily. "I suggested Papa, since I knew he would be available on a moment's notice."

Plus, she didn't want to chance anyone else learning that she'd already dealt with Lucien before or that Lucien knew she was Nightshade.

"I would wonder why you chose Soren, except that you are right about his availability versus mine." Al said, with only a little irritation in his voice. "But he said nothing about the nature of the meeting? Do you want me to send extra men to the office?"

Selia rolled her eyes. "He didn't mention anything other than he wanted to see me." She paused, trying to figure out how to dismiss his suggestion of more men without making Al even more paranoid or annoyed. "If you want to send Alex and Bernie, I wouldn't object. If Lucien wants to speak with me, surely it can't be anything important? Or anything dangerous. I mean, I'm just Soren's daughter. What could he possibly want with me?"

"That is precisely the question," intoned Al. "I can send the Caruso brothers and trust them. I would prefer to have as many people as I can trust at this meeting." There was a pregnant pause. "I'll tell you what we're going to do: I will have a small battalion of men outside the building. However many Lucien brings with him, I will have the same number of my men enter the building after him."

"As you wish, Uncle," Selia replied smoothly. "Do you want me to call or drop by your office after the meeting?"

She knew Lucien wouldn't have anyone other than her, Soren, and himself in the meeting, but that wouldn't placate Al.

"Yes, come by my office and we'll have a debriefing." That seemed to be all that he had to say on the matter.

"Okay. I'll see you later, Uncle," Selia replied, ending the call before he could. She turned to Wil. "Well, that went rather well, didn't it?"

"Better than I expected," Wil replied. His manner didn't seem relaxed at all. Wil was looking at a fixed point on the wall. Selia knew the look: he was pondering something.

"What?" She asked, putting the phone back on the nightstand.

"Hmm?" Wil looked at her. "'I'm trying to formulate the most likely scenarios that Al would run with. My biggest concern is Al overreacting and trying to take Lucien out while he's on Lascari territory. Hell, he'll be at Lascari Central, for that."

"Lascari Central would actually be Al's office," Selia corrected him. "Papa's office is a little office building on Eighth Street. He moved there after he brought me to New Campania." She sat up in the bed, curling her legs around her. "Al might be a paranoid nitwit, but he isn't that stupid."

Wil rolled his eyes. "I am well aware of where Soren's office is. But you should be aware that the majority of the Lascari business and money flows through that building. If Lucien were to disrupt business by, say, killing everyone on your floor, it would cost the Family major profits, as well as show the Lascari to be weak and foolishly trusting." He looked at her with cold eyes. "Al could be thinking that the perfect time to strike against his biggest adversary is when he has surrendered all of his advantages."

"It sounds more like Lucien is wanting me to investigate something." She paused and then groaned. "Bloody hell. It has something to do with my not returning to Temeria, which means he wants Nightshade. He's probably also wanting to do a little fishing to try and get an upper hand on Soren."

"And you just said yes to the meeting. But I don't think it's as bad as that." Wil rubbed her neck. "Lucien would know how Al thinks, and might show up alone, or only with enough men to not appear suspicious. He's going to be trusting that you want to keep your secret, and therefore protect him while he's on enemy territory."

"It's not like I had much of a choice," she said with a heavy sight. Glancing at the clock, she rolled over onto Wil and smiled impishly down at him. "We've still got an hour or so. Know a way to kill the time?"

# Chapter Eleven

Fifteen minutes to eleven, Selia made her way to Soren's office. The office was busy with people coming and going, and it felt good to be home again. The familiarity of the building, the bright lights, and smiling faces of people she knew only reaffirmed her decision to not remain on Temeria. Taking the elevator up, she studied her reflection on the mirrored interior.

Despite the changing fall colors, and Halloween only being a couple weeks away, the weather was still warm during the day. She had chosen a light-weight business suit-jacket, a snug sleeveless white blouse, and a black skirt just a few inches shy of her knees. Three-inch black heels gave her a few extra inches and her hair was pulled back into a simple black clip. It was as close to 'business' as she was going to get for the day. The only piece she had that wasn't completely business-like was the simple leather purse she carried. She doubted anyone would search her purse and ask why she had three phones inside it.

Adjusting her jacket, she turned slightly in the elevator, making certain her M&P's shoulder holster was hidden from sight. After everything that had happened, Selia didn't feel as safe as she used to and had taken to wearing her weapon whenever she went out. The elevator dinged and Selia continued into Soren's office.

A secretary's desk was situated at an angle in front of the door to Soren's innermost office. A reddish-brown wooden paneled wall separated the two rooms, with a closed door granting the only access into Soren's haven.

"Hey, Maria," Selia said, pausing by the blonde secretary's desk. The woman had cherubic features and sharp blue eyes. "Can I go on in, or is Papa in a meeting?"

"Papa?" Maria asked; amusement in her voice that had a strong Southern accent.

"Soren," Selia clarified, only a little annoyed.

Maria chuckled. "I knew who you meant, sweetie. I just haven't heard you call him that."

Selia shrugged. "I gave up trying to pretend he doesn't mean so much to me. Amazing what almost losing someone can do to you, huh?"

"Very true," Maria agreed, pursing her red lips. The woman loved tanning and her blood-red lipstick. "But that was two months ago."

"I haven't been around here lately, what with joining Soren on his trips," Selia explained. She glanced over Maria's shoulder into his office.

Maria nodded in agreement. "Yeah, we've missed having you around here. It's been sort of boring, actually." She grinned. "Go on in. Maybe you can get him out of his grumpiness."

"I'm not a miracle worker," Selia teased, turning and entering Soren's office. Soren looked up from his desk, positioned directly opposite the door, and Selia grinned. "So, when are you going to want me to return to work?"

"Considering that you're here on business, I'd say today." Soren grunted. "But if you mean your full-time appointment, you can return whenever you want. Your formal training as the new Trade Master with Temeria begins in two weeks."

"Really?" Selia asked, not hiding the excitement she felt. She crossed the room to him and dropped into one of the two chairs opposite his desk. She couldn't resist teasing him. "Does that mean I get a corner office, too?"

"You can have my office, for all of that," he retorted. "It doesn't matter where you take your calls for that job."

Frowning, Selia tilted her head to the side. "Care to share what's wrong?"

"Al's got the whole building and the street outside swarming with extra muscle. I found the electronic listening devices someone planted in this office when I arrived an hour ago." Soren growled. "I find it perfectly unacceptable that I don't know if Lucien is trying to undermine our ranks, if Al is questioning our loyalties, or if everyone is just running paranoid during normal business practices."

"Lucien called, asking if my trip was successful. I told him I was glad to be home. His response consisted of that was good, because it coincides with what he has in mind." Selia squirmed in the chair, not happy with anything. "As far as Al is concerned, he didn't like Lucien calling me, which is understandable, and I'm supposed to report to him after this damned meeting."

"I hadn't heard about you reporting to Al after this." Soren almost spat. "This is just improving by the second."

"You expected less?" Selia countered. "Lucien requests to meet with me- a female and your adopted daughter who happens to be from a land of warring women- and has been using you as his unofficial liaison for two months. If anything, Al probably will suspect us of setting up a coup, so Lucien can waltz in and take over everything." She drummed her fingers against the arm of her chair. "The balance must be kept, and I intend to keep it. Regardless of what Al or Lucien ultimately want."

Hearing Soren say almost the same things Wil had was beyond worrying. It was downright frightening. She'd been forced to turn to Lucien for help when she'd been targeted by Alfi, and now it seemed Lucien was creating problems for Soren. If it had just been her being placed in danger, she wouldn't have worried about it but so much.

No, Lucien was coming close to crossing a line and she was prepared to meet him in their favorite meeting place and ask him just what the Hells he thought he was doing by not contacting Al first. He was a freaking don, for gods' sakes! He knew the channels and the proper way to do this stuff, and none of it started with calling her from a phone that had been delivered in the morning by a florist's shop.

"Here's hoping it can be managed." Soren observed.

"Agreed," Selia said as the intercom buzzed.

Sandy's voice came from the speaker. "Mr. Lascari, Mr. Vaschetti is here for a meeting." It was said more as a question.

"I'll greet him," Selia said as she stood and crossed to the door. Pasting a smile on her face, she took a deep breath and opened the door. "Mr. Vaschetti. Good morning."

"We'll hope it is, and work towards that end," Lucien declared sagely.

He was dressed in a dark blue suit that had to cost as much as a small compact car. He had two men with him. Both men were just over six feet in height, broad shouldered, wearing identical gray suits and military style haircuts.

"Will they be joining us in the meeting, sir?" Selia asked, stepping to the side of the door. She paused before adding, "Can I get any of you anything?"

"They were my escort to this office." Lucien explained. "But I have no concerns for my safety once I am in the office. You may feel free to have more men in the room, if it makes you feel more secure."

"We will be joined by two other gentlemen," rejoined Soren. "Extra witnesses to alleviate Angelo's concerns and interests."

"As long as they remain outside the office door, I have no qualms about that arrangement," Lucien said.

Lowering her eyes demurely, Selia replied, "That is for Papa to decide."

"Will you submit to a search by those men? Are you comfortable with being recorded?" Soren asked Lucien.

"Are we going to be videotaped?" Lucien countered, raising an eyebrow.

"Audio only," Soren replied.

"I would be fine with that and the body search as well."

Soren nodded and pressed a button next to the intercom on his desk.

"Send up the brothers. They will be keeping Mr. Vaschetti's escort company outside my office," Soren instructed before releasing the button.

Delight flashed briefly in Selia's eyes before she glanced away from Lucien and to her adopted father. A genuine smile on her face, Selia turned back to the outer office. Not even five minutes later, Bernie and Alex Caruso entered the outer office; both dressed in business attire.

The brothers were both dark haired, dark eyed, and had handsomely chiseled features, but that was where the similarities stopped. Alex, the older of the two, wore a charcoal gray suit that emphasized his tall, model-perfect frame. He reminded Selia more of an accountant than a deadly enforcer. Bernie looked the part of a rough-and-tough enforcer, even in the dark blue suit, with his wide-shoulders and short stature. Leaning slightly to the side, Selia nodded to the pair, her smile broadening just a little.

The Caruso brothers had often been her 'babysitters' when she'd first arrived in New Campania, and she adored them both, even if Alex was her favorite of the two. Both had been assigned to check up on her daily two months ago, when she'd been stuck in a so-called 'safe house'.

She'd somehow managed to sneak out past the pair, keep them from suspecting she was in cahoots with the Sandman, and keep her own secret identity a secret. Not an easy feat, but she'd managed it and had also managed to reconnect with the pair. Seeing the brothers again, she decided that it'd been too long since they'd hung out.

"Gentlemen," Soren addressed the brothers, and gestured as he spoke their instructions. "You will be searching Mr. Vaschetti for weapons, and you will be respectful as you do so. After the search is complete, you will join Mr. Vaschetti's escort in the waiting room. You will be respectful to them as well, unless, of course, they become disrespectful."

Lucien smiled and nodded once to Soren, even as he put his arms out to either side and stood with his legs apart.

The brothers took two minutes to body search the Vaschetti godfather. They turned up a compact five-shot revolver which was handed to Soren, and a smartphone that wasn't supposed to be on the market for another two months. Soren gestured for the phone to be returned to Lucien. Other items, like the platinum money clip that was packed with cash, sunglasses and a slim wallet, were not taken from him, but replaced respectfully.

The folder that Lucien held in his left hand was not opened. Alex ran his hands over the folder to make sure nothing metallic or thicker than a credit card was inside. It obviously wasn't, since he handed the folder back over without a word or pause. The brothers nodded at Soren. He nodded back, and they exited the room, closing the door behind them.

Soren moved Lucien's revolver to the end of the desk furthest from the godfather. He glanced at it, then at Lucien.

"Pretty hefty for a five-shot," Soren observed.

"It's a .44 Special. I've had it longer than your lovely assistant has been alive," Lucien Vaschetti replied. "It has never let me down."

"Fair enough." Soren reached into his coat and withdrew a similar revolver. "I prefer this one. It's chambered for the .45 long Colt round. It's currently loaded with frangible rounds. Figure two-hundred and fifty shotgun pellets per load."

He pushed it down his desk towards Lucien. Lucien nodded at Soren and smiled. He lifted the weapon up with his free hand.

"I imagine this would create quite a mess," the Vaschetti godfather commented. He placed the weapon back down on the desk but did not push it towards its owner.

"We often have messy business," rejoined Soren.

"But not today," Lucien finished.

Selia suddenly realized that this had been something akin to a ritual: Both men were now clearly more relaxed, even though each of them had quick access to deadly weapons. The weapons belonged to the other man, but still... They seemed pleased, now.

Soren opened a drawer in his desk and removed a small tape recorder. Selia hadn't seen one of those since she'd graduated high school. Soren placed it on the desk and pressed the "record" button. He and Lucien were smiling at each other.

"Lucien, if you will take a seat across from me, and, Selia, you sit at my side. Then we can begin business."

Lucien took the single seat across from Soren. Selia moved around the desk, discovering a chair that was really more of a piano stool. Leaning against the desk, next to the stool and out of Lucien's view, was a sawed-off shotgun. It was an old one from the look. Double barreled and sawed down to where it could almost be concealed in a suit coat, it nonetheless shone brightly and gleamed with gun oil. Selia sat on the stool beside Soren and wondered what was going to happen next.

"I am here to propose that Selia replace you as the liaison between the Vaschetti and Lascari families, and that the part of the liaison be a more active role than it has been as of late." Lucien held up his hand to prevent responses from either Soren or Selia. "I do not say anything in disrespect. Soren, you have risen in rank since you first took the role, and you have far too much to do. If our families are to grow and work together in peace, we need a more active... buffer, if you will, keeping us in check. We need someone who is not wholly of your family, or mine, and someone that all can respect. I consider Selia to be, truly, the only person who fulfills these requirements."

Selia folded her hands on the desk and kept her face slightly bowed, her gaze aimed towards her fingers. She glanced at Lucien from the corner of her eyes, a frown marring her features. There had to be some ulterior motive for Lucien's actions. Not when he'd told her previously he was looking forward to the carnage she would bring down upon the city.

"She's a woman." Soren commented casually.

"Ah, but in this matter, I believe our 'old ways' work to her benefit, and thus to ours!" Lucien seemed excited by the point that Soren had tried to make. "Perhaps you are concerned, Soren, that because she is a woman, no one will take her seriously. But I see differently. Women do not actively seek war, unless they feel they are wronged. Even then, they do not seek war. Then, they seek the utter dominance or destruction of that who has wronged them. They care nothing of obtaining their adversaries' possessions or power. Only the suffering and total defeat of whom they would destroy."

Selia pondered Lucien's words, thinking of her homeland. The queens of the clans didn't just bring about death and destruction to their enemies. The fights were always over territory and power. The queens coveted what each other had and would do anything in their power to obtain it. However, she'd never witnessed a ritual such as she'd seen in this office between two queens. Well, to be honest, she'd never seen it between any two women on Temeria.

Lucien smiled at them both. "Also, think of our so-called old fashioned code: Do not harm or threaten women. True, there are women that must be taken out from time to time, but they are the ones that threaten our livelihood. Selia is not, nor would she have any reason to be, such a threat. If one of us were to harm or threaten her, would the other not race to punish the insolent cur who was so disrespectful?"

At that, Selia glanced upwards towards the ceiling, as though asking to be saved. Despite the desire to do so, she didn't shake her head in disbelief. Somehow, she highly doubted Lucien would be quick to draw a weapon against someone who dared to threaten her. Soren definitely would, but Lucien? That was a bit tougher to swallow.

Soren, to Selia's surprise, laughed. Lucien did not respond badly to this, either. He smiled and nodded at Soren.

"Yes, we are rather quick to defend a woman's honor, aren't we?" Soren asked, still smiling. "Depending on the woman, of course."

Lucien waved his hand in the air as if brushing something away.

"We all have those moments, my friend," offered Lucien. "But you know what I say is true. You have grown too high in the ranks to give the job of liaison the time and effort it deserves. War would not benefit either family. It would only benefit the jackals and coyotes that snap at the scraps we discard. To keep both families honest, as cliché as it may be to say so, I believe we require a good woman."

He nodded to Selia.

"That may be so," Soren said. "But how do you propose we make this change? What assurances do you offer that you will not feed disinformation to the new liaison, or try to sway her?"

*Been there, done that, he failed,* Selia thought as she glanced sharply at Soren.

"Ah, the heart of the business." Lucien smiled. He opened the folder he had brought in with him. "I have a contract that covers her duties and obligations. It is already signed by me and my underbosses. It will be complete when you, your *capofamiglia*, and the rest of his *sotto capos* have signed. And Selia, of course."

Lucien leaned over the desk and held out the opened folder. There was a contract several pages long inside it, but on top of those pages was a photo. A clear, high definition photo that was facing Selia and Soren.

The photo was of Nightshade. She stood over several dead and unconscious *soldati*, brandishing a gun even as she was checking a body. Selia recognized the bodies and alleyway from when she and the Sandman had been patrolling right before she had left for Temeria.

She took long, quiet breaths before taking her eyes from the picture.

Lucien was staring at Soren. When Soren looked at Lucien, the Vaschetti godfather nodded at the picture, and then nodded at Selia.

Selia grimaced, her face flushing as she looked at Soren and nodded. She shrugged, pointing at the picture. Turning, she glowered at Lucien. Internally, she wanted to grab both men's revolvers and empty them into the godfather's torso.

Lucien smiled and looked at Soren. Soren had a very sour expression on his face and looked at Selia with a single eyebrow raised.

She rolled her eyes and pointed at Lucien with her thumb. She mouthed, "Yes, he knows."

It was so very tempting to call Lucien a variety of names, none of which were polite.

Soren rolled his eyes, then looked to a very satisfied looking Lucien and held his hand out for the folder. Lucien gave the folder to Soren but kept the photograph. He slipped the photo into an inside jacket pocket.

"I will have to take this to my *capofamiglia*, of course," Soren said. He didn't even bother to look at the contract's contents. "Are you expecting me or Selia to argue in your defense?"

"No," Lucien said brightly. "I do not. I expect *il mio pari* to read it over and be satisfied with the content and restrictions for all parties concerned. If he is not, he can call me directly. No need to go through *il legame*. He can tell me any reservations he has, and I will deal with them."

"Why?" Soren said through clenched teeth.

"As I have said: I consider Selia to be the perfect candidate. She has... the most to lose, should things go badly."

Lucien offered this last bit of wisdom with a charismatic smile and spread his arms wide. He mouthed the words "no disrespect" and gestured to both Selia and Soren.

*No, you bastard, you do*, Selia thought. If things went badly, she'd have no problems carving Lucien's heart out, and not in a figurative manner, either. She kept her hands folded together. Well, more like clenched together.

She'd kept her end of the deal, and then some, by restoring the balance between the families. She wasn't a cold-hearted murderess, not really, but Lucien was getting pretty damned close to her threshold. Clenching her jaw, she kept silent as she glowered at Lucien.

Drawing a deep breath, she closed her eyes, thought of Wil, and let her breath out slowly.

"I will do as my uncle, the *capofamiglia*, and my father desire," she managed to say.

Selia was pretty damned certain her tone could have frozen boiling water, but that really didn't matter. If Al questioned her, she could always say she didn't like being forced into working with the enemy.

"Well, hopefully *l'altro individuo* will see the wisdom of this arrangement and agree to it." Lucien commented.

*Gods*, Selia thought, *I want to smash that smile of his into the back of his skull.*

"We will present this to Angelo Lascari, and someone will contact you as soon as he has made his decision." Soren offered.

"Just have *il nuovo legame* arrange a time to bring it by." Lucien shrugged. "If Angelo feels the contract is unacceptable, he can contact me directly; as I have said."

Lucien stood up and pushed Soren's revolver towards him. He laid a business card on top of it and waited.

Selia peered at the card even as Soren reached over to retrieve his weapon. Handwritten upon the card were the words "*Meet me at the usual club at 8pm tomorrow.*"

Selia turned her steely gaze to Soren, a single brow raised. Hopefully it wasn't her and Lucien's usual spot, which happened to be just outside a freaking graveyard. Soren nodded to Lucien as he put the card in his own jacket pocket. Holding his weapon, Soren pushed Lucien's revolver back towards him.

Lucien promptly holstered his weapon. Soren did the same. Lucien bowed slightly and said "*è un piacere che facendo affari con lei*" to them before heading to the doorway.

When he opened the door, four men rose to their feet. The brothers moved past Lucien and looked at Soren for instruction. Soren held up one hand and shook his head slightly. The brothers turned and watched Lucien and his two men walk casually to the elevator and get in. When the doors closed, the brothers entered the office and looked, a little anxiously, at Soren.

Selia reached over and hit the 'stop' button on the recorder before muttering, "So *not* a pleasure doing business with you, you bastard." She raised her gaze to Soren, her eyes dark and furious. "I am going to need either a good strong drink or a bottle of sedatives before visiting Angelo."

Soren tapped his ear and pointed towards the ceiling. The meaning was clear- Al's listening devices were still on. He smiled at her, though, and looked to Bernie.

"Break out the twelve year old scotch. I think we can all use a stiff drink."

# Chapter Twelve

The trip to Al's office building was quick, despite it being in the heart of the city. They had taken Soren's car, with Bernie and Alex following in a gleaming black Mercedes Benz. There was no conversation. The fear of the car being bugged was enough for Selia to keep quiet. Well, that and she wanted to think about what had occurred.

Lucien had forced her into a precarious position, but there had to be a reason. The man wasn't nearly as paranoid as Al. Ruthless, yes, but Lucien wasn't a paranoid schizo. The four of them entered the elevator and she slid her hand into Soren's. He glanced at her, and she smiled. Returning the smile, Soren gave her hand a squeeze, but didn't let go.

Al's office was on the top floor of one of the oldest buildings in the city. It had its heyday in the sixties, and rumor had it that the Family had acquired it from an advertising agency that folded in the seventies. The outer rooms and hallways had been upgraded to more *avante garde* shades of grays and blues, along with black and lots of white coloring the furniture, carpet, paints and wall art. Al's office was the throwback.

Wood paneling adorned most of the wall space, along with muted yellows and reds. The carpet was deep red, and the furniture was vintage. The wide oak desk that Al was pacing behind was at least a century old. The chairs and couches all seemed to have been transported from the Sixties. Shining steel and brown leather was everywhere. A topical map of Italy seemed out of place, taking up most of one wall. But it still fit the office better than the modern intercom, iPhone dock and speaker system, along with the tablet sitting on the antique desk. Al glared at them both when they entered his office.

"You wait outside." Al instructed Soren, jabbing a meaty finger at him. "I'll talk to you individually."

"Papa?" Selia asked softly, turning her eyes imploringly to Soren.

She might not have felt in fear of her life, but she sure as hell couldn't let Al know that. Nope, she had to act the part of docile, frightened wallflower who had been thrown into the middle of a fight. It really sucked, too.

Soren squeezed her hand and smiled. "I'll be right outside. Don't worry." He let her hand go and shut the door after her.

Slowly Selia turned to Al, her gaze cautious and uncertain. Deep down, she wanted to roll her eyes and scold Angelo for being so damned paranoid. If she'd wanted to stage a coup, she could have done it long before now, and without Lucien's assistance.

"Well, what did Lucien want?" Al got right to the point. He continued pacing, barely looking at her.

"He wants me to be his liaison between the Families," she replied, following him with her eyes. "He claims Soren is too busy to be effective. That it's important for the families to work together more in order to keep peace and grow." She shrugged slightly as she stared out the window, recalling the words Lucien used. "He said I'm not wholly Family and I'm someone all involved could respect."

Al snorted but kept pacing. "Everyone would want to protect you, that's what he meant. Fine, fine. Did your proposed appointment as Soren's replacement in Temerian trade come up?"

"No," Selia said, stifling a sigh. "Lucien apparently only wants me as liaison between the Families. Nothing was said about my position within my Family or about Temeria." She paused, and then added with a shy smile. "Other than the fact I'm a woman, of course."

"Well, he's got guts and he's thought this out." Al grumbled. He stopped in front of his chair. Pulling it out and dropping into it, he barked a laugh. "So, what do you think about his proposal?"

"I'm not happy about it," Selia said honestly. She tucked a strand of wayward hair behind her ear. "But I will do as you and Papa tell me."

Al stared at her hard for a few moments, and then exhaled heavily through his nostrils. "Do you even really know what the job entails?"

Selia shook her head. "My guess would be I'd be the go-between for you and Lucien, or whoever else is involved." She shifted her weight to her left hip and asked, "But does that really matter? Lucien wants me and it depends on you as to whether or not I'm made the liaison. Despite being a woman, I'll still obey you, Uncle, since you are the don. My personal feelings, my dislike for this, have little to do in the matter."

Al threw one hand into the air as if he were tossing something into an imaginary wind. "What the job mostly entails is being available to communicate messages and desires between the *capos* and the *sotto capos*... the bosses and the underbosses. It was supposed to be only the bosses, but that became impractical after a while. You don't deal with the captains." Al rambled on. "You act as the buffer at those rare meetings when both Families are present. You point out when one side is gaining undue advantages in a discussion. Kind of a... what do you call it... mediator, or counselor. *Capisce?*"

"*Capisce*," Selia said with a nod.

Lucien, she was certain, had other ideas, though. The Vaschetti don, she suspected, also wanted her because she was Nightshade. Not that Selia could tell Al that tidbit.

"I take it you agree with Lucien's... request? I might also add that Papa has a contract for you that I'm supposed to sign as well, if I'm to be the liaison."

"I'm sure he'll present it when I see him." He waved his hand dismissively. "Now, I have agreed to you becoming Master Tradesman for Temeria. If you take on this additional responsibility, you'll barely be in the office. But your burdens will be greater. I will... be watching to see how you handle all of it. If I allow the liaison job, of course."

Selia nodded and waited.

"Knowing that bastard Lucien, he'll have it tied up in a bow so saying no will be a bigger problem," complained Al. "If you become liaison, someone will have to be assigned to take on your duties in that capacity when you are trading with the lovely people of Temeria."

"I understand, Uncle," Selia declared. "If you choose to give me both positions, I will take them. Thank you for appointing me to Master Tradesman of Temeria."

"Didn't seem like I had much choice on that, either," Al growled. "All right, send in Soren. We'll talk again soon."

He stood and began pacing again. Selia took her cue and made her way to the door. When she opened it, she found Soren sitting comfortably on the expansive couch that cost as much as a small car. Soren picked up the folder that Lucien had given him and rose to his feet. He met her halfway between the couch and the open door.

"It went okay?" he whispered.

"Good as could be expected," she acknowledged in a low voice.

He nodded, kissed her on the cheek, and went into Al's office. Selia took the spot Soren had used on the couch and waited. About fifteen minutes later, Soren opened the door and beckoned for her to enter.

Al was sitting at his desk scowling. He shoved the contract across the desk to her along with a pen. An 'x' was next to a line where she guessed she was supposed to sign and date it. She did as silently bid and slid the folder back to Al, who shut it. Soren touched her shoulder, and she got the message. Turning, they quietly left the office. Neither spoke until they were outside again.

"I'll visit you tomorrow, Papa," Selia said. "I plan on going out tonight and having fun. Maybe spend the night with my beau, for a change." She kissed him on the cheek. "I'll stay out of trouble, I promise."

"If by that you mean you won't get caught, I hope you're right," countered Soren.

She murmured softly, "Where do you think I got the name?"

"I honestly have no idea."

"Belladonna," she said, keeping her voice low. "Who do you think calls me that?"

Soren narrowed his eyes at her. "No wonder he's fixated on you. Lucien loves to be an influence on lovely ladies."

"He's known ever since that first meeting. The first picture to land online was taken after I'd finished talking with him." She kept her head bowed as she walked beside him. "There's more going on than what Lucien said. I just have to figure out what it is. It can wait a day, though."

Soren rubbed his eyes. "Let's hope you're right about that."

# Chapter Thirteen

Selia felt alive as she crossed the rooftops of the buildings. She and the Sandman had taken his electric motorcycle across the city to the warehouse district. Wil, in his disguise as the Sandman, had parked it in one of the waterways before taking a fire escape to the top of a building. From there, they had traversed the rooftops of the warehouses.

The air was cool and crisp. The breeze from the ocean, only a few blocks away, teased at her senses, reminding her of the voyage to Temeria. Thoughts of her homeland brought forth memories of her new position as Master Tradesman, which snowballed into her thinking of Al, followed by Lucien. Lucien and his conniving ways reminded Selia about why she was out enjoying the cool autumn air and not Wil's warm bed.

She needed to release her pent up frustrations on someone. Since neither Wil nor Al, let alone Lucien, were an option, she was going to take her anger out on some hoodlums. The group that had been plundering the warehouses was good enough, in Selia's opinion. Since Wil had needed her help to tackle this group of jackals, Selia was more than happy to go after the group tonight. A small part of her had thought Wil would have had all the fun while she had been gone, but apparently more trouble had just popped up with 'Nightshade' AWOL.

It was good to be missed, Selia thought with a malicious smile beneath her scarf.

As they neared the edge of the building that was to be that night's target, Selia tapped the Sandman on the shoulder, gesturing for him to wait. Peeking over the edge, they could make out forms moving below, but not how many were below them. Wiggling her finger, she moved away from the edge and waited until the Sandman was standing next to her. Holding her left hand out, she whispered the words to a spell she'd learned on the ship back from Temeria. In fact, she'd learned the spell specifically for her nights out as Nightshade.

Magic surged around her, coursing through her body as the spell built before coalescing in the palm of her hand. Small blue dots, barely larger than the eraser on a standard pencil, formed around a large square and two smaller rectangles. The square was, obviously, the warehouse, and Selia guessed the smaller rectangles were trucks of some sort, since the dots were moving from the rectangles to the square and back again.

Waving her right hand across her left, the dots paused, and she favored Wil with an extremely smug expression. Counting a total of twenty, she raised a brow to Wil, who nodded. Clenching her fingers into a fist, she flicked her wrist, throwing her hand outward as though casting a spell. Instead of throwing magic, the spell vanished, the dots seemingly tossed into the air before dissolving.

"With or without glamor, my love?" she asked softly.

"With," Wil replied in the deeper voice of the Sandman. It sent shivers of desire down Selia's spine. He continued, his mask pulling into what was probably a knowing smile. "Take every advantage possible."

Selia rolled her eyes. After dealing with the aberlin, the idiots below would seem like a walk in the park. Even with their weapons. But she wasn't going to argue. Not when it meant she'd get to enjoy terrifying them. With a gesture of her right hand, a shimmer fell around them. At some point, she'd have to ask him if he could see it like she could.

Kodachi or M&Ps, she pondered as they began down the fire escape. She could always use the pair of batons the Sandman had given her. Blood, broken bones, and bruises. Yeah, that sounded like fun. She pulled the batons free from her utility belt and gripped them cheerfully in her gloved hands.

The Sandman glanced over his shoulder at her, his brows furrowing slightly. She raised her own in reply. He paused and lowered his glasses for a brief moment. She rolled her eyes, dropping her head to the side.

"Are we going to do this or stand here all night?" Selia hissed.

"You weren't this impatient before you went back home," Wil said. "Maybe I should get you a giant walking lizard suit and let you run rampant?"

"Nah," Selia replied, laughing. "I just figured it'd be better to take my anger out on those bozos, instead of my dear so-called 'uncle' or the one who has tossed me into the fire."

"That's all well and good," Wil replied. "Should I paint a target on your chest and butt to make it easier for the bozos to aim?"

Selia snickered. "I think I'll pass. Would you prefer I use the M&Ps, then? Because I can do that, too."

"Do the fabled Amazonian warriors have no grasp of tactics? Do you just charge each other and not worry about taking losses?" Wil sighed dramatically. "Geez, you go home, skin a saber tooth tiger, and suddenly you want to go Rambo on everything. So much for estrogen, eh?"

Selia laughed softly, forcing herself to keep quiet, which made her sides hurt. "Oh, not fair." She giggled. "You can blame Lucien for this. If the sorry bastard hadn't pulled me and Soren into Angelo's line of sight, I wouldn't want to maim, cripple, and kill."

"I'm starting to wonder if you shouldn't make use of a certain test which requires you to pee in a cup. Or maybe you're heaving those amazing bosoms more than usual. Giving the illusion of growth."

Shaking her head, she smacked him on the chest. "Very funny. Now can we please get rid of the idiots down there?"

"It's going to be cold bodies and no exceptions with you, isn't it? Fine. Yes, my tactic has successfully delayed you enough for them to get in the perfect positions for our attack."

She saw his balaclava stretch around his cheekbones, and she knew he was grinning fiendishly at her. He had probably dropped her a wink behind those infrared sunglasses. She swatted him again and he laughed as he turned and continued down the fire escape.

Selia paused on the bottom landing and studied the scene below them. There were two men in jeans and t-shirts with shoulder holsters at the car on their left. Ten more were to the right, which left eight people inside the warehouse. Pulling her M&P with her right hand, she cast a silencing spell onto the weapon. Aiming at the men on the left, a cold smile on her lips, Selia held a breath, squeezed the trigger, carefully lined up the next shot, and squeezed again. Both men slid down to the ground, minus an eye and a considerable amount of brain matter.

Raising the weapon, Selia nodded to herself, before dropping a stun grenade down over the edge. Wil had already vanished inside the building, which was a good thing, since she was more than happy to take care of the ones outside.

Hopping up on the edge of the rail, she counted to five. The grenade went off, and she dropped down in the center of the men. Pulling the batons, she bashed the weapons against the temples of the pair on each side of her. Their skulls gave in, and they dropped like lead weights. Turning, she brought the batons around under the neck of another, crushing his larynx, and brained another as she completed the turn. Sliding the batons into her pockets, she unsheathed her beloved swords and took two steps into the group. One had dirty blond stubble on his head, and the rest all had dark, slicked back hair.

Twirling the blades, she sliced another in the stomach with her left hand, as her right swept across the chest and neck of another. There were still four left, who scrambled, trying to pull their semi-automatics. Rolling her eyes, she walked over to the dirty blonde, and brought his head down onto her knee before bringing the pommel of her sword against his left temple.

The man collapsed.

She ducked and rolled, avoiding a poorly-aimed shot from one of the other remaining men. Rolling into a crouch, she dropped her left blade, pulled her M&P and placed a nearly point blank shot in the temple of her would-be attacker. With inhuman speed, she sprinted to the last thief. He managed to get one shot off at the start of her sprint- the bullet stuck in the protective armor she wore- which did not improve her mood. She grabbed him by the neck of his shirt, and promptly pummeled his face with one fist.

"Just kill him already," Wil said from behind her after she had delivered the twelfth blow.

Snorting, Selia dropped the unconscious body onto the ground. She turned to look for her blade, only to find Wil standing there with it. He was shaking his head and looking at the carnage around them.

"Awww, did you take out all the ones inside?" Selia teased him. "No more to pummel?"

"I'll go hire some people and have them meet us here, if that will make you happy," Wil retorted.

Selia laughed and crossed to him, taking her blade from him. "That's okay. I'm sure there will be plenty more opportunities later."

She tilted her head and held her hand out, palm down, over the bodies. A bright golden glow rose from the ground, reaching for her hand and filling the air. Brighter than a spot light, it illuminated the unconscious bodies and motionless corpses scattered about her.

"Do any of these look familiar to you?" she asked, twisting her mouth into a frown.

"I see two of Lucien's captains and at least four of his goons," Wil replied, studying the bodies.

"That's what I thought," Selia replied, tapping her foot in frustration. "What in the Hells is going on here?" Wil gave her a shrug and she released the spell. "Looks like I'll be visiting Lucien tonight, after all."

# Chapter Fourteen

L ucien's penthouse was at the top of one of the older buildings in the city. It was a gorgeous brick building with a circular covered entrance. The building had an old-world charm to it, or at least Selia thought it did. The architecture reminded her of Palladian style structures, with its symmetrical, temple-like construction.

Wil parked the small Bug two blocks from Lucien's apartment building. Dressed in all black with her shoulder holster in plain view, Selia drew a deep breath and cast her spell. Her usual earbud was nestled in her ear, and she smiled at her beloved.

"I don't like this," Wil muttered.

"It's not like I have a choice," she countered. "No one will pay attention to me. Nor will they be able to describe me or even remember me. Well, except for you." He snorted. Selia smacked him lightly on the head. "Not my fault my magic doesn't work on you."

"Sure it does," he retorted, a devilish grin on his face. He'd chosen a short black wig with a matching goatee to go with his t-shirt and jeans. Not exactly something that would stand out, which was the point.

Rolling her eyes, she gave him another brief kiss before hopping out of the car and walking the two blocks to Lucien's building. The bellhop nodded to her, opening the door before turning back to the street. She spotted no less than three of Lucien's men in the lobby. Sauntering over to a chair, she glanced at her watch with a frown before looking around, as though she were supposed to meet someone. Choosing a chair barely within sight of the penthouse elevator, she sat and picked up one of the magazines and began leafing through it.

About fifteen minutes passed and Selia was starting to wonder if she'd need to just pick the pockets of one of the men already in the lobby when the elevator door opened, and another of Lucien's men stepped into the lobby. Calling up a little more of her magic, she felt her necklace pulse beneath her blouse, and she added a touch of power to her spell.

Standing, since no one was even looking towards her, she moved towards the man who had just exited the elevator. Walking past him, she dipped her hand into his right pants pocket and removed the pass key he'd just dropped into it. Continuing on to the elevator, she allowed the magic to drop back to where it had been and swiped the keycard. The doors opened, and she stepped inside. Breathing a sigh of relief, she allowed herself to relax against the back wall of the elevator after pushing the button for the penthouse.

"So far so good," she breathed just barely above a whisper.

"You aren't in the penthouse yet," Wil's voice said in her ear.

She gave a non-committal murmur of agreement when she felt the elevator slow before stopping. "Ah, hell," she grumbled. "This should be interesting."

The door opened even as Wil asked what was going on. Two of Lucien's men stood with .45s pointed at her. Dressed in perfectly tailored dark blue suits with black ties and shining boots, she was tempted to ask where the sunglasses were.

"You're coming with us," the one on her right said. She stifled a snort, feeling more threatened by the amount of hair gel he used than his physical presence.

Selia raised her hands slowly, palms out. If needed, she could use a little magic to slip away from the pair, but she'd rather not do that if she could keep from it.

"That all depends," she said with a slow drawl. "Where are you taking me?"

The second guard frowned at her. "You'll go wherever the boss wants you to go." He bent to the side and spoke to his partner. "Call the boss and let him know we've got her."

Interesting, Selia mused. Perhaps Lucien knows more about Alfi's conspirator now, than he did two months ago.

Mr. Gelled-Hair pulled out a phone, his weapon never wavering. Selia gave him a few bonus points for that. He put the phone on speaker and dialed a number. "We've got her, boss." There was a pause and Selia could hear Lucien asking who it was. "I, uh… we don't recognize her. She's… uh… around five feet?"

The pair exchanged confused expressions and Selia smirked.

"Tell him it's Bella," she suggested, leaning forward only slightly.

"Bella? What kind of name is Bella?" The guard asked. His face contorted into an expression of complete confusion.

"Bella?" Lucien's voice came over the phone. "Bring her to me. Don't disarm her."

The pair looked at each other in surprise.

Mr. Gelled-Hair replied, "Uh, sure, boss."

Selia placed her hands on the metal rail at the back of the elevator, crossing her feet and giving them a very relaxed pose. "Well, you heard the boss."

The pair stepped into the elevator, as far from her as possible. The guard with the phone punched the button for the penthouse. Neither lowered their weapons. Selia leaned her head back against the wall and merely smiled. When the elevator doors opened, the pair motioned for her to exit first, by way of waving their guns at her. Shrugging, she pushed away from the wall and stepped into the foyer.

It definitely wasn't what she'd expected. Thick plush carpet that just begged to be walked on barefoot. Wooden paneled walls in shades of black, grays, and browns met her at every turn. The furniture was a combination of soft crushed velvet grays and blacks, while the tables and shelves were made from cherry, mahogany, or walnut wood. Bright paintings of landscapes broke up the dark monotony, as well as elegant antique lamps.

Lucien was sitting in a tall, antique chair that looked remarkably uncomfortable, with its hard cushioned back and seat. It was dark brown and had been reupholstered with equally dark gray fabric. Selia vaguely remembered seeing one with a distinctly fire engine red covering at one point, but she could have been wrong. She'd never been one for antiques, after all.

"Good evening. To what do I owe this pleasure?" Lucien asked, waving dismissively to the guards.

Selia glanced over her shoulders and suppressed a snicker at the glares coming from the pair of guards.

"But, boss-" the hair-gelled guard started to say.

He didn't get to finish his objection, because it was cut off abruptly by the discharge of a gun. Blood pooled and flowed from what remained of the bridge of the guard's nose. His eyes rolled back in his head, and he collapsed to the floor.

Selia's brows rose as she turned back to Lucien. He tucked away the same revolver she'd seen in Soren's office. "Impressive."

Lucien made a sweeping gesture with his fingertips. The remaining guard, as well as two others on guard at the sides of the room holstered their weapons and carried the dead guard from the room.

"We'll send up the cleaning crew when you're ready, boss," one of the other two guards said.

"Fine," Lucien said. The guards left, and Lucien waited until the elevator doors closed before speaking again. "You could have just called me, belladonna."

Selia dropped her magic, and crossed to the plush sofa, opposite Lucien. Dropping into it unceremoniously, she smiled. "Some things require a personal touch. I'm actually rather surprised you, or was it your people that were able to figure out what was going on? Either my magic is slipping, which I highly doubt, or you have some interesting safeguards in place."

"It's the latter," Lucien explained. "But it wasn't built with you in mind."

"Discovered Alfi's accomplice, did you?" Selia said, snuggling into the softness of the couch. Maybe she could coax Al into giving her something similar as a Christmas present.

"Nice, very nice," Lucien said, getting up and walking over to a panel. It flipped out revealing a full bar. "Care for a drink?"

"No thanks," Selia replied, with a smile.

"Refusing a drink shows a serious lack of trust," scolded Lucien. "Of course, so does attempting to break into a person's home." He waggled a finger at her. "Not the best way to begin your job as liaison."

"I said before that I don't drink. What makes you think that isn't true?" Selia countered, still smiling. "I'll get to the rest, after you answer that."

Lucien smiled as he poured himself a glass of what looked like scotch. "Nightshade has crashed every kind of party from a black market *bar mitzvah* to a rave. Does she just happen upon the loudest places in a city block? Are you saying you did no recon beforehand, ever? Wouldn't you be conspicuous as the only hot woman drinking a sparkling water?"

Laughing, Selia shook her head. "Yes, well, I prefer Shirley Temples when I'm out and about." She shrugged, trying to not giggle. "Is it so odd that a person doesn't like to drink anything alcoholic?" She couldn't exactly say she only drinks with a select few, now could she? "I'm actually here due to my 'new' job as liaison. No, that isn't quite right." Her voice dropped a few degrees as she continued. "I'm here to ask you what in the Hells is going on. You didn't request me to become your liaison out of the goodness of your heart."

"No, I didn't," Lucien retorted. "I did it for the reasons I stated and… because someone is trying to undermine my Family's power, and very likely, your Family's power as well. The intelligent adversary would try to make both

Families blame the other and squabble. Wasting resources and pointless revenge against each other. I want someone I can trust to work against such events occurring."

"Yes, because who else would work towards keeping the balance and not trying to topple one or the other," Selia said with not a little sarcasm. She leaned against the back of the sofa. "Have you looked inwards, in regard to this… problem?"

"I am working every angle, but I am, admittedly, too close to the problem."

Tapping her finger against the arm of the sofa, she tilted her head to the side.

"That brings me to why I'm here tonight, and why I didn't just call you. I'm certain that if you haven't already received the call, you will. Some of your captains, and their men, will be found either unconscious or dead… at least a dozen are dead, I believe." She bowed her head, even as she raised a hand against an argument from him. "Somehow I don't think you'll mind their demise, considering they were working with others and looting one of your warehouses."

His outrage was immediate and vicious. He swore fluidly in Italian, bringing a heavy fist down on the surface of the bar. Bottles and glasses rattled from the impact. It took him a full minute to collect himself. His face flushed a bright shade of red and she was certain she could see steam rising from his scalp. He looked at her, breathing heavily, fighting back the rage.

"I apologize, *mia belladonna*." He all but gasped. "It is as bad as I feared. You may wish to inform your other 'friend' that there will be shipments coming into the docks that are likely to be ambushed. Since I am not sure which of my men can be trusted, I must rely on… outside parties to intercede in everyone's best interests."

"Your apology, though not needed, is accepted, Lucien. I will pass the knowledge along, should I see him," Selia said. "I presume you have a method to ensure that I can contact you without having a repeat of tonight? Or previous occurrences?" She paused before adding with a sly smile. "Somehow I don't see Al allowing me to be a frequent visitor to your office, let alone any clandestine meetings, like before."

"I gave you a cell phone as a direct contact for me." He drained his glass, carefully and set it aside on the bar.

"Hopefully further… meetings won't become necessary," Selia replied.

"Until the moles and threats are bled out, we will have to work collectively for the benefit of everyone in our respective Families," he said as he began making a second drink.

"Well, while I'm here," Selia said with a nod. "I have a question about this whole liaison thing." She didn't bother waiting for permission. Instead, she plunged ahead. "What about when I am no longer an asset to the family; or I decide to distance myself, as much as is possible? Eventually, I will wish to start my own family. I highly doubt a mother would be welcomed by any member of the Family as a close, full-time employee."

"The position as liaison moves you further out of the day-to-day illegal trappings of the business and allows an exit strategy to begin for you, actually. You are supposed to remain impartial, the further you distance yourself from either Family, the better you should be able to do your job."

"The position is appreciated, as well as the opportunity it allows," Selia conceded. "I am curious as to why you're helping me obtain an exit strategy from my Family. I know why *I* would desire such, as well as why Papa would desire it. But why you?"

"Soren and I are not so different," Lucien admitted. "We want to provide our living by means that does not require the constant threat of police vigilance." Lucien smiled. "Real estate, politics, pharmaceutical companies… all are ways to amass vast fortunes while still retaining some semblance of legality."

"Would you be approaching me now, had I not come to you during the whole fiasco two months ago?" Selia asked, remembering a similar question Lucien had asked of her.

Waving dismissively, Lucien said, "I don't dwell on such thoughts and what-if's. A successful business person recognizes an opportunity and works towards making that happen to their advantage."

Selia nodded, reluctantly getting up from the sofa. She ran her fingers along the arm of the sofa one last time before flashing Lucien an innocent smile. "Should anything more occur, please do give me a call. Any insight or suspicions you may have, however slight, could be very beneficial to solving this problem."

"I'll keep you posted on any information I obtain." He handed her a Shirley Temple. "I trust you will do the same."

"Indeed I will," Selia replied with a smile, accepting the drink. She took a sip and gave a satisfying sound of pleasure. "Perhaps we can enjoy a drink together, and discuss the best way for me to exit without raising suspicions?"

# Chapter Fifteen

The next morning, Selia swept into Soren's office building, waving a greeting to the receptionist before stopping in front of the elevator. Her hand paused over the button before she clenched her fingers into a fist. Shaking her head slightly, she crossed to the door to the stairwell and pressed her thumb against the pad. The door clicked and she entered the stairs. There was a safety feature to unlock the stairs, should it detect smoke, carbon monoxide, or if any alarm went off; but otherwise, she and Soren were the only two who had access to the stairs without a key card from Soren.

Selia had chosen a flirty black skirt that swished with each step, a deep emerald blouse, with a black and silver chain belt. A pair of knee-high black boots and a lined leather jacket over her shoulder holster pulled the outfit together. Her intent was to make sure she was noticed for her feminine attributes and not much else. Especially the weapon she had concealed. Pausing on the top landing, she checked her outfit, made certain her jacket hid her holster, and opened the door.

Once off the elevator, she'd taken two steps into the small hallway to the left before hearing the distinct sound of a baton being snapped open. She ducked, bringing her hands together above her head, crossed at the wrists, barely having time to conjure a shield. The shield didn't completely form before the baton came down upon her left wrist and she snarled at the pain. There'd be a serious bruise there, but she didn't take the time to react to the discomfort.

Reaching up, she grabbed her assailant's wrist, bringing it down as she stood, her leg coming up in the same motion. The man gritted his teeth as the wrist broke. Selia caught the baton as it tumbled from his fingers. Turning, she brought the baton around and down with the full momentum of the weapon onto the back of the man's head. He collapsed to the floor. Kneeling, she dropped the baton to the floor next to the body and quickly searched the pockets of her attacker.

A cell phone, wallet, and curiously enough, a keycard were pulled from various pockets. She tucked them into her right jacket pocket and checked the fallen man's pulse.

Whoops. There *was* no pulse. Maybe she shouldn't have hit him so hard, Selia inwardly pondered. Her body count was growing, and too often it was growing without intent.

She opened the door to the stairwell and shoved the body onto the landing. Out of sight, out of mind. At least for the moment.

Turning and holding her aching wrist, she scurried through the office door and ignored Maria, who was saying something about Soren being in a meeting.

Opening the door, she barged into the office and let the door shut behind her. Soren's eyes narrowed and he frowned darkly.

"I… I'm sorry, Papa," she began, her voice breaking. She held her wrist up, turning it so Soren could see the black, purple, blue, and yellow bruise that was quickly forming.

"Selia, what in the name of all that is holy happened to you?" Soren demanded. His voice was barely below a roar as he jumped up from behind his desk.

"I was attacked," Selia said softly. "Good thing for those self-defense classes you made me take." Her smile wavered as she played the part of frightened victim.

Soren's jaw tightened as he came out from behind his desk. She moved forward towards him, meeting him halfway. He carefully grasped her arm and gently touched it. Selia hissed in pain, and Soren's frown deepened. He turned towards the man sitting across from his desk.

Selia glanced at the blonde-haired client. The man was frowning and had a concerned look on his handsome face. His features were not quite boyish, and his bright blue eyes narrowed as he watched her and Soren.

"Please ask my secretary to reschedule this meeting," Soren said dismissively.

"Of course," the man said, standing. Nodding to her and Soren, the man quickly left, leaving them alone.

Selia looked pointedly up at the ceiling, not knowing where the bug was kept. Dipping her hand into her pocket, she pulled out the contents from her pocket and handed them to Soren. She gave a wicked smile and made the universal sign of 'dead' by drawing a line across her throat with her right hand pointer finger before pointing to her wrist.

Soren sighed heavily and shook his head. "It's off. Where did this happen?"

"It was near the elevator, Papa. The body is currently in the stairwell." Selia replied, dropping the act. She grimaced as she turned her eyes back to her wrist. "This hurts like hell, too."

Pulling out his phone, Soren dialed a number. "Alex, you and Bernie come to my office. There's a body to dispose of from the stairwell. You still have the override keycard I gave you, yes?" There was a pause and Soren nodded his head. "Put Bernie in charge of it. I want you to follow us." Another pause. "Selia was attacked. Her wrist is injured, but she's otherwise okay. Once you two get here, I'll be taking her to get checked out and I'll inform Al."

Selia walked over and sat on the edge of Soren's desk as Soren dialed another number. "Do you really have to call him?" Soren turned around and raised a brow. She waved her right hand. "Ignore that question. Any way could you have someone bring an ice pack?"

"Call Alex and ask him," Soren retorted as he held his cell phone up to his ear.

Selia leaned over and turned Soren's office phone towards her and dialed Alex's number. "Hey, Alex! Yeah, I'm fine. My wrist hurts like hell, though. Could you bring an ice pack with you?"

"No problem, Lia," Alex replied before relaying the request to Bernie, who was apparently driving.

She couldn't resist teasing Bernie. "Oh and tell Bernie I could really use a teddy bear." Alex laughed and she heard Bernie asking a question followed by him swearing at Alex's reply. She giggled. "Tell Bernie I'm not serious, okay?"

"Sure thing, Lia," Alex replied with a laugh. "We'll take care of you."

"Thanks," Selia said before hanging up. She turned back to Soren, who was finishing up his own call. Once he'd hung up, she said, "Alex and Bernie are bringing an ice pack. We can just stay here until they arrive, right?" Soren chuckled and nodded. "So, how angry and paranoid is Al about this?"

"Oh, he's livid. But he isn't so paranoid that he thinks you or I arranged the attack to draw away suspicion. He knows me better, and he doesn't give you enough credit."

"Oh, good," Selia replied, almost cheerfully. "At least he isn't trying to blame Lucien, also." She rolled her eyes and tapped her wrist experimentally. "Well, I don't think it's broken, but it's definitely badly sprained."

"Not that I ever mind seeing you, dear, but why were you coming to my office?" Soren asked, walking back around to his chair.

"Oh, right," Selia said, hopping off the desk and sitting in the chair that had been vacated by the client. "I had a nice chat with Lucien last night." Soren's brows rose and she rolled her eyes. "Don't worry, Papa, no one saw me, other than Lucien. It seems he has a problem with his own people undermining his Family."

"Go on," Soren drawled, settling into his chair behind the desk.

"We caught at least two of Lucien's captains and several of his thugs cleaning out one of his warehouses. They were working with some other thugs we didn't recognize. I had a nice visit with Lucien afterwards and it seems that is why he strong-armed me into being liaison. He thinks someone is trying to tear down his Family, and figured we were having the same problems. Well, that and apparently to help me form an exit strategy."

Selia shifted in her seat. Her wrist was starting to throb in perfect time with her heart. Soren seemed to be waiting for her to finish talking.

"I came here to ask you about it. To ask if our Family is having the same problems or if it's just Lucien. I can contact him easily, without Al knowing about it, due to him sending me a phone under the radar."

"You want to know if we have traitors in our midst." Soren almost laughed. "My dear child, every successful business has them. People who are unwilling to bend to rules to get ahead, people who want someone to pay them for laziness and betrayal. If you are wondering if we have had an increase in the number of rats in the nest, then the answer is no." He looked levelly at Selia. "If we did, I would know it, and I would tell you. Our materials and businesses, aside from the seedier aspects that I do not approve of, are thriving and safe. We have not lost goods or men due to espionage or similar acts. At least, no more than usual."

"That's refreshing to hear," Selia replied. She shifted in the chair, trying to find a comfortable position for her wrist. "Whoever attacked me, Papa, knew I took the stairs, not the elevator as I normally do."

Soren didn't reply, but instead pulled the dead man's wallet out of his pocket and looked through it. He pulled out the ID, nodded, and held the picture out to her.

"Your attacker was Paulio. He was security for my floor. He's had that assignment for two weeks now, and it was at Al's insistence. I tried to tell the old man that Paulio was on the take, but he wouldn't listen to me." Soren walked over to his lamp, where Al had gotten someone to place a micro-transmitter and microphone bug. Soren spoke loudly at the bug beneath the lamp's shade. "Maybe Al will listen to me next time!"

Soren threw the wallet and ID onto his desk, disgust clear on his face.

"If Paulio knew where you were coming from, then he had someone on the ground floor inform him, either by cell phone or via the security earpieces that our guards all wear." Soren growled and picked up his office phone. He punched three numbers and when he spoke into the phone, his voice was hot and rough.

"Get me the security camera tapes for the lobby from the past hour." He barked at whomever had answered his call. "Also, I want the transcriptions from the security com center, delivered by the head of security, *now*."

"It won't take long to figure out where the other mole is," Soren reflected, pulling a silver case out of his pocket. He withdrew a single cigarette, lit it with a silver lighter from another pocket, and put both items away. He inhaled deeply and blew smoke through his nose.

"As I said, Selia," Soren continued. "There hasn't been an increase in treachery, but it does seem those prone to treachery have been put on your scent. Any guesses as to why?"

She shrugged, a tight smile on her lips. "Perhaps because I've been placed in a position where the Families are likely to form a truce? If a certain person who managed to survive the last failed coup is back, trying to cause havoc, I'd say that's reason enough to want me out of the picture."

"The necromancer is certainly one possibility, but not the only enemy. Nor is she the only person we have to deal with that has a high level of ambition." Soren sighed. "You have to ask yourself what the necromancer would gain by this. She also knows your abilities. Probably better than anyone, including me. Why would she send a lone person, who would have to be very lucky to gain the advantage, to capture or kill you?"

"I don't know," Selia replied honestly, shaking her head. "Perhaps it's whoever is causing trouble for Lucien? If the families talk more, and ally themselves, whoever is trying to undermine Lucien obviously would want me out of the picture. He used a baton, Papa. Not a gun or a knife. The intent was probably to injure me enough to put me in the hospital."

Oh, hell. She needed to inform Wil what had happened. He wasn't going to be too happy about the attack, either. With a sigh, she reached into her jacket and pulled out a phone. Her phone, the one she used for personal needs, was attached to her belt. She slid the slender phone across to Soren. It was a chance, and she prayed she wasn't making a mistake. This phone had been a gift to her.

"I need that back, but I think there's a number there that could possibly be of help." She followed Soren's gaze to the phone before meeting his gaze again. The name on the screen said "Sandy" and Selia gave her beloved father a tight smile and single nod.

# Chapter Sixteen

Sitting on the edge of the highest place on the dry-docked ship, Selia peered through her night vision binoculars. She'd cast a cloaking spell over her and Wil, in his Sandman disguise, as soon as they reached the docks. None of the night watchmen paid any attention to her or Wil, so she counted the spell a success. She had healed her wrist after visiting the doctor, who had proclaimed it wasn't broken. They were safely tucked away beneath her neoprene gloves, though Wil was watching her as though she'd broken it. Sweet, yes, but not needed. There had been time for her to rest from that exertion before this evening's activity.

"Bernie brought me a teddy bear, this one dressed up as Nightshade," Selia said, breaking the silence. She heard Wil snicker. "It was a joke! I didn't think Alex would really let him buy me one. Not that I can argue with his reasoning."

"What was that?" Wil asked, crouching down beside her. He, too, was searching for thieves and vagrants using a pair of night vision binoculars. "How did you keep from laughing?"

"He said that he'd rather see Bernie spend his money on a woman worthy of it," Selia replied, trying to match Alex's Italian accent and partially succeeding. Wil snickered again and she couldn't help but chuckle. "I didn't bother trying to hide it. I laughed and gave him a hug. I promised to keep it in whatever office Soren gives me, as protection from would-be attackers."

Wil laughed softly, shaking his head. "Nice."

"Well, it's not like I can tell him we designed them and put them on the market, now can I?" Selia asked, trying to sound offended and failing miserably.

Wil owned every copyright and trademark possible on both her alter ego and his. She'd made a joke about a teddy bear to cuddle instead of him, and it had snowballed into a pair of Nightshade and Sandman teddy bears, complete with plush weapons and utility belts. There was currently a pair of the toys in their bedroom at Wil's place. The toys had become a hit with kids and adults, and Selia had left her income from the toys to Wil. Somewhere she had a nice investment portfolio, courtesy of Wil's amazing talents and lawyers.

"Very true," Wil drawled out. He sat beside her. "The accomplice got away. Nothing at his house and no pings on his cards."

"Makes you wonder if Bennie didn't meet with a fatal fall, doesn't it?" Selia asked knowingly.

Wil turned his head at her in a sharp, sudden motion. "Speaking of 'fatal falls', Soren gave me a call today."

Selia ducked her head, grimacing a little. "He's not going to betray you. There's no way he could do anything without risking me or him. It's bad enough Lucien let Soren know that *he* is aware that I'm Nightshade."

"You're a powerful ally, and Lucien can use that knowledge as leverage against Soren," Wil stated, waving dismissively. "I don't mind Soren knowing. He can't tell who I am without involving you. Since he loves his little girl, he's not going to break her heart. He'll just wait for me to do that."

Selia rolled her eyes.

The balaclava stretched as Wil smiled beneath the fabric as he said, "I'm not sure if I'm glad you got me involved in this mess, though."

"Uh huh," Selia said, turning towards the opposite side of the docks.

"Yeah," Wil replied. "Soren wants me to ferret out whoever the mole is. That means I've got to become a made-man and work in the building." Selia stiffened and turned back to Wil, lowering the binoculars. Wil nodded. "That means, my lovely lady, you won't be able to flirt with me, or hit on me, or threaten to ravage me."

"You're going to make my life hell, aren't you?" Selia asked, the smile hidden by her scarf evident in her voice.

"Every chance I get," he replied mischievously, enunciating each word.

Selia turned back to the dockyard and the ships. Life was going to get even more interesting, it seemed. Not only that, but she'd soon find out just how good an actress she really was, because knowing Wil was going to be near her would only make her want him that much more. Maybe she'd get lucky and be too busy to think about her mate. Nah, she decided. Not likely. No matter what was going on, she always ended up thinking about him.

"I wish I had a better idea about what was going on with Lucien," Selia said, changing topics. "It's the only reason someone would want to scare me off."

"I don't think they are just trying to scare you," Wil retorted, nodding at her wrist.

Selia gave a half-shrug. "I can take care of myself. Otherwise, I wouldn't be here with you."

"Says the woman who I had to rescue… How many times has it been? Three? Four? More?" Wil asked.

"Yes, well…" Selia trailed off, saved from trying to wiggle her way out of that corner by spotting a group of black-clothed men moving towards a cargo ship. "Oh, lookie! Our playmates have finally decided to show up!"

There were a total of thirteen people on the dock; six workers, six henchmen, and a leader. Nightshade inspected the silencers that the Sandman had purchased for her M&P .45s while the Sandman checked the new toy he'd brought along: A fully automatic shotgun machine gun. The silencer for the weapon was almost as long as the gun's barrel and it had been built for him by the gunsmith he favored. The fifty round drum held non-lethal rounds; shotgun rounds that fired small beanbag-like projectiles. They would hurt, they would incapacitate, but unless someone fired several rounds into another person's head at point-blank range, there would be no killing with this weapon.

The Sandman nodded and chambered the first round into the shotgun machine gun. "See you down there. Remember, I will take out the dock workers. Then you can have all the fun you want."

It would take some time for him to get down there, encumbered by the oversized weapon. He made his way cautiously. Nightshade felt three full minutes pass before there was a rapid coughing rhythm. The sound was drowned out by the "thump thump thump" of the beanbags hitting flesh, sounding very close to a body being struck in the stomach repeatedly by a baseball bat. Workers cried out, groaned, and crumpled. The henchmen had their guns out, looking for a target at dock level. The leader had found cover behind some tall crates, and Nightshade could not see what he was doing.

Knowing she had her own part of the mission to do, Selia trusted her partner to go after the leader. Grabbing the rappelling rope they had tied to the main deck, Nightshade went over the side of the docked ship. Controlling her descent with one hand, she began picking off henchmen with the other, using one of the silenced .45s. Shots were fired by the remaining two before she could get to them, but the men had no idea where she was and had been firing blindly.

Just before she sighted in to finish them, the sound of the silenced shotgun came twice. There was a horrible, agonized scream. The two remaining henchmen turned towards the large crates, affording Nightshade a perfect view of the men's left-side temples. A beanbag round went into the side of each, and the men dropped lifelessly to the ground.

Running up to the crates, the Sandman had the shotgun out in front of him, aiming at something or someone. He fired once, and another scream was joined by the sound of something plastic breaking and bouncing along the paved hardtop of the dock. Nightshade hurried to where the Sandman was, pulling her other M&P and checking all around for further problems. She was back-to-back with him in under a minute. She glanced over her shoulder to see what was going on.

The leader was sniveling, lying on his side. One knee was bent at an odd angle. Both appeared swollen and useless within the man's overpriced trousers. The trousers also had a large wet spot in the crotch. He was in his early thirties, at least seventy pounds overweight, with dark hair that had receded to almost his crown. A scraggly widow's peak tried to prevent the man from looking ten years older, but it didn't work very well. He hadn't even attempted to unholster the large automatic that hung from his left shoulder. His right hand was a mess of broken fingers. The cell phone he had been trying to use lay in pieces over a stretch of ten yards.

"So, you kneecapped him with the beanbag rounds, and then shot the cell phone out of his hand?" Nightshade reasoned. "Nice shooting, Tex."

The Sandman grunted and spoke with a thick Irish accent. "Warned him he'd take the next two rounds in the face if he went for the gun, I did. I remember this guy from ten years ago. Got made at an early age and it just over-inflated his already gargantuan ego. Used to terrorize a lot of neighborhoods. Though all the girls wanted him. He is rather fond of his face." The Sandman pushed the end of the silencer against the man's cheek. There was a slight hissing as the man grimaced. "Aren't you, Jimmy-Boy? But he won't cry like a girl in front of a woman. It would ruin his image."

"I'm not impressed," snorted Nightshade, glad her scarf hid her amused smile. "You figure on getting information from him?" she asked the Sandman.

"Not going to talk, pretty lady," Jimmy said through gritted, smiling teeth.

"We're going to have company, and soon," the Sandman interjected. "He was calling reinforcements from the boat. I figure another ten to twenty seconds." He nodded at Jimmy. "After we're done here? Yeah, he's the one."

"Not happening," Jimmy said defiantly.

"You'll talk or I'll cut your best friend off, while you watch," Nightshade said pleasantly, looking around the boat for the back-up Jimmy had called for.

"I hope you brought a big saw, pretty lady," Jimmy replied, his confidence returning. "If you want a keep-sake, we could-"

Nightshade pistol-whipped Jimmy across his left shoulder. Something broke with an audible *snap*. Despite his best intentions to the contrary, Jimmy yelped, and tears streamed. He sobbed for a second before containing himself.

"I don't care if you've got a third arm for a dick." Nightshade continued in the same pleasant tone. "One swipe with my sword and it's gone for good. But you'll get to keep it. You'll die choking on it. If you talk, I'm sure there will be plenty of girls with low self-esteem to feel sorry for you and pay it attention. Or a gold digger or twelve, but I'm none of those."

"Fucking lesbians." Jimmy nearly spat. "Trying to be a guy. Makes sense."

Nightshade holstered her right hand gun, turned and promptly grabbed the Sandman's crotch. Her hand could not hold even half of the contents. She squeezed and looked at Jimmy. His expression was priceless.

"I don't need what you've got." She put just enough porn-star breathlessness in her voice to make sure she had his attention. "I've got plenty. Any time I want it."

"I hope you don't intend to want it while I'm holding this shotgun," the Sandman deadpanned. "I might accidentally shoot Jimmy in the face. Besides, we're about to be interrupted."

"Later, then, lover," she purred, letting go and pulling out her gun. There were ten more men coming from the boat, all heavily armed. None were wearing working-class clothing.

"I've got this," the Sandman proclaimed.

Stepping out from behind the crates, the Sandman emptied the fifty round drum, moving the weapon methodically left and right, pausing when the recoil pulled his aim too high. It took only a matter of seconds and sounded like bowling ball-sized hailstones were pounding into the men and the ship. Before the gun ran empty, all ten men were down, some moaning pitifully. He turned and walked out of the cloud of gun smoke he'd created. Nightshade could see where his body armor had taken a few hits. He didn't seem to notice that he had taken rounds. He crossed to her, leaning the shotgun against his right shoulder to free up his left arm. He used the free hand to grab her at the waist and pull her close.

"Don't take long to get what we need," the Sandman advised. "You got me all hot and bothered. I wanna take you to a cheap hotel and treat you like you're pretty."

Suppressing a laugh, Nightshade pressed against the Sandman and said, "You know what? I'd rather have that over anything he could give us."

Stepping away, Nightshade whipped out the sword near her right hand. She walked purposefully towards Jimmy, swinging the sword to get momentum for the strike.

"I'll talk! I'll talk! *I'll talk!*" Jimmy screamed.

# Chapter Seventeen

Selia followed Wil through the tunnels that had become extremely familiar over the past two months. The winding path led into the sub-basement, up a short flight of stairs, and into the basement of the Sandman's lair. It looked more like a man-cave or a family room, with a sofa, coffee table, and television. There were cabinets along the far left wall and a full-length bar against the wall behind the sofa, opposite the sub basement's stairs. A flight of stairs leading up into the true lair were against the far right wall. It had been the first room Selia had seen, and she knew the sofa was very comfortable.

The pair headed up the stairs to the first floor. There was an office, complete with a vanity that held every type of make-up and wig possible, along with several closets full of clothing of every type imaginable. William Brendan Fredricks, her beloved mate who was nothing short of a chameleon, had been taught by his grandmother on how to adopt any role and where to get the best props. His grandmother had been a legend in the theatrical scene and was still loved by many in the arts. Selia had seen a photograph of the woman in her heyday and had to admit she'd been a beauty. A more recent photograph, with a teenage Wil, showed the woman had aged with a magnificence few could possibly claim.

Selia followed Wil towards the office, and they began undressing. Though Selia didn't mind silence, there were too many questions to be left unspoken. Placing her green-tipped blonde wig on a foam head, she removed her swords and slid them into another set of sheathes. Those she placed on a pair of wooden stands.

"So, what do you make of what Jimmy-boy had to say?" she asked, walking to the closet and opening the door. Grabbing a wooden hanger, she hung the trench coat up as Wil began removing his own outfit.

"He says a capo called him and offered him a hefty sum to go lift Lucien's goods," Wil observed, pulling off his balaclava. "It makes sense. There used to be a lot of that kind of undercutting between the Families. Even within them. When you're the next to the lowest rung on the ladder, you probably figure the old ways might work better for you. At least in the short term." Wil pulled off his gloves and continued. "It doesn't tell us much as far as the scope of this whole goes. We don't know if it was one capo in his family or more, we don't know if it goes any higher than that. We'll need to investigate further."

Selia pulled off her blouse, followed by her Kevlar top before tugging off her boots. Wiggling out of her pants, she picked all her clothing up and turned to him.

"Nope, unfortunately it doesn't," Selia agreed. She shook her head as she moved towards the mannequin in the far corner of the room and began dressing it. If the outfits weren't kept on a form of some sort, they would lose their shape and become even more cumbersome to put on. "Maybe I can dig around some tomorrow and see what comes up. If nothing else, I can go visit some of Lucien's establishments as liaison and see who comes after me."

"Oh, yes," he replied sarcastically. "There's no concern of danger in doing that." He rolled his eyes. "You want to borrow the shotgun?"

He pointed to the arsenal wall, where the shotgun sat on its hooks.

Selia laughed. "If I go out in broad daylight, I can assure you I'll have a slew of my Family's people shadowing me." She finished dressing her mannequin and turned to Wil, who had begun doing the same to his mannequin. Leaning against the wall, she sighed. "You have a better idea? Want me to dress up as a blonde or redhead and snoop around Lucien's office?"

"No," he said with a sigh. "I just wish there was some way I could go with you, other than as one of your many boyfriends. You know, to watch your back."

"If you would start the job as a made-man in the Family," Selia drawled out slowly. "Soren would certainly put you on guard duty. Or, as his beloved daughter, I could tell you to join me."

"Yeah, I suppose that idea does make a great deal of sense. I just need to figure out…" He trailed off smiling. "Yeah, I think I'll talk to Soren about that tomorrow."

Selia gave Wil a sidelong curious gaze. "I'm almost afraid to ask what you have planned."

"You'll find out soon enough," he teased.

"Oh? I can't… coax it out of you?" She purred, pushing away from the wall and slinking towards him, one foot carefully placed in front of the other.

Reaching up, she began pulling the pins from her hair, letting the strands fall down in curly, messy waves. Running the tips of her fingers along his jawline, then down his chest, her hand paused at the waistband of his boxers. Her lips curved upward into a seductive smile as she ran her fingers from one side of the waistband to the other.

"You can coax a lot out of me. But you're not going to get my little surprise until I'm ready."

Selia pouted and gave a put upon sigh. "Well, I suppose I'll just go take a shower, then." She turned and began to walk away, a smile on her lips.

"Awww, you don't want company?"

"I didn't say *that*," Selia retorted, glancing over her shoulder, her eyes sparkling with mischief.

"Good." He removed his boxers. "I'll join you then."

# Chapter Eighteen

The theme to *Jaws* began playing, and Selia rubbed her eyes as she reached for her phone.

"Couldn't you call at a decent hour, Uncle Al?" Selia asked, sleepily, answering her phone.

"You kids don't appreciate 'early to bed, early to rise'," Al countered. "Now quit complaining and get to work. You're needed in the office."

Wil looked over and rolled his eyes. He smiled slowly and ran a finger down her spine. Selia inhaled sharply.

"Papa said I wasn't supposed to start for two weeks," she said, looking over her shoulder at Wil.

"On a regular basis, that's true. However, your position needs to be engaged now. Get it taken care of, and you can go back to sleeping late for a little while."

Wil's hands slid around, and she smothered a moan as they began exploring other, more sensitive parts. She was so going to find a way to get even with her mate. Somehow.

"*Which* position are we discussing?" Selia asked, trying to keep her mind on the conversation, which was becoming more and more difficult.

"The position of liaison between the families," Al replied, and Selia could hear the growing annoyance in his voice. "Do I need to send the brothers to chaperone you?"

"No, no, that's quite all right," Selia replied quickly. "I'll be at the office shortly." There was no way she was going to tell Al she wasn't at her apartment. "How long do I have to get there?"

"I expect you within an hour."

Selia glowered at the phone. "As you wish, Uncle." She didn't bother hiding her annoyance and hung up the phone. She rolled over, dropping the phone back on the nightstand. "So much for having fun."

"How long do you have?" Wil asked.

"I'm supposed to be at the office in an hour, to take up my position as liaison." Selia rolled her eyes and glanced at the clock. It wasn't quite eight o'clock yet. "And here I was hoping to enjoy another week of laziness."

"I guess we'd better get going then," Wil said, giving her a quick kiss.

"Guess so," Selia said with a sigh, before rolling out of the bed.

Thirty minutes later, Selia walked into Soren's office building and headed into the elevator. She had left twenty minutes before him, so that they wouldn't look as though they were coming in together. No need to raise even more suspicions or jeopardize his new job.

She'd chosen a simple, short black leather skirt and snug teal blouse. A short black business jacket was buttoned at her waist hiding her M&P, which was now her constant companion. Since Wil was going to be working for Soren, she only needed the bare minimum of accouterments.

Maria looked up as Selia walked into the office. Surprised, she waved Selia on into Soren's office, not pausing as she clicked around on her computer. Selia guessed she was talking to a client and continued into Soren's office. For once, no one else was there and she gave her father a bright smile.

"Good morning, Papa," she said, dropping into the chair opposite his desk. "Do you need to call Al and tell him I arrived with thirty minutes to spare?"

"I'm glad you did, since it's his office you have to report to, not mine," he replied in a dour tone.

"What?" Selia asked, not quite shrieking. "He said I was supposed to report to the office for the job as liaison. Why in the Hells would it be with him?"

"Because you're not really reporting for work," he grumbled. "He has slightly different plans that mirror the duties of your job, but do not include them."

"I'm not going to like this, am I?" she asked, trying to not clench her hands into fists. She looked pointedly at where the bug was positioned.

"It's off for now. He doesn't know I'm in my office."

"Can you tell me what it is he wants of me?" she asked cautiously.

"I intend to tell you, since it will give you time to calm down and not do something exceedingly rash. Or, at least, only do it in my office." Selia nodded and he continued. "He plans to use you as bait, under the guise of doing your job as liaison."

Selia frowned, clenching and unclenching her hands a few times. The desire to burn something or kill someone was exceedingly strong, but she kept it contained. Barely.

"He wants to use me as bait? Two months ago, he wanted to keep me safely tucked away where no one could find me. Have I suddenly become 'disposable' to him? Or has he finally snapped?"

Soren eyed her warily. "It's due to you showing how tough you are lately. He figures you can handle yourself in a minor risk situation with an escort."

She muttered a curse. "The attack. He knows I took out my attacker. Son of a…" She sighed. "So who gets to choose my 'escort'?"

"Fortunately, me," Soren replied.

"Thank the gods," Selia said with a relieved sigh. "I might have been able to trust Alex, but I prefer a certain other… person. Who happens to already know all my dirty little secrets."

"Funny you should mention him. He thought you might be comfortable with a familiar face." He paused for effect. "Smarmy little bastard thought *I* would appreciate a familiar face, also. He'll join us soon."

"As long as I'm not late getting to Al's office," Selia grumbled. "Are you going with me to the meeting?"

"No, I'm not supposed to be here. I was only called as a courtesy." Soren ground his teeth. "He let me know what his plans were so I would be aware. I didn't have a say in them."

"I'm going to have to tread very carefully, aren't I?" Selia said slowly.

"Yes," was his only reply.

There was a knock at the door.

"Come," Soren called out for whoever was at the door.

The last person in the world that Selia expected to see, came in. He was dressed in a very dapper dark blue suit with no tie. His hair was a floppy but well-coiffed strawberry blonde. Freckles adorned his smooth cheeks and his full, but not over-sized lips, broke into a boyish grin.

"Well, hi-ya, Miss Selia. Long time, no see! How've you been?" he asked as he shut the door.

Selia just stared at her beloved. It took a few minutes for her to be able to speak.

"You were the doorman!" She squeaked. If it hadn't been for the very literal magic that let her sense him, the magic that had bound them together as mates, she'd have never believed it was Wil. "Billy... you were Billy?" Disbelief rang in the air, and she turned back, wide-eyed to stare at Soren. "He worked here! For... not that long! How... when..." She turned back to Wil and just stared at him, slack-jawed.

"Quite a surprise, isn't it?" Soren commented in a droll tone. "I didn't even realize it was anyone but Billy until I tried to tell him we had no positions within the Family, and he said-"

"Gee whiz, Mr. L," Wil interrupted, using the 'boy next door' voice of Billy the former doorman. "That's a shame. I hope Selia isn't too upset that you're turning me aside, what with us sleeping together and all!"

"I almost shot him," groused Soren.

"You almost got to your gun, is what you mean," Wil corrected.

Soren's expression soured further. "Yes, I went for my gun and your darling here, whipped out one of his batons and pinned one of my hands inside my coat, before I realized I'd been duped."

Selia tried to not smile as she looked at Wil. "What happened then?"

Wil spoke as the Sandman. "I told him, I put him in a hospital once as a sign of mercy and peace. I'd hate to put him back for over-reacting."

"So I hired him on the spot," Soren cheerfully proclaimed. "He's now a low-level made-man and your bodyguard… ummm… your assistant."

Selia chuckled softly. "Wonderful! He can come with me to Al's office!" She smiled slyly. "I promise to not break him."

"At least one of us does," Soren retorted.

Standing, Selia slid her hands down her outfit, making certain the jacket fell into place. "Come on… Billy. If I'm late, Al will have a fit."

"Yes, ma'am!" Wil replied in Billy's exaggerated, excited voice. At Soren's irritated groan, Wil looked between the two of them and explained "I can't change this character's voice or mannerisms much. It would be suspicious, and the whole point of 'Billy' was to be too ridiculous to be considered a threat at first impression."

"I hope there is another… character, in that mind of yours, that I don't want to kill on sight." observed Soren.

Instead of answering, "Billy" smiled while opening the door for Selia.

# Chapter Nineteen

Selia ignored the beauty of Al's office and headed straight for the elevator with Billy at her side. Knowing what Al was planning helped her anger but having Wil in disguise at her side helped even more. The fact that Wil had fooled everyone with his doorman-disguise for weeks made her proud and honored to have him as her man.

She punched the button for Al's floor and leaned against the wall of the elevator. Glancing at 'Billy' from the corner of her eyes, she smiled.

"What's the beautiful smile for?" Wil asked.

"I'm actually enjoying myself," Selia replied, barely remembering in time to stay 'in character'. "I'm glad you're my bodyguard."

"I'm pleased that I didn't have to argue with Soren about it," Wil replied.

"So am I," Selia agreed. She glanced away from him and at the buttons as they lit up. They were nearing Al's floor. "Don't be surprised if you're told to wait in the outer office. Al won't harm me."

Angelo wasn't that foolish. At least not yet. Plus, she was never completely 'unarmed'. Magic wasn't something a person could simply stop. It would be like trying to stop a heart from beating without killing a person. It was impossible. Selia wasn't stupid. She knew that if Al believed she was a threat, or believed Soren was a threat, he would move against them. It was why she had adopted the persona of Nightshade and why she walked on eggshells around the godfather of her Family.

She hoped that he never became dumb enough to move against her or Soren. If that happened, there were only three true options: Run, die, or kill.

"I'm expecting to, actually." Wil shrugged. "It suits me fine. I intend to plant a few bugs while I'm waiting."

Selia laughed. "Somehow, that doesn't surprise me." She leaned over and kissed his cheek. As she moved away from him, the elevator chimed, and she smiled. "Top floor, everyone out!"

Leading the way into Angelo's office, she paused at Sandy's desk, then glanced at the clock on the wall and grinned. "Ten minutes to spare! I'm improving."

Sandy laughed as she buzzed Al's intercom and said, "Sir, your niece is here."

There was a long pause, long enough for Sandy to look at Selia as if to say "I don't know what's taking him so long."

Finally, the intercom clicked, and Al's voice said, "Send her in."

"Shall I send in her guard as well?" Sand asked brightly, but Selia saw the impish gleam in her eye.

"No, just her," Al replied.

"Suits me fine," Sandy said, giving an appraising glance over to Wil. "What's the hunk's name?" She asked Selia.

"Billy," Selia said impishly. "No distracting my bodyguard." She glanced at Billy, a sly smile on her lips. "At least, not while he's on duty. After work... well..." She dropped a wink and chuckled.

"I can be perfectly professional in my distracting," Sandy offered a little louder than needed.

Giving a brief wave to Sandy, Selia turned and walked into Al's office, shutting the door behind her. Wil was so going to pay her back for that, but she hadn't been able to resist. Trying to stifle her giggles, Selia turned to face Al. Though she managed to keep from laughing at Sandy's teasing, she couldn't remove the smile from her face. She crossed to the chairs in front of Al's desk.

"You wished to see me, Uncle?" She asked.

Al would tell her if she was to address him formally or not. He always had in the past. Plus, she was enjoying reminding him that she was truly Soren's daughter, even if it wasn't a blood connection.

"Have a seat," Al instructed.

Selia took a seat in the chair to her right and studied him. "You said this is about my job as liaison," she began. "You have a message or something that I need to take to the Vaschetti Family?"

"I've been talking with the other heads of the five families. Specifically Anthony Carenzo, Carmine Pavanello, and Vincent Scarlatti." Al began. "I have approached them about you being the liaison between all the families. They have agreed to give it a go."

He swelled with pride and smiled at her.

Selia could feel the blood draining from her face and she swallowed hard. This was not what she wanted to hear.

"I, um..." She drew a deep breath and let it out slowly. "When and where am I to meet them?"

She wasn't just any bait: She was shark bait. Now she knew what that goat felt like before the t-rex came and chomped down on it.

"The details are up to you." He casually tossed a small note pad across his desk. "Here is their contact information. I am trusting in you to open communications and for things to go smoothly."

Selia leaned forward and took the notepad, not caring if her jacket revealed she was armed or not. Well, at least she had something that might help with Lucien's problem. She raised her eyes to Angelo. He wasn't worthy of being called 'uncle', she decided. Anyone who cared so little about her well-being didn't deserve to be considered family.

"Is there anything else?" She asked. She winced inwardly at the sharpness of her tone, but she refused to apologize for it.

"I expect a progress report every Friday. Made to me, not Soren." He gestured to his main office door. "You can schedule a time with Sandy."

Selia tore off the paper with the contact information and tossed the pad back to him. Standing, she folded the paper and tucked it into an inner pocket of her jacket.

"As you wish," she replied. "See you next Friday."

Turning, she strode out, not bothering with waiting for a dismissal. Closing the door behind her, she hissed a curse in Temerian under her breath before heading to Sandy's desk.

"I need an appointment to see Al next Friday. Make it as late in the day as possible," she told Sandy, a malevolent gleam in her eyes. Trying to sound cheerful, she asked, "So, did you two stay out of trouble?"

"She has been very engaging," Wil replied in his best "Billy" voice. He was wide-eyed and nearly hopping with energy.

"This one is such a treat," Sandy said with a sly look at Wil. "You let me know if you ever get tired of him, Selia."

"That might take a while," Selia said with a laugh. "He's a lot of fun." She gave a put-upon sigh. "Not that I could get away with dating him. You know how Papa is with me and anyone in the Family."

"Oh, I can imagine so," Sandy replied. Her eyes narrowed at Wil and Selia could see the woman shifting her legs. "Too bad for you."

"That's okay," Selia said with a sly smile. "I've got more than my hands full with my lover."

"Is it that hot British guy? The rocker?" Sandy said dreamily, still undressing Wil with her eyes. "He's a catch, too. But hey, whatever keeps your nights full."

"Why do you think I was groaning over Al's call this morning?" Selia joked. "It's as though he's gotta interrupt any fun I want to have." She rolled her eyes and tilted her head at 'Billy' before asking, "So, what times do I have to choose from for next Friday?"

"Well, look who we're talking about," Sandy replied as she finally tore her eyes away from 'Billy' and pulled up Al's calendar. "There's a two thirty and four forty-five opening."

"Put me in the four forty-five slot," Selia replied smugly. "He can wait until the end of the day for his report." Sandy chuckled as she began typing in the information. Selia grinned as she said, "See you next week, Sandy."

Sandy looked up and sighed. "You bringing him with you?"

"Probably."

Sandy smiled and shifted in her chair. "I'll be looking forward to it."

*I'm sure you are*, Selia thought, trying to not laugh. "See you later." She turned to 'Billy'. "Come on, I want to see if Papa is at his office. If he is, I plan on seeing him.

Otherwise, we'll be going home… errr… that is, to Papa's home."

She could hear Sandy giggling as the elevator doors opened and they stepped into it. Giving Al's secretary a wave as the door closed, Selia sank against the wall and pulled out the slip of paper. She handed it to Wil.

"I'm not just any bait, I'm shark bait," she said with grim humor. "I don't know if I should be *flattered* by Al's confidence or want to *flatten* him. As it is, I've got to call Lucien and inform him of Angelo's wonderful new idea."

"It might go over well, but I wouldn't count on it." Wil consented. "It seems to me, Al is treating you like a new guy in the office. Someone who has to prove their worth."

Selia turned her head to look at Wil. "You say that after Papa... wait... did Papa tell you Al was planning on using me for bait?"

"I have a listening device planted on your clothing," he admitted. "Heard the whole conversation."

"Good thing I love you, darlin'," Selia drawled. She sighed and shook her head. "It doesn't matter if I'm bait or if I'm supposed to prove my worth. This throws me right into the middle of the problem and definitely gives me... us... the opportunity we need." She tipped her head back and stared up at the ceiling of the elevator. "We're taking a detour on the way to Papa's office, though."

# Chapter Twenty

The trip to Soren's office was uneventful, aside from the quick side-trip to pick up the heavy bag that Wil was now carrying. Maria, on the phone as usual, waved Selia and her bodyguard through to Soren's office. 'Billy' opened the door for Selia, and she smiled her thanks to him.

"That was an interesting… meeting, Papa," Selia said after Wil shut the door behind him. She crossed the distance to Soren, who met her at the edge of his desk. Kissing his cheek, she gave him a hug before taking the seat he offered. "I behaved… unless you include the side-trip back to McLeary's where I placed an order for myself."

Soren hitched a hip onto the edge of his desk. "Not a bad idea. I should place an order myself. What do you think of his 'proposal'? Do you think you can handle it?"

"Being liaison between all the families? It'll be interesting, to say the least, but nothing I can't handle." Selia smiled impishly. "They'll never know what hit them. Figuratively, of course."

Soren laughed until tears were streaming down his face. "Good to know they haven't intimidated you yet, my dear. What's your plan?"

Selia shifted in the chair. "I plan on getting an office, stashing away the booze I just ordered, and getting settled here. Al was generous enough to give me the contact information to all the godfathers, along with the demand to report to him, not you, every Friday." She rolled her eyes as she added, "As though I'm not going to tell you everything, anyway."

"He doesn't think that far in regard to most people, especially you," Soren replied.

"Why am I so special? Or should I be thankful for his foolishness?"

"You've made yourself a bit of a problem. You act too much like a male for Al's satisfaction. Being able to handle yourself without his help has you on his 'bad' list." Soren explained. "Or at least on his shit list."

"Let's face it, Papa. I became a 'problem' when he first suspected me of being Nightshade," Selia countered. "That's when I stopped being just another pretty face and became something that could unseat him."

"Not that you ever would unseat him…" Soren trailed off, peering at her closely. "Or am I wrong about that?"

Selia raised her gaze to meet his. She'd never lie to Soren. At least not consciously.

"Only if he threatened the people I love," Selia said softly, though her tone was firm and honest. "If he came after you, my beloved, or even me, I wouldn't have a problem reminding him of exactly who and what he is up against. I don't need an army, like he does."

"No, just me and my armory," Wil interjected sarcastically.

Selia snickered and turned slightly in her chair to face Wil. "Hey, Al doesn't have the same security measures that Lucien does." She waggled a finger at him. "We both know that I could take out that paranoid nutcase with ease if I had to."

"Do you hear anyone in the room debating you," Wil retorted. "Because I haven't heard anything to the contrary in this room. I just hope you don't think you can take out everyone with ease."

"My god, are you two just going to get married or what?" Soren bellowed.

"He hasn't asked," Selia retorted, giving Wil a smirk before turning back to her father.

"Well I wish you would get on with it," Soren nearly roared.

Wil shrugged. "Gee, I hadn't really thought about it. But if you're going to push me, I guess I'll just have to start, won't I?"

Selia stiffened in the chair, and she narrowed her eyes at her father. "It isn't like we have to get married any time soon, is it? It's not like I want to be forced into a marriage." Not that she'd allow it. "I don't want him to ask simply because you demand it."

"Oh, it's all in good fun," Wil assured her.

Soren sighed. "I swear you're all raising my blood pressure."

"Send the bill to Al," Selia quipped. "Now, what about that office?"

Soren actually had an office ready for her. It wasn't exactly a corner office, but it still had a nice view. The office also happened to be at the end of the central hallway where the rest of the offices on the first floor were located. She didn't know who it had belonged to previously, and she didn't want to know.

About half the size of Soren's, the office was still larger than most of the others in the building. A large mahogany desk that gleamed in the light sat in the center with a very plush executive chair behind it. A banker's lamp sat on what would be her right side and a monitor, keyboard, mouse, and docking station for a shiny new laptop sat on the other. A multi-line phone universal to almost every office sat to the left of the docking station. It seemed she was getting a very nice collection of laptops. Across from her chair was a pair of plush and very comfortable-looking chairs.

Behind the desk were wall-to-wall windows with venetian blinds and thick, heavy red curtains that were currently shut, giving the room a somewhat romantic lighting. Cabinets lined the wall nearest the lamp and a small wooden shelf, complete with doors that locked, were against the other wall.

Her nice selection of high-label gin, rum, tequila, scotch, and bourbon were currently tucked away out of sight behind the locked doors of the shelf. She'd never been much for vodka but had a small bottle for anyone who wanted it. A sterling silver ice bucket and martini glass set, along with tumblers and snifters, however, had been set out on the shelf. The Nightshade teddy bear Bernie had given her, was currently sitting opposite of the glasses.

"I really need to get out and have some fun," Selia declared, after an hour of exploring her new office. "I want to buy a few things to decorate my new office. Maybe get a poster of *Swimming with Sharks*?"

"To remind you of what you're up against?" Wil guessed. Selia nodded. "I think it would be a nice touch."

"Wonderful! I'll buzz Papa and let him know I'm leaving for the day and to not worry about me." She leaned over and dialed Soren's extension. He answered on the first ring. "Hey, Papa, I'm leaving since I really don't have anything to do at the moment and need to burn off some energy."

"Well, how do you like the office?" Soren asked.

"I love it! I think I might actually enjoy working in an office," she teased.

"I have one question." Soren continued. "What kind of couch would you like?"

Selia blushed and kept her gaze on her keyboard. "Um, Lucien has a couch that is so soft and comfy. I would love to have one like it."

Soren chuckled. "I know the one. I'll have it delivered today."

"Thank you, Papa!" Selia exclaimed. "What time do I need to be in tomorrow?"

"Make it eleven o'clock. Sleep in a little bit," Soren replied, and Selia could hear the smile in his voice.

"Thanks, Papa," she said, grinning. "I'll see you tomorrow!" Soren bid a farewell and she hung up. Turning to Wil, she grinned. "So? Feel like some shopping?"

# Chapter Twenty One

Two hours and twice that many stores later, Selia and Wil made their way back from her car. They'd just finished dropping off another couple bags and were trying to decide where to go for lunch. It wasn't often they got to enjoy a quiet day out together. Not wanting to be annoyed by members of her family, Lucien's, or anyone else, she and Wil agreed on Salvatore's.

Salvatore's was a small, independently owned Italian restaurant. The owners spoke fluent Italian and made fresh-baked bread daily. Choosing a small booth, they sat and chatted quietly about the day's events while they waited for the waitress.

A man approached their table, but he wasn't a member of the restaurant's staff. Vincent 'Vinny' Scarlatti wore a charcoal gray Armani three-piece suit and immaculate Italian leather shoes. He was just under five and a half feet tall, sparse, with an expensive hair cut meant to accentuate his features. Unfortunately, the suit and hair style did more to accentuate his thin over-tanned rat-like appearance.

Wil shifted subtly in his seat. Selia withheld the urge to do the same as Wil, which was preparing for battle in close quarters. Vinny smiled as he noticed they were both looking at him and held out his hands in a friendly gesture.

"How you two doing?" he asked in a thick Italian accent. "You know my club on the Upper West Side, the Ice Room? I would like to have the pleasure of your company tonight. Just tell the guys at the front your name and they'll let you in to the VIP area, no charge."

Selia glanced at Wil before turning her attention back to Vinny. "To what do I owe the honor of such an invitation?"

"The chance for us all to get to know each other better, before official meetings and politics get in the way," Vinny replied, his cheerful voice never wavering.

"Can I bring a boyfriend, or should I bring the muscle?" she asked, nodding towards Wil. "Or should I bring both?"

"Bring whoever you want," Vinny said, spreading his arms wider and shrugging. "You'll be coming under a banner of truce and peace. Nobody will search you at the front door."

"That's very generous. I appreciate it and would enjoy the opportunity," Selia replied smoothly, lifting her chin a fraction.

It could prove to be an interesting fishing trip for her and Wil, after all. Plus, if anything happened, there would be two Families gunning for the bastard. If he survived, that is.

"Great! I'll see you tonight, say eight o'clock?" Vinny asked.

"Sounds wonderful," Selia replied with a smile. "I presume my date won't have a problem, either?"

"Not at all," Vinny said and then turned, and promptly left.

Selia watched until the door closed behind him. Dropping her voice to just above a whisper, she said, "Well, things just keep getting better and better, don't they?"

"What do you say we not worry about it and enjoy our lunch?" Wil suggested.

"Lunch, and then home," Selia agreed. "Though, I suppose I should make a couple phone calls first."

"Go ahead and make them," Wil suggested. "I already know what you'll want to order off the menu."

"Sounds like a plan," she replied, pulling out the cell Lucien gave her and dialing the number to his office. Three bars of music later, Lucien answered. She beat him to a greeting, though, and said, "Such a pleasure to hear a friendly voice."

"What's happened?" Lucien demanded.

Selia snorted. "What hasn't happened, you mean. I presume you already know of the, ah, run-in I had at Papa's office. Are you aware that I'm now to become liaison to *all* the families?"

"What?" Lucien hissed. "What idiot put that into play?"

"Guess," Selia drawled. "You should get it on the first one."

"Is it Angelo Lascari?" Lucien spat. "He's the only one with enough power and so little brains to come up with it." There was a pause. "No, it's not lack of brains. It's a complete lack of concern for your well-being."

Selia smiled. "See, I knew there was a reason I liked you. I might not like your methods all the time, but I can definitely respect them, and you have yet to try to play me for a fool."

"I have respect for you. Even before you decided on a wild nightlife, I respected you, belladonna. Has the idiot bothered to ask anyone besides you, concerning this large hook he wants to hang you on?"

"Papa wasn't informed, and I wasn't given an option. He did contact the other three dons, and Vinny has already extended a personal invitation to a meet and greet at his Ice Room," Selia replied.

There was a long wait before Lucien answered. "I ought to carve out that senile old bastard's heart."

Selia snickered. She couldn't help it since she'd had a similar thought, only it had been towards Lucien at the time.

"I ought to put that smarmy horn-dog's balls into a wine press," Lucien continued, causing Selia to snicker even more. "Belladonna, you need to proceed with more caution than you ever have in your life. Even your… nocturnal activities haven't prepared you for this."

Selia's amusement ebbed. "I think that needs to be explained in a bit more detail. Believe me, I'm fully aware I've been thrown to the sharks, but what you just said makes it seem even worse than that."

"Every gesture from anyone in the Families is suspect," explained Lucien. "This isn't something you can forget. The inability to trust anyone is going to weigh heavily on your shoulders."

"So should I take bodyguards with me, despite his declaration that I'll be arriving at his place under, and I quote, 'a banner of truce and peace'?" she asked with a heavy sigh.

"No," Lucien replied. "Take your boyfriend with you. That should be enough. I don't believe anyone will be stupid enough to make a direct, blatant, physical attack on you."

"Great," Selia groaned. "I'll just have to hope no one slips a Mickey into my drink." She shook her head, hating where things were heading. "I thought this was supposed to distance me from the Families, Lucien. It feels as though I'm being pulled further into them."

"If you can weather through this, it would actually work out that way." Lucien sighed. "I would have suggested something akin to what Al's thrust upon you after a year or two of liaison work just between our respective families."

Selia stared across the table at Wil. "So far, there have been a handful of people who I've found I can trust. Care to guess who has just been added to that very small list?"

"Good to know I've got your trust," Lucien said. "I'll do my best to remain worthy of it."

"So far, you're doing a hell of a lot more than Al is," Selia admitted. She chuckled. "Do me one favor?" There was a non-verbal sound and she continued. "Let me know if you plan on keeping those threats. I might want to watch."

"You got it." Lucien replied, and Selia could hear a smile in his words. "*Caio.*"

The call ended and Selia sighed. Turning in the booth, she leaned against the wall and stretched out on the seat and dialed Soren's number as the waitress showed up.

Instead of English or Italian, she spoke in Temerian. "Hey, Papa. I have some good news and some bad news. Which do you want first?"

"Bad news, as always," Soren said with a sigh, also in Temerian.

"Better fix up a stiff drink," Selia said, continuing in her native tongue. "I just got extended a personal invitation to do a meet-and-greet at Vinny's club, the Ice Room. Supposedly under a banner of truce and peace. I'm to show up at eight tonight, and I'm taking my boyfriend."

"That's more than a little suspicious," Soren observed. "But you already knew that. As long as you have 'Billy' with you, I'll only worry a little bit."

"Lucien wasn't too thrilled about it, either. In fact, he's a bit furious with Al about making me liaison between all the families. No, he's not going to do anything, despite the desire." Selia smiled as the waitress brought their drinks. Thankfully, it wasn't unusual for other languages to be spoken in New Campania. She took a sip of her sweet tea and gave Wil a grateful look. "Busting heads is a lot less stressful, you know that, right?"

"You're the only person I know who would like to retire from a criminal syndicate to pursue vigilante justice." There was a snort over the phone. "At least you can make a living in the syndicate."

Selia laughed softly and changed back to speaking in English since Wil had finished placing their order.

"I love you, Papa. I'll get through this, and everyone will be in one piece. Well, except for the traitors. They'll just wish they were in one piece. If they survive."

"That's my girl. Take care and try to enjoy your lunch."

"I am going to enjoy lunch, and then hide in my apartment with my beau until the appointed time. Even then, I'm going to come back home in time to relax."

# Chapter Twenty-Two

By the time Selia and Wil arrived at the club, there was already a line forming outside the Ice Room. Wrapped up in a thigh-length trench coat and knee-high stiletto boots, she was thankful they hadn't had far to walk. She loved the winter, but even after a decade of living in the city, the cold air still chilled her to the bone. Snow and ice was gorgeous to look at and fun to play in, but it was hell for driving. The slush when the snow and ice melted was horrible, and she ended up freezing more often than not. It probably had something to do with living on a South Atlantic island that rarely got colder than the mid- to low-fifties

Wil wore a black polo shirt under his light gray Italian suit. His face had neatly trimmed stubble that wasn't quite a beard, and his parted hair was a medium length iron gray mixed with dark roots. It was also immaculate. His persona for the outing would be that of Dorian Porter.

He was packing his other favorite handgun, the Walther PPQ, in a shoulder rig. The Walther was loaded with Glaser blue safety slugs. Bullets designed to empty over two hundred shotgun pellets into a body but not over-penetrate.

Wil had placed two Walther PPK handguns, similarly loaded, elsewhere on his body. Selia believed he was carrying at least one knife, one baton, and probably a flash bomb somewhere.

He had an arm wrapped snugly around her waist and they walked in perfect sync, bypassing the line for the normal patrons for the bouncer at the door. The bouncer, almost six feet tall and the size of a professional football player nodded towards the winding line.

"The end's that way," he said gruffly.

Selia smiled demurely. "I'm expected, by Vinny."

The name caught the bouncer's attention and he suddenly straightened, giving her and Wil his undivided attention. Another man appeared from the inside of the club's small threshold.

A few inches over five feet with short cut wavy black hair and green eyes, he wore typical high-end club wear with a casual ease.

The newcomer asked, "What's your name?"

"Selia. Selia Lascari. Vinny said you'd let me and my boyfriend in without trouble and we'd be taken to the VIP area." She gave Wil's waist a squeeze. "Do you need to see my ID?"

"Nah, I recognize you," the newcomer said. He gave her a charming smile, flashing a set of pearly white teeth as he unhooked the rope and stepped to the side. "I hadn't expected you to be on time."

Selia laughed as she and Wil crossed through the opening and waited for him to hook the rope back into place. "I can be on time if it's necessary. Unusual for a woman, I know. I had some encouragement."

"Been a while, Chuck," Wil said in a steady, almost passionless tone. "Good to see you got the club back together after that New Year's Eve fiasco."

"Hey, Dorian," Chuck, the newcomer, said cautiously. "Yeah. It's been a while. Nice of you to pay for the replacement bar after that night."

"It seemed only fair. I put your two bouncers and that idiot bartender through it, after all."

Chuck cleared his throat.

"Yeah," he replied nervously, trying to smile. "Well, that's what they get for messing with a world-class merc. I've gotten wiser about my employees: They don't start shooting at my customers who are taking cover, understandably, behind the bar."

Keeping his gaze on Chuck, Wil continued. "That's good to hear. I hope you've gotten better bartenders."

"I didn't have much of a choice, did I?" Chuck replied, still smiling. "No one is going to water down your drinks this time."

"I don't care about that." Wil answered. "I care about anyone I call out on doing so, not trying to stab me for it."

"Not gonna happen!" assured Chuck. "It's all in the past!"

"Outstanding. Care to escort the lady and me to our assigned place?" Wil asked. The smallest smirk showed at the corner of his mouth.

"You know it. Right this way." Chuck gestured for them to follow him.

Selia shook her head as they followed Chuck. She gave a soft sigh and raised her brows at Wil. It seemed he had a reputation of some sort everywhere the Families were located. Not surprising, but a little warning would have been nice. Wil just winked at her.

Of course, she also knew why he spoke in a flat tone and wasn't likely to have extended conversations with anyone at the club. Part of his disguise was a prosthetic worn against the upper plate of his mouth. It changed the shape of his face subtly and made him look more like an Irish actor well known for action films.

Chuck led them through the back of the club, along a wall to a set of stairs. Glancing briefly at Wil, she followed the man up the set of stairs. She glanced over the rail at the writhing, undulating bodies below. The music was loud and typical of a club. The lighting was dark, with strategically placed colored lights.

The upper floor was open, though there were several bouncers blocking the area off from intruders. All of them, Selia noticed, were armed. Of course, so was she.

The bouncers moved to the side, letting her, Wil, and Chuck past them.

It was a good bit quieter above the thudding music below, and there were more lights. There were also sofas, chairs, curtained windows, and over a dozen men milling around.

Every single one of Vinny's underbosses, his advisor, and a handful of his captains were in the room, along with a handful of the staff from the club. Vinny was standing near the windows, talking quietly with his *consigliere*. She hadn't met his advisor but recognized the man by the descriptions she'd heard.

Selia smiled sweetly and unbuttoned her trench coat. Wil, or rather 'Dorian', stepped behind her and slid it from her shoulders. The quiet thrum of conversation dropped a few notches more as the men noticed her. Or rather, what she was wearing.

She'd chosen a slinky red gown that stopped two inches above her knees. It had a plunging neckline and was almost backless, showing more skin than was probably appropriate. What wasn't seen was the small Keltec automatic that was wrapped around her upper thigh. The wispy, flirty skirt swished with each step, allowing plenty of skin to show, yet kept her weapon hidden from sight.

A win-win situation in her opinion.

"Thank you, Dorian," Selia said, smiling at Wil as he handed the coat off to a staff member.

"You look amazing." Vinny announced across the room. "Thank you for accepting my invitation. What would you like to drink?"

"Do you have hot chocolate?" Selia asked with laughter in her voice. "If not, a cola would be wonderful."

There was a low rumbling of laughter from the men, except Wil.

"Hot chocolate for the lady," Vinny agreed, smiling slyly. "What for you, Mister...?"

"Porter. Dorian Porter," Wil declared.

That caused some uncomfortable shifting in the room. Vinny kept his smile, but he had recognized the name, at least. The *consigliere* had gone pale.

Wil looked over the room before answering. "Bombay Sapphire, neat. No ice."

Vinny nodded to Chuck, who had stayed in the room. Chuck nodded and sped out.

"Can I offer you anything to eat," Vinny asked. "We have the best food in the city."

"A generous offer, and greatly appreciated, but I'm afraid we dined before coming," Selia replied, not moving from where she stood.

"Suit yourselves. Now, how do you propose to initiate communications between all five families?" Vinny asked, getting to the heart of the matter.

Selia shifted her weight. "Angelo gave me your contact information, as well as that of Carmine Pavanello and

Anthony Carenzo." She smiled sweetly. "I have already spoken with Lucien Vaschetti. I will be contacting the others in the coming days, to speak to them of Al's offer."

"Ah, I was hoping to speak with you before all others," Vinny said, throwing his arms up dramatically. The smile never wavered, though. "The Vaschettis beat us smaller families to the punch, yet again. An old story and a boring one. Well, I'll just have to show more hospitality."

Selia merely smiled. It wasn't as though she could burst out laughing. The fact that Vinny had remained on the opposite side of the room spoke more for his thoughts on the matter, than his verbal proclamation. Odd that of the three godfathers she'd dealt with so far, Lucien was the only one who had treated her as a respected guest, or equal.

"What I'm concerned about is that you, or whomever was going to take the position of liaison between all the families, see each boss as the leader of a family. Not just an individual. An individual is someone you have to deal with or choose not to deal with. People forget that there are people under that boss, and they have importance as well. I want to make sure you know everyone." He dropped a wink. "Or at least everyone that matters, when you're dealing with me. Perhaps you'll be inspired to do the same with the other bosses: Even if they aren't as charming as me, and their men aren't as loyal!"

This garnered a hearty round of laughter from Vinny's men. Vinny shrugged as if being modest, but the shit-eating grin was plastered to his face. He looked to her, almost telepathically screaming "the ball's in your court, now".

"It's even better to know how many you'll have to deal with in a war." Wil observed in Dorian Porter's flat, emotionless tone.

That quieted the room in a hurry. Vinny's smile even faltered.

"True," Vinny said, trying to recover the room. "But most people aren't constantly thinking of strategy and how to conquer."

"No, it's only those who plan to survive and succeed." Wil countered.

Shrugging, the eldest Scarlatti focused on Selia.

"I'm curious. Have you employed this gun-for-hire as your personal bodyguard?" the mobster asked.

"No, we're… seeing each other. Socially." Selia admitted with a smile.

Several of the men, including Vinny, looked surprised by that statement.

"What could you possibly see in-" Vinny began to ask.

"She's got a great ass." Wil cut in.

Blushing, and trying not to giggle, Selia gave a shrug of her own and gestured to 'Dorian' while saying, "He's honest, and comes straight to the point."

Considering this, Vinny nodded. The waiters came in at that moment carrying trays filled with appetizers, entrees, salads, and enough drinks to ensure a four-digit bill for the night. Everyone waited and was served. Vinny asked Selia again if she wanted something to eat, claiming he would feel bad about eating in front of someone, but she politely declined.

Instead, she took a sip of her hot chocolate and declared it delicious. There was so much whipped cream on top she thought she could almost make a meal out of it, though she didn't say it aloud. Vinny ignored his food for the moment, however, and addressed her.

"All right. How about I do the same for you? Let me introduce you to the movers and shakers of the Scarlatti family."

Vinny did the round of introductions in a style that was half proud father, half bad game-show host. Selia dimmed out his chatter after the second of the underbosses had been introduced, along with yet another story of why Vinny "loved this guy". She knew all the underbosses' names and wasn't too worried about the identities of the captains, or *capos* as they were typically called. Wil had detailed files and pictures of each in his database.

She looked over at Wil to see what he was doing. He sat ramrod straight, on the edge of his seat. His coat was unbuttoned, and his right hand sat on his right leg. Aside from the drink being methodically brought to his lips, a person could have mistaken him for a statue… or a man ready to start a firefight. His eyes scanned everyone in the room slowly, like a predator. Selia knew he was taking in data about each man, each story, to file away for later use.

Once the introductions and unnecessary tales were concluded, Vinny sat down to his dinner plate. He took a large bite of an inch-thick steak, looked at her, and asked, "Well? What do you think of the family?"

"I think you are a lucky man to have such loyalty," Selia rejoined. "They are fortunate to have a don who spends time on the front line with them."

This seemed to please Vinny, and some of the others. The advisor and a few of the captains did not seem particularly pleased. The remaining ones were just too interested in the food before them to react.

"I'll only ask one more time," Vinny promised. "Are you sure I can't get you something to nibble on?"

"Actually, I have a better plan," Selia said in reply. "We'll go spend time in the club while you eat. That way, no one feels pressured to speak to us while eating, and we don't feel like we have to eat something to be polite."

"I don't want you to feel like you're unwelcome," Vinny objected.

"No, not at all," Selia assured him. "You've been very hospitable. But I'd rather listen to some music and sit at the bar, instead of forks, knives, and chewing."

Vinny consented, and Selia had to shake hands with every member of the Scarlatti family before she and Wil could leave the private room and head for the bar.

"What do you think?" Selia stage whispered as they walked.

"Not sure. Seems he wants you to think of him as a good guy," Wil whispered back.

"Can you get us the hell out of here? I really don't want to spend more time listening to the 'Vinny Scarlatti Show'. I can stand it a little longer, but much more and I'm going to set fire to the place."

Wil grunted a laugh.

"I might have something planned. Let's give it a few minutes at the bar, shall we?"

Selia sighed and consigned herself to her fate.

At the bar, the two of them began a pleasant conversation with the bartender. This one apparently had nothing but sympathy for Mr. Dorian Porter, who had demanded his predecessor pour a real drink instead of a watered-down one. The fact that he had killed the bartender when the man had tried to threaten him with a knife over the watered-down drink was of no concern to the fellow.

This opened a wonderful communication about alcoholic mixtures and recipes. It was interrupted twice by members of Vinny's family, who had left their plates to come down and try to engage them in light conversation. Both men said they were just making sure that the two of them felt at home and were being provided for. Once they were satisfied to that end, they returned to the private room and their meal.

As the third member, the advisor, was approaching the bar, there was a loud bang from the kitchen, and a great deal of smoke. People were hurried to the exits as the situation was checked out. Most patrons stayed on the streets outside the club, either eager to get back in, or hoping for something interesting to happen. Probably so they could take pictures to post online.

Selia and Wil used the situation to slip away and head down the street. When they were two blocks away, she stopped him.

"Did you cause that?" she said, peering suspiciously into his eyes.

"I might have hired one of the kitchen workers to put something behind the least-used oven," Wil admitted. "Something I could trigger with a device in my pocket."

He pulled a wireless triggering mechanism from his right jacket pocket. His left hand was still occupied by his second Bombay Sapphire. Wil smiled and wiggled the glass in front of her nose. The glass tumbler was inscribed with the club's logo.

"I really like the glasses they use," he added with a smirk.

"I love you." Selia laughed and took his right arm as they made their way back to her car.

# Chapter Twenty Three

The next morning, Selia awoke to an empty bed. Glancing at the clock, she yawned and stretched. It wasn't quite nine yet, which meant she still had time for a shower and to pick out something fun to wear. She wasn't certain where Wil was, but she wasn't worried. The last couple days had been a treat, since he typically got up early and checked the news.

Despite their relationship, he hadn't changed his routine. Nor did she have any desire to disrupt it. Well… not too much.

A quick shower and breakfast later, Selia parked her car in the parking garage next to Soren's office. It was odd, how after two months, she still got chills at the reminder of parking her car in the same spot before finding out Alfi had turned traitor to her family. In a round-about way, she had the now-dead jerk to thank for setting her up with Wil. Collecting her purse and a few items she planned on decorating her office with, she headed into the office. Wil, in his disguise as Billy, the Now-Made-Man held the door open and followed her inside, swiftly taking the shopping bag from her hand in one graceful motion.

"Thanks, Billy," she said as they headed towards her office.

"No problem, Miss Selia," he replied in his chipper, eager voice. He opened her office door and sat the bag just inside. "Anything I can get you, Miss Selia?"

Selia smiled impishly. "A lot of push pins or something else to put those up with." She nodded towards the posters poking up out of the bag. "You know where the storage room is?"

Wil grinned and nodded. Of course he knew. He had probably memorized the layout of this building, Al's office building, and every office the dons used. Just one of the many reasons he had managed to succeed as long as he had as the Sandman.

"I'll return in a jiffy, Miss Selia," he replied, staying in character.

Selia chuckled and after 'Billy' had left, promptly picked her bag up and began emptying it onto her desk. The door opened and she glanced over her shoulder to find Soren. A bright smile lit up her face and she turned to give him a hug.

"Good morning, Papa!" She said cheerfully. "Billy is off getting some push pins for me. Are you here for work, to ask how last night went, or to keep me company while I decorate my new office?"

"All three, actually," Soren replied. "Do you like your new couch?"

Selia turned and grinned at the soft black sofa nestled against the wall to the left of the door. "I love it, Papa! Thank you!" She gave him another big hug and kissed his smooth cheek. Dropping a wink, she added, "I promise to behave with it."

"No, you won't," he contradicted her. "I had it treated to repel stains. There's also a cover for it tucked in between the couch and the wall."

She giggled and blushed. "Thanks, Papa."

Giggling again she sat on the edge of the desk and crossed her legs, feeling more like a teenager with every passing moment. She'd chosen to wear a pair of black wool dress pants, white blouse, and black business jacket, instead of a dress or skirt. The outfit had been tailored to her curvy figure and the blouse was unbuttoned just far enough to show a hint of cleavage.

"Last night was actually pretty boring. Vinny played 'proud father' and introduced me to each of his underbosses and advisors, along with a handful of his captains and a few thugs," Selia said, not bothering with hiding her true feelings or picking her words. She didn't have to care about being diplomatic with Soren. "It was more of a 'meet my family and be welcomed to my table' type thing."

"That cannot be everything," Soren said, settling onto the sofa.

Wrinkling her nose, she added, "He asked how I planned on communicating with the Families. Which reminds me, I still have to talk with Carmine and Tony. Hopefully they'll be a bit more interesting."

"I am a little surprised by Vinny's approach." Soren admitted. "He's always been flashy, trying to show style to make up for his lack of substance. But the whole 'Ward Cleaver' approach, or perhaps 'Seventh Heaven' is a better reference for you, is odd." Soren shrugged. "Perhaps he's trying to grow up. As far as Tony and Carmine go, Tony has always been his own man. Carmine is a character."

"I'm looking forward to finally meeting them," Selia admitted. "I know you've always tried to keep me shielded from the other dons, but I have to confess to being curious about them." She gave a slight sigh. "I also need to let Lucien know how the meeting went. I'll admit to being tempted to walk into his office and demand a meeting with the old man." She gave a wink to show she was teasing.

"Then you should do exactly that." Soren said with a somber face. "Don't let any of the dons think they own you."

"You mean I can?" Selia asked, her face brightening. Then it dawned on her. "Al couldn't even argue or complain, could he? Because I'm doing my part as liaison between the Families, and I have a contract with Lucien, unlike with the others."

She sat straighter on the desk, suddenly liking her position just a bit more than she had previously. "I think, Papa, I'm going to enjoy my new position and Angelo Lascari is going to grow to really despise his bright idea. The best part is, he can't complain, argue, or try to backpedal."

"No, he can't. He might try. Don't give him the ability to make any room for it," Soren advised.

'Billy' entered the office and smiled at both of them.

"Am I interrupting a touching family moment?" he asked with the hyper optimism of his character.

"Don't worry, Papa, I won't give him the satisfaction of that," Selia said softly, a malicious twinkle to her eyes. She turned to 'Billy' as she slid off the edge of her desk. Soren rose from the sofa in an easy fluid movement she couldn't help but admire. "Nope, not at all, Billy. Just discussing business. And speaking of business, we have a meeting to go to."

She offered her hand to her father. "Care to walk me out to the lobby, Papa?"

Soren took her hand, and they walked the short distance to the lobby. The lobby was bustling with activity. It was just before the lunch hour and there were packages waiting to be signed for and people trying to get in meetings before daring traffic and gastronomic tragedy.

"Oh, hold on a second!" Wil exclaimed loudly. He pulled a small box out of his jacket, and a long envelope.

"One of your boyfriends, Liam, told me to give this to you, Miss Selia!" Wil said, and he was talking loud enough to have the attention of the whole room. "Said you should open the envelope first."

Selia opened the envelope, which held two plane tickets to Paris. She felt her eyes growing as wide as they could at the sight of the tickets. She looked at the small black box, her fingers going numb as she opened it.

A ring sparked against the velvet interior of the box. At least two carats of diamond were surrounded by a quartet of small opals. The band was likely made of platinum.

Silence pressed in on her, and Selia vaguely realized that everyone in the lobby was looking at her... and waiting. She thought her eyes couldn't get any wider. Yet it seemed they had, and she couldn't take them off the ring and the tickets.

"He said you can call him anytime with the answer, by the way!" Wil said in his most chipper 'Billy' voice.

"Ummmm..." she began awkwardly.

"This is quite a prank." Soren mumbled to her. Then he caught a look in her eye that changed his demeanor slightly. "Isn't it?"

"Ummmm..." Selia didn't think her mouth was going to work at all today. She was going to kick Wil's ass for this.

*"Well?"* someone in the lobby screamed.

Most of the people jumped and then chuckled. Then, they went right back to staring at her.

"It's... a joke." Selia said loud enough to be heard in the back. "It's from Liam, the rock star guy? He's trying to stun me into running off to Paris with him for a week of debauchery when he knows I'm so busy with my job... er, jobs, here."

There was unhappy silence from the crowd.

"He's not asking me to marry him, people," Selia said, trying to sound amused. "He's just trying to manipulate me. You know bad boys and their games. What do you do?"

"I'd love a week of debauchery and manipulation from that man!" one of the well-dressed men in the lobby blurted.

That erupted laughter from everyone. Selia, sensing her way out, waved the tickets at him and hollered, "You want the tickets?"

"Honey, I'll take that ring!" the man replied, and the laughter in the lobby doubled.

Even as she laughed, she passed the tickets and rings over to Soren, whispering "please put these in my desk" before kissing him on the cheek. Soren stowed them away, and Selia and Wil made their way through the lobby, enjoying the teases of "congratulations," "can I have him if you're too busy" along with well-meaning chuckles and waves of affection.

Out of the lobby, the two of them turned and went to the parking deck next to the office. Once they were in the shadows of the deck, Selia turned and slapped Wil in the chest.

"You asshole!"

Wil tried to look offended, but the veil only lasted a second, then he started giggling.

Selia smacked him repeatedly in the chest and biceps, calling him "asshole!" with every strike. Wil brought his arms to his chest and giggled more like a kid as she did it.

Stopping to take a break, Selia barked, "What in the hell were you thinking?"

Wil just grinned at her, staying in his mockery of a defensive position. Selia could only laugh.

"Well... 'Papa' said I should make an honest woman out of you." Wil dropped her a slow wink. "He didn't specify which one of me should do it, though."

She couldn't help but laugh. "Point to you, dear sir."

"I decided to go with Liam-" Wil said, but stopped suddenly, as if about to say too much. "Because he would be one of your 'boyfriends' that wouldn't be taken seriously."

Selia just shook her head, laughing softly as they continued to her car. There wasn't much she could say to that. She glanced at him from the corner of her eyes as she said slyly, "At least he didn't threaten to shoot you... again."

"Oh, I am certain there will be ample reason, and opportunity for Soren to threaten me again, given time." Wil shrugged as he deactivated the security alarm on Selia's car with the remote control. "It wasn't a concern of mine."

As they got into the car, Wil started up the ignition, and put on his seat belt. Instead of engaging the transmission, he pulled out his iPhone, tapped the screen a few times, and handed it over to her.

There was a picture of her, slack jawed and bug-eyed, looking at the ring and tickets.

"It was so totally worth it," Wil observed as he pulled the car out of its parking spot.

# Chapter Twenty Four

As usual, Wil knew exactly where she wanted to go. He pulled into a parking garage near Lucien's office building. Selia took a moment to gather her thoughts as they stepped from the car. A small part of her wished the proposal had been a genuine offer, but she wanted it to come from Wil, not some alter ego he pretended to be. Until that happened, she was content being his girlfriend and lover. Besides, once a ring was placed upon her finger by him, there was no chance of them going out without Wil needing a disguise.

She shoved the thoughts away and stepped from the car, taking a moment to adjust her jacket. She might have a right to carry a weapon, but there was no need to advertise it. Walking around to Wil, she didn't tuck her arm through his, or even take his hand. Instead she gave him a nod and began to walk towards Lucien's building.

Ten minutes later they were entering the luxurious lobby. Potted plants and a huge receptionist's desk were the main objects of interest. There were chairs and small tables piled with magazines scattered about and abstract art hung on the walls, but all were of muted colors.

The receptionists, one on each side of the desk, spoke with the gaggle of people moving through the lobby and answered phones. Both were pretty blondes and wore tailored business suits. Selia chose the receptionist to the right and strode forward as though she owned the place.

"I'm here to see Mr. Vaschetti," Selia said briskly.

"Do you have an appointment with Mr. Vaschetti?" the receptionist asked, clicking around on her computer.

"No, but he'll wish to see me regardless," Selia replied, her lips curving into a smile. "I'm Selia Lascari, liaison between his companies and those owned by the Lascari Family."

"I'll inform his secretary, she'll be expecting you," the receptionist said quickly. "Please, take the elevator to the top floor."

"Thank you," Selia replied before turning and striding purposefully towards the elevator. Minutes later, she smirked at Wil in the elevator. "I really shouldn't be enjoying this so much."

"I can't think of a single reason you shouldn't," Wil replied in his own voice.

"Somehow, I don't think Al or Lucien are going to feel the same," Selia said with a grin. She paused before asking, "Feel like going to a club tonight? I have a sudden desire to torment a couple other dons by visiting one of their establishments. I'm open to suggestions, too."

"Sounds good. Who do you think is likely to be behind the attacks on Lucien's holdings?" invited Wil.

"I'd absolutely love to say it's Vinny and proceed to give him a double tap," she replied, leaning against the wall of the elevator. She adopted a talk-show host tone, openly mocking Vinny from the previous night. "However, Jimmy was one of Tony Carenzo's boys. The only problem of blaming Tony, is we both know money is a powerful corrupter. I wish to point out the now-twice-dead Alfi for reference." She chuckled at Wil's expression and shrugged. "I'm doing this more to annoy Al and do as Papa suggested. To show them that no one owns me. Lucien, I'm pretty sure, won't care. If he does, he'll at least respect my reasons behind this move."

"Good enough," Wil declared. The elevator doors opened onto Lucien's floor. A large reception desk in a C shape faced them, along with a very pretty, well dressed blonde. She smiled and greeted them.

"Hello, he's waiting for you in his office. Please go in." She said, speaking with a slight Welsh accent. "Sir, you are expected as well."

Selia glanced at Wil and raised a single brow. Turning back to the secretary, she said, "Thank you."

Wil merely shrugged and opened the office door, allowing Selia to enter before him.

Lucien's office was an amazing study in retro-modern design. The walls looked like wooden paneling at first glance, until one moved and saw the lines of metal mesh that were the actual construction material. Both the desk that Lucien sat in and the oversized couch that took up the other third hat of the office were of bulky C shapes. The desk was topped with mahogany, and the rest was steel that was so shiny that it might have been polished aluminum.

The couch was bright red, and looked comfortable enough for sleeping, sitting, or anything else. There was a black glass coffee table in front of it, and two black lounge chairs on the other side of the table. The carpet was short, and a deep red that could have been called blood. Two pieces of art adorned the walls. One was a large oil painting of the four horsemen of the apocalypse rendered as ghostly, graphic characters riding out of a nuclear power plant. The other painting was a face painted in shades of blue. The eyes were closed, and the open screaming mouth was formed out of the various hues.

The paintings weren't what Selia would have expected, but they appealed to her and seemed oddly fitting for the

Vaschetti godfather. Almost reluctantly, she turned her attention back to Lucien.

"Thank you for seeing me on such short notice," she said, moving forward towards his desk. "Also, I'd like to extend my appreciation for allowing my… assistant to join me."

"I've been wanting to see your assistant. Some of my best snitches work at the Ice Room. They told me Dorian Porter came with you. I wasn't sure if he was your assistant or one of your boyfriends. I see he must be of the boyfriend-variety, because this cannot be the infamous Dorian Porter."

*What a laugh it would be*, Selia thought, *if Lucien were told the man with her was all of the above.*

Smiling with genuine amusement, she sat gracefully in one of the chairs in front of Lucien's desk. "I see Dorian on occasion, socially. I thought he would be perfect as a date and a bodyguard, while visiting Vinny in his den. Dorian certainly created a stir and kept anyone from making any unwanted gestures."

"Ah," said Lucien, and there was a touch of disappointment in his body language. "I was rather hoping you had hired him as your full-time bodyguard. I would rather you had someone protecting you at all times, who-" he looked significantly at Wil, "-isn't on a Family payroll."

Leaning against the back of the chair, which was remarkably comfortable, Selia smiled sweetly. The man did love his comforts and making sure his guests, and clients, were comfortable, also.

"I'm quite capable of taking care of myself, Lucien." It took everything she had to keep from snickering because she knew exactly what Wil was thinking. "However, Papa appointed Billy here, and I'm quite satisfied that he can, and will, keep me safe."

Tilting her head to the side, she thought for a few moments, before she met Lucien's gaze. Her eyes twinkled with mischief as she said, "I will ask Dorian if he'll be interested in playing bodyguard until this fiasco is over and done with. I'm fairly certain he won't object to my request. But I didn't come here to speak with you about my interest in men. I came to speak to you in the capacity of liaison."

Lucien settled back in his chair. "Very well, go ahead."

"As you're aware, I spoke to Vincent Scarlatti last night, at the Ice Room. I met his advisor, underbosses, a handful of his captains and their underlings." She settled more comfortably in the chair. "He was quite the 'proud father' in introducing the men and hoping I'd see his Family *as* a family. Not just a business organization. He questioned how I planned on communicating with all the Families and was a bit annoyed by the fact you had already contacted me."

"There is little I can do that doesn't annoy Scarlatti," mused Lucien.

She smiled slyly as she said, almost apologetically, "I somehow neglected to mention the fact you had initiated the idea of a liaison between the Families. I don't know how that could have slipped my mind."

Lucien frowned. "You do plan on meeting with the other two dons, don't you?" He looked apologetic as he continued. "I don't mean to seem selfish, but this new position that's being forced upon you actually gives you a perfect opportunity to discover who is behind the power-plays that are plaguing, if not both our families, then certainly mine."

"Oh, I plan on meeting with Carmine and Tony. I have every desire to do so, for multiple reasons. Finding out who's behind the troubles is merely one of them." Her smile grew colder as she lifted her chin ever so slightly. "Angelo gave me little choice in the matter. I plan on… making certain I do my job as liaison to my fullest abilities, and we both know what those are."

Lucien nodded somberly. He looked over to Billy. "Would you excuse us for a few minutes, Billy? There are a few things I need to speak to the liaison about that no one else needs to hear."

Wil looked to Selia for confirmation that she was alright with the request. Selia nodded.

"Sure thing! I totally understand." He nodded to Selia, stood and left the room.

The Vaschetti godfather waited until Billy had closed the door. He looked at her levelly. "Play me straight here, Selia. What else do you have in mind as far as your 'duties' as liaison go?"

"My plans are to keep the balance in this city. Angelo threw me into the fire without a care for my wellbeing. Something you, at least, are concerned about. If I can make him rue giving me this job, distance myself from the family, and come out on top? Then I plan on doing just that." She narrowed her eyes at Lucien. "If the Families want someone to play Switzerland, so be it. But you are the one I have a contract with. That means you're the one who will get more than the basics. Vinny hasn't had me sign anything, and I doubt the other two will, either. Foolish, perhaps, but it gives me leverage and the right to decide what I do and don't tell them. I can also move against them easier, without fearing as much reprisal."

He nodded again, seeming to be a bit more satisfied. "I only have one more thing to ask, then." He leaned in close and Selia was suddenly nervous about what he might ask. "Is Dorian Porter the Sandman?"

Selia burst out laughing. When she finally had collected herself, she put on the most serious expression she could muster and said, "Lucien, you know I can't give you that answer. I'm sworn to secrecy."

"That's… not a denial."

Selia suppressed a laugh. "No, no, it is not."

Lucien slumped back in his chair. Speaking in a lower tone, he said, "So that's why you're not worried about having a bodyguard. Does anyone know? Has anyone else figured it out?"

"No, Lucien, I don't think anyone else knows. Though, I wouldn't be surprised if Papa does. He is my father, after all," Selia replied, trying to not burst out laughing again. She swallowed back another laugh. "May I ask a question of you?"

"Of course! Sure! Anything, *mia belladonna*!"

"May I have a drink?"

Lucien appeared momentarily stunned. After a moment, he recovered and said, "Yes! Of course!" As he approached one panel of his wall and touched a button, he said, "Don't worry, I'll tell no one."

"I greatly appreciate that, Lucien." She grinned impishly. "Instead of a Shirley Temple, could I have a Bombay Sapphire?"

He paused and then said, "Nothing else? Nothing to mix with it?"

"Over ice," she replied innocently.

"Okay, because… until you said the ice, that's *his*-" Lucien emphasized the word as though speaking of a deity or demon, "-drink of choice."

Selia shrugged, enjoying herself way too much. "Why do you think I don't drink in a social setting? Besides, I trust you." *At least for now.* Though she wasn't about to speak that aloud.

"I'm very grateful that you do," Lucien replied. He handed her the drink.

Selia smiled and raised her glass to him. Yep, she was definitely enjoying her job way too damned much.

# Chapter Twenty Five

Shortly thereafter, Wil and Selia were in her car with Wil driving. Wil took alternate routes to avoid the still-bustling downtown lunch-time traffic.

"So, feel like some lunch?" Wil asked.

"Would love some," Selia replied, still immensely amused by her chat with Lucien. "What do you suggest?"

"Fortunately, in this costume, I can eat just about anything." He sighed. "Unlike Dorian, who's pretty much regulated to sushi and soups."

"Guess it's a good thing you love sushi, huh?" Selia teased.

"One of my favorite foods, and still really good for you," Wil replied.

"You aren't going to believe what Lucien asked me," Selia said, dropping her voice to a conspiratorial level.

Wil chuckled and said, "He didn't hear about the wedding proposal already, did he?"

"Oh, no, nothing so boring," Selia retorted smugly. "He asked if Dorian Porter is the Sandman."

There was a microsecond of stunned silence and then Wil laughed so hard he couldn't keep his eyes entirely open and watching traffic. Selia watched him laugh because it was his true laugh, not any of his characters.

"Oh, no," Wil gasped. "What did you tell him?"

"I told him I couldn't answer that because I'm sworn to secrecy," Selia replied. Though her tone was innocent, the smile on her face was full of mischief.

Snickering until tears streamed down his face, Wil said, "Please don't tell me anymore until we get out of the car. I'm going to wreck the vehicle if I laugh more."

"Yes, dear," Selia replied demurely.

Selia looked over to smile at Wil when she noticed his eyes shifting from the side-mirror to rear-view mirror rapidly. His face, while not dour, certainly had less of the happily amused expression she'd expected. Just before it happened, Selia caught a glimpse of the large SUV coming too fast and too close. The car shook and lurched to the right, protesting the SUV striking it on its left flank.

Wil regained control of the vehicle almost immediately, but said, "Hang on. This is going to get ugly."

Selia glanced into her side-view mirror at the SUV but couldn't see much. The passengers were wearing black ski-masks that hid their features and were clothed in all black.

"Guess someone didn't like me visiting Lucien," she remarked. "I wonder if I should send the bill to him or Al for this."

"Let's worry about getting through this, first," Wil said through gritted teeth as he pulled the car into an alleyway.

"Sweetheart, this is a dead-end!" Selia exclaimed.

"That's the idea," Wil growled. "If they're trying to trap us or kill us, time to change the game to our advantage.

He floored the accelerator but stopped a good twenty feet from the brick wall that capped the alleyway.

"Hang on!" Wil warned Selia.

Selia relaxed her entire body, knowing that tensing up would just make it worse. The impact and the sound exploded against her a heartbeat later. The car lurched forward, Airbags expanded and pushed against her and Wil's bodies. Since the front of the car didn't go crunch, she figured they hadn't been pushed far enough to take that hit as well.

There was a small pop, and the airbag began to rapidly deflate. She heard a second pop, looked over, and saw Wil extracting a large switchblade out of his now-punctured airbag. With his left hand, he worked the seatbelt's release.

"Out," he commanded. "Sorry about your car, but you can't go Nightshade on them."

"Does that mean I can't kill them in revenge for ruining my day?"

Wil opened his car door, grunting with the effort. "Nope. Just means you can't get exotic. Go Dirty Harry on them. Try to leave one alive."

"Sounds good to me," Selia replied, opening the door with one hand as she drew her M&P .40 with her other. She made it a habit to not carry the exact gun in her personal life as she carried in her persona as Nightshade.

There were four passengers in the SUV, plus the driver. All wore masks and each was armed with a blunt instrument, although the driver had a large automatic in a shoulder holster.

Wil threw his switchblade, and it landed in the throat of the attacker nearest to the driver. He then jumped the driver, slamming his body into the half-open door. The door slammed against the driver's legs, breaking them with an audible snap. Selia wasn't so kung-fu. She shot one attacker in the face with a quick double-tap. The second was hit in the hip, crippling him. The third, she shot in the right shoulder, causing his weapon to fall from lifeless fingers.

"Feeling lucky?" Selia asked with a smirk on her lips.

The remaining attacker turned to see where Wil was located. Wil, still leaning against the driver-side car door, had his Walther PPQ in his left hand. It was aimed at the attacker's head.

"Run, little rabbit," Wil advised.

The attacker ran like his ass was on fire.

Selia snickered and walked towards the fallen men. Turning, she sighed dramatically at her poor demolished car.

"What was your plan, exactly?" she inquired.

"To not have to drive all through the town at reckless speed, or allow ourselves to be trapped," he replied. "By forcing them into a collision, one that we were prepared for, we gained moments to take back control of our situation."

"Not the best planning you've done," she observed.

"Any crash you can walk away from is better than the alternative," Wil countered.

"Looks like I'll be needing a new car," she stated before turning towards the men. "Shall I call Papa?"

"Definitely call Soren," Wil advised. "Would you like a hybrid, or a BMW?"

"After this? I want a Beemer or Benz... SUV or Hummer," Selia replied.

"Cool!" said Wil, finally taking his weight off the car door. "We get to go shopping! I love shopping."

Selia rolled her eyes, bent over with her foot on the crippled man's hip, and jerked the mask off, ignoring his screams of agony. Narrowing her eyes, she gestured towards the others and asked Wil, "Care to remove their masks and see if you recognize anyone while I call Papa?"

"I recognize that one, already," Wil admitted. "But I'll check the rest."

As Wil began unmasking the others, Selia pulled out her cell phone and began dialing Soren's number. She glanced over at Wil in time to see him frown. Almost faster than she could track, he brought up his Walther and fired twice.

She looked down to see the crippled attacker that Wil had recognized flinch his last living moment away. There were two holes overlapping in his temple from Wil's 9mm. In the dead man's right hand was a small automatic: a hold-out gun that she had not been aware of.

"You have to appreciate an adversary that doesn't know when they've lost," Wil observed. "However, I wasn't going to let him shoot you."

Swallowing hard, she drew a deep breath and let it out slowly. "Yet another I owe you," she murmured, a tight smile on her lips.

"I don't keep track anymore," Wil said with a wink.

Laughing, Selia shook her head. "Of course not." Soren's voice finally came over the line and she held the phone to her ear. "I'm going to need a new car, Papa, and there's a mess that needs to be cleaned up."

"Where are you? Are you alright?" Soren demanded.

"I'm fine, thanks to Billy," Selia replied, as she crossed to Wil. "I'm in the dead-end alley across from Laurel Avenue. There are three dead, one escaped, and one passed out from being a wuss."

There was a snort of laughter from the phone and then Soren replied, "I'll notify the police station and send the clean-up crew. They'll have a car with them."

"Thanks, Papa," Selia said, leaning against Wil. "I'll tell you about the meeting later, but I want lunch, a car, and some relaxing time first, though. Can I come over for dinner?"

"Absolutely," Soren replied. "See you in a little while, *piccolina.*"

Selia ended the call and turned to Wil. "Dinner should be a lot of fun, don't you think?"

"Probably so, and I recognize all of these characters," Wil said.

Selia raised her brows, silently urging him to continue.

"They're a group of hirelings from one of the local gangs. Instead of making their money selling, making, or transporting drugs, they're relatively cheap muscle-for-hire." He paused, wrinkling his nose in disgust. "The nastier the work, the happier they are."

"So we're no closer to figuring out who is behind this than we were before," Selia murmured. "Anyone could have hired them."

# Chapter Twenty Six

Later that night, Selia and Wil, in his disguise as Dorian, entered the nightclub, the Blue Moon, which happened to be owned by Anthony 'Tony' Carenzo. She hadn't been issued a personal invitation from anyone. But considering Al had informed Tony of her being liaison for the Families, her going to Tony's club wouldn't seem odd. Not that Al would probably approve, but at the moment, Selia didn't give a damn about what Al did or didn't approve of.

She had chosen black leather pants, a black bustier-type blouse and a leather jacket, with a built-in holster. She had no plans on removing the jacket, and she doubted anyone would dare question or search her.

Considering the bouncer gestured her in with only a curious look at Dorian after showing him her ID, she guessed her name had been added to the 'allowed without question' list. Brushing her hair behind her ears, she slid onto a bar stool and ordered a Shirley Temple, even as Wil ordered his characteristic Bombay Sapphire, neat, with no ice.

Leaning over towards him, the music was loud enough to injure ear drums; Selia said in Wil's ear, "I thought this was Carenzo territory."

When Wil looked at her and she glanced pointedly down the bar from them at a handful of Tony's men, who were laughing it up with a couple of Carmine's people.

"We've got a lot of interesting coincidences; must be a sale going on," Wil replied.

Selia smiled as she accepted her glass with a nod to the bartender. Once the bartender moved down the bar, she said, "A few too many, if you ask me." She leaned over towards him. "You *do* dance, right? I mean, this is a club and I do plan on having some fun."

"Classically trained in ballroom and swing," he assured her.

"I've got to take you to one of our functions at some point," Selia said emphatically.

"As long as they serve sushi, I'm fine."

"How about mashed potatoes?" she asked impishly.

He shook his head. "Get stuck in the prosthetic. A pain in the ass to clean."

"Sushi it is, then," Selia whispered in his ear, her breath warm against his earlobe.

He made a pleased sound. "Careful or I'll be too distracted to protect you."

"Oh, so I guess I shouldn't nibble," Selia said with a sigh. She took a sip of her drink, smiling sweetly at him over the rim.

"Later for that, business for now," he advised.

The bartender walked over and said, "Excuse me, but the owner is requesting the pleasure of your company at his private table."

The bartender then pointed to one of the back corners where a larger ornate booth, complete with a large curtain available for privacy, was located. There was a large group consisting of made-men from both the Carenzo and Pavanello Families. The big man of the Carenzo Family himself, Tony, sat in the middle. He was waving and gesturing for them to come over.

"Of course," Selia replied with a smile. "We'd be delighted to join him."

Shirley Temple in hand, she slid off her barstool and began towards the booth, with Dorian Porter the Mercenary at her side. Glancing around, she noticed several of Tony's underbosses, captains, and his advisor scattered about the club, along with an equal number from Carmine's Family. Exchanging a sharp look with Dorian, she turned her attention to Tony, a bright smile on her face.

"How you doin'?" Tony asked, with amiable charm.

Of the dons, he was certainly the most casual. He wore a loud purple suit with a black t-shirt and was a large man in nearly every sense. Over six-feet tall and approximately forty pounds overweight, he had hands big enough to arm wrestle a gorilla. Nearly bald with neatly trimmed brown hair at his temples and crown, he was clean-shaven with beady brown eyes. Large rings adorned two fingers on each hand.

Young, beautiful girls sat on either side of him. Whether or not they were old enough to drink, was questionable. The fact they were drinking, was not. Both girls had large steins of dark beer in front of them, at least a third full.

"We're doing very well, thank you." Selia replied, her smile not wavering. "It's a pleasure to finally meet you."

"So how you feeling about dealing with all us lowlifes?" Tony asked.

Selia chuckled. "It's a change from my usual duties, definitely, but I'm enjoying it so far."

Tony's laugh was low and earthy. He tilted his head back when he laughed, and his eyes narrowed into twinkling impish slits.

"Getting bored over there," Tony inquired, "with all that big money?"

"Bored? Not hardly." Her eyes narrowed as she wrapped her hands carefully around her glass. "Al might have placed me in my current position, but it wasn't he who told me to come here." She gestured around the club with her left hand. "I was raised by Soren Lascari, and I was taught by him. I can assure you, I know my way around and can certainly handle myself and this job."

Tony chuckled, looking at her a little differently. "Tough broad, eh? I can respect that. You gotta work twice as hard to do the same thing. Well, you won't find any trouble with me. I'm all about teamwork and communications. You tell me what you need-" he shrugged, "-I'll do my best to help out."

"That's good to hear, especially since I've spoken to Lucien Vaschetti and Vincent Scarlatti already," Selia replied with a polite nod. "I'll certainly keep your offer in mind."

"Yeah, how is old Lucien doing these days? I hear he's having a time getting his shipments in," Tony said.

"I wouldn't know anything about that," Selia lied. "He was faring well, the last I spoke to him, and is interested in opening communications between the Families." She hadn't learned to spin the truth for nothing. Her expression never wavered, and her eyes remained fixed upon Tony.

Tony smirked, saying, "Well, you'll start learning the Families' businesses soon enough. I heard about that little incident at that momma boy's club: Some idiot nearly blew up an oven in the kitchens. Did Vinny bore you too badly? The man hardly knows when to shut up."

Selia laughed and held her hand up in defense. "I can take no credit for that." With a genuine smile, she added, "I'm the neutral one. I'm not going to play favorites or anything like that. The meeting with Vinny was interesting. He introduced me to his, ah, family."

"Yeah, I'll bet he did. Always sticking his nose in, that's Vinny. If he treated you okay, he's doing better than the last time I dealt with him."

That piqued Selia's interest. "Interesting. I was treated just fine. I'd be happy to take any message or request you have for him, Lucien, or Angelo to any or all of them. Once I've spoken with Carmine, and if he agrees to my position as liaison, the offer will stand with him, also."

"Think I'm going to like you," Tony said with a soft smile. "You seem to have your head on straight. Well-" he put his hands up as if in surrender, "-I'm no showman like Vinny, but a lot of my Family is here. If you want to meet them, I'll have them introduce themselves."

"I'm sure as the time goes by, I'll have a chance to meet those with whom I'll be dealing," Selia replied, smiling. "I'm more than happy meeting those you deem necessary, when you feel it's a good time."

Tony laughed his deep laugh once more. He picked up his tumbler of what was most likely either scotch or bourbon and toasted her. "Salute! You and your very dangerous boyfriend there, pop a squat at our table and join us for food and laughs. Anything you want on the menu, food or drinks, on the house. And," he held up one little finger, "I just might be able to help you, little lady."

He winked at her then pointed at the people on his left and made a shooing gesture. The two people on the end got out of the booth and insisted that Selia and Wil take their place. Selia noticed Tony pointing to someone on his right and nodding. A burly man with a well-trained mane of silver-gray hair nodded and excused himself from the table.

"Now, before you get too far into your job," Tony began. "You ought to know my position. Your poppy, he's a solid guy. I like him. The man shows respect. But Al and Lucien?" Tony shook his head, almost sadly. "They forget where they come from. Those of us still close to the streets, we know how things are. Soren never forgot. Al, he occasionally shows some sense. Lucien, he's been taking too much of the pie for too fucking long."

"How do you feel about Vinny?" Selia asked, keeping her tone neutral.

Tony grunted. "He doesn't know how to run a club, let alone the big Family business. He likes to think he knows the streets, and where he ought to be in the grand scheme. Lots of ambition, not a lot of brains."

"What about Carmine?" Selia asked, suspecting she already knew the answer.

Tony broke into his widest smile yet. "How do I feel about Carmine? Same way he feels about me. Isn't that right, Carmine?"

There was a soft parental laugh from the front of the booth. The laugh came from Carmine Pavanello. Around five and a half feet tall, Carmine was broad and fit. He looked like a man who enjoyed going to the gym to work off the calories from the drinks he had at the clubs he frequented. Light brown hair was cut into a neat, slicked-back style and his eyes were a pale, pale blue. He wore a polo shirt and khakis, which gave him an even more relaxed appearance than Tony. The only thing stereotypical about Carmine was the large ruby pinky ring on his left hand.

"He's a lazy, loud-mouthed bag of hot air, that lets everybody else do all the work while he spends all the money and scarfs up all the pretty girls," Carmine said, smiling broadly. Tony roared with laughter. Carmine chuckled and nodded then stuck out his hand to Selia. "Pleasure to make your acquaintance."

She held out her hand, expecting it to be shaken, when instead Carmine lifted it to his lips and gave it a gentlemanly kiss. He released her hand, looked to Wil, and nodded. Wil nodded back.

"It's some dangerous company you're keeping, little lady," Carmine commented.

"Don't give yourself so much credit, old man," Tony quipped.

Carmine chuckled again. "Your reputation precedes you, Mr. Porter."

Wil nodded and took a sip of his drink.

"How much do you charge for a job, anyways?" Carmine asked with no pretension of hostility.

"Depends on the job," Wil replied sagely.

"Fuck me dead. You mean that's Porter? Dorian Porter?" Tony exclaimed.

"You ought to read the important stuff we intercept from the government, Tony." Carmine dropped a wink at Selia before addressing Tony again. "Or at least learn to read."

"Ohhh, the old man, he's got a million of those smart-ass remarks."

"Got to do something to ease the boredom," answered Carmine. "It gets boring watching you struggle all the time,

Tony. Up the stairs, making money, in your old lady's bed…"

Wil almost laughed, Selia felt him tremor slightly and saw him smirk as he brought the glass to his lips.

"Ah, you're gonna get yours, old man," Tony said, pointing a finger at Carmine. "I'm going to get mine, and soon. Then you're going to be in trouble."

Carmine rolled his eyes. "Big talk. Always with the big talk. When are you going to show, *Vinny?*"

"Hey! No need to get nasty now," Tony shot back.

Carmine smiled and spread his arms wide. "And that's called sweet victory, young 'uns. Enjoy your moment of basking in my glory."

There was laughter all over the table, even Selia joined in.

"Now if you'll excuse me," Carmine said, "I'd like to get back to my splendid little birthday party, courtesy of Tony and his boys." He pointed a finger at the other don. "Don't you come over and stink up the place, Tony."

"Nah." Tony waved a dismissive hand. "I want them to know who really stinks. Have fun, you dirty old fuck."

Carmine lifted an imaginary glass and toasted Selia and Wil. Wil returned the gesture, as did Selia, with their actual glasses. Carmine nodded one last time to Tony and made his way off.

"As you can see," Tony said with a grin. "We can't stand each other at all."

Selia said, "Well, my job just got more interesting."

"That's what we do here. Make people happy," Tony said with a measurable amount of smugness. After Carmine was out of sight, Tony leaned towards Selia and asked, "You doing okay? I heard about those punks trying to cap you."

Selia raised her brows. "I'm here, I'm safe, and I'm well protected." She let a smile grow across her lips as she added, "Papa has made certain I'm watched over, and I've learned to take care of myself." She gave a significant look towards Dorian. "I've also got people who I can trust to watch my back. I appreciate the concern, though. I'd also enjoy learning why they were coming after me." She tilted her head to the side. "You wouldn't happen to have any theories, would you?"

"Your new position, most likely. Not everyone wants somebody new poking around in their business. You just watch your back and keep the right kind of company," Tony advised.

"Sound advice," Selia replied thoughtfully. She finished her drink and glanced at the watch on her wrist. "As much as I'm enjoying this, we need to be going."

"What? Already?" Tony balked. He shrugged, saying, "Ah, well. You young kids go and have fun. You're welcome here anytime. Come by when you can sit a spell. I've got plenty of stories about us dons."

"I look forward to hearing them, and working with you and Carmine," Selia replied, smiling as she and Wil stood. She gave a sly smile towards 'Dorian' before looking back to Tony. "Have a good night."

Tony nodded and bid them a good night once last time and, hooking her arm through Wil's, they exited the club. Knowing word would travel that she was growing affectionate towards 'Dorian Porter' was certainly going to make her life more interesting. She couldn't help but wonder what her father was going to say when he found out.

# Chapter Twenty Seven

Selia arrived at her office an hour early the next morning, wearing more casual clothing than normal. The day was a bit cooler, and she had decided upon a pair of black jeans, a white silk blouse and black jacket. She felt somewhat safe at Soren's office, but she wasn't willing to push her luck. Wil was waiting for her outside, and as they entered the lobby, she spotted Alex and Bernie.

She waved to the pair, who waved back as they headed up to Soren's office. They continued to her office where Wil, in his disguise as 'Billy', opened the door to her office and set about searching for bugs. Finding nothing, he nodded and slipped the gadget back into a pocket.

As her laptop booted, Selia turned to Wil. "Any thoughts on last night?"

"Other than Tony having a deep-seated dislike for Lucien? That he and Carmine are good friends and have already formed their own alliance?" Wil asked, his eyes closed as he stretched across the sofa.

"He doesn't seem to like Al or Vinny, either," Selia mused, "Though he doesn't mind Papa. He also seems to know a lot about what's going on. But his and Carmine's people definitely don't associate with Vinny."

A knock on the door brought Wil to his feet. Glancing at Selia, she nodded, and he opened the door. The mail clerk stood in the doorway, smiling at Selia.

"Oh, hi, Amy," Selia said.

"Moving up in the world, huh?" Amy asked with a grin.

A petite woman with unruly curly red hair pulled back in a tight ponytail with laughing green eyes, she had a thick

Irish accent. She had graduated two years ago, applied for the job when the last mail clerk had retired, and had immediately become well-liked by all the staff.

Selia shrugged. "It had to happen eventually."

"True that," Amy replied. She pulled out a stack of envelopes and handed them to Billy.

"I've got mail already?" Selia asked, intrigued.

"Maria said to bring them to you from now on," Amy explained. She gave a shrug. "She said if you had any questions to talk to Soren."

Billy glanced at the envelopes briefly before handing them to Selia.

"Thanks, Amy," Selia replied, taking the stack.

Amy nodded and turned around, pushing the cart in front of her, so she could finish her rounds. Wil closed the door and crossed to Selia's desk, hitching a hip up on the edge.

"Fan mail?" he asked, his eyes sparkling with mischief.

Removing the rubber bands, she flipped through the envelopes, her brow furrowing in confusion. The envelopes weren't your usual business-letter envelopes, and each had Soren's name and the address hand-written across the front. They were either large square or rectangle shaped envelopes and many felt like there were cards inside them. Or, at the very least, paper heavier than what your typical business-type letter arrived on.

"These are all organizations," Selia said, completely confused. "Why would Soren be sending me these?"

"Why don't you ask him?" Wil asked.

"Good idea," Selia agreed. "Come on. It'll look odd if you don't escort me to Papa's office."

Collecting the envelopes, she wrapped the rubber band around them again. Together, they headed up to Soren's office.

"I'll wait out here for you, Miss Selia," Wil said in his eager, hyper, 'Billy' voice.

Maria's eyes lit up at Billy's words, but she said to Selia, "Soren's in a meeting with Nicky."

"Oh, well," Selia replied. "I'll take all the blame for intruding upon yet another of his meetings. Besides, he hasn't technically removed me as his assistant yet."

Maria chuckled and waved Selia on, knowing it was pointless. "Go on. You're probably the only one around here who can intrude on Soren and come out with your head attached."

Laughing, Selia entered Soren's office, shutting the door behind her. Stepping to the side, she leaned against the wall as Soren finished talking to Nicky.

Nicky was the Family's lead hacker. He wasn't that bad looking, if one went for conspiracy theorists. He had black hair that he kept spiked, a weak chin, and a gangly build just shy of six feet. She doubted he weighed an ounce over a hundred thirty pounds soaking wet. Nicky was, however, a wiz at what he did.

"Hey there, beautiful! Miss me?" Nicky asked, turning in his chair to see who'd come in the office.

"Hi, Nicky," Selia replied with a smile. "Like a toothache." She shot Soren an amused look. "I'm not interrupting anything, am I, Papa?"

"You probably are, but this kid loses me two minutes after he opens his mouth," Soren said demurely.

"You're getting better. It used to be one minute," Nicky shot back.

"Need me to sit in?" Selia teased Soren. "I can usually follow him, and when I can't, I remind him not everyone speaks 'Geek'."

Nick shot up from his chair. "Feel free to sit in! You're always welcome!"

Soren rolled his eyes. "Had any more attacks or marriage proposals, Selia?"

"Yeah, I heard about that," Nicky said, sounding concerned. "You're seeing someone other than me? I'm crushed! I'm wounded! You may have to salve my damaged ego."

"Yeah, and I'm thinking of adding another to the list," Selia shot back. "He's hot, handsome, and dangerous. I'll have my assistant send you a bouquet of roses and box of chocolates to ease the pain, later, Nicky." She paused as though considering something. "Or would you prefer a fruit basket?"

Sighing, Nicky shook his head. "You can only live in denial so long, Selia. You've succeeded in making me jealous, you've got me hooked, now claim your prize."

Selia rolled her eyes and looked at Soren. "He doesn't give up, does he? How come you haven't threatened him, Papa? Or are you waiting for me to do it?"

"There's no reason to threaten him. He'd faint if you so much as hugged him. All the Viagra in the world won't help him when he's unconscious and drooling."

Nicky suddenly decided to change topics. "So, what's the name of this new boyfriend I keep hearing about?"

"Dorian Porter," Selia replied smugly.

"Are you serious?" Nicky laughed. "Sounds like a character from a daytime soap."

"Feel free to look him up," Soren suggested.

"Oh, I intend to," Nicky assured him. He turned to Selia. "So, what brings you here to see me?"

"Actually, I came to ask Papa a question about these," Selia replied, holding up the stack of envelopes and wiggling them in the air. "I didn't even know you were here. To be honest, I had expected to see Alex."

"I thought you'd like to take over the charitable contributions aspect of business here," Soren replied smiling. "I'm having all the correspondence from the organizations we have contributed to in the past forwarded to you."

Glancing at Nicky, who had a sullen, pouty expression, Selia bit back a laugh. "This should certainly keep me occupied for a while." She dropped Soren a wink as she added, "Might keep me out of trouble, too."

"There are other ways to keep you occupied," Nicky suggested, trying to come out of his pout.

"Nicky," Soren said gently, as he opened a drawer in his desk. "Don't make me shoot you in the face."

Nicky shut up immediately. He put his hands in his lap and sat quietly.

Selia crossed to Soren and kissed his cheek. "Thanks, Papa. I'll get started on these now." She giggled. "If I didn't know better, I'd say you're trying to tie up my night life."

"Me? Never. How could you think such a thing?" Soren asked, laughter sparkling in his eyes.

"Of course not. Perish the thought!" Selia replied with a laugh. She turned to Nicky. "See you around, Nicky."

Nicky gave her a smile and polite nod, not saying anything, as she exited Soren's office. Wil, or rather 'Billy', was having a lively chat about a television series with Maria but excused himself when he saw Selia.

"Thanks for keeping him entertained," Selia said to Maria with a grin.

"Anytime," Maria replied, her eyes not leaving Billy. The phone rang and she gave a dramatic sigh. "I'll talk to you two later."

"See you later, Maria," Selia said, heading towards the elevator.

Billy nodded to Maria and followed Selia into the elevator. Once the door closed, he chuckled. "Is every woman in this building looking for a new boy toy?"

Shrugging, Selia leaned against the wall of the elevator. "I don't know. I've never seemed to have that particular problem." She gave him a smirk. "Oh, I should mention that Nicky asked who my new 'boyfriend' is… I told him 'Dorian Porter' and he didn't seem to have a clue as to who he is."

Wil shrugged. "Technically, neither do you. Nicky might find out, he might not. He's cute. For your biggest stalker."

Selia laughed. "He's harmless. I think. But you have a point. Are you going to clue me in on why everyone that hears the name 'Dorian Porter' freaks out?"

"If you want to know, sure, but it'll take all the mystery out of it." Wil admitted.

"I'm not asking for the nitty gritty details, love," Selia assured him. "Just the basics so I know why everyone wants to run in fear upon sight of Dorian."

"Early in the Sandman's career, I accidentally interfered in a CIA-FBI operation against a cell of terrorists in the city," Wil explained sheepishly. "Despite that, all the terrorists were… ehh, stopped. It was quite a mess, and the government boys were trying to make each other take the heat for the damages. I was dressed as Dorian that night, under the mask."

Selia stared at him in a mixture of awe and admiration. She hadn't heard anything about something like that happening, though she also wasn't surprised. There was plenty that occurred in the city that she didn't know about having happened.

Wil shrugged and blushed a little. "I suggested that they use my fake persona, calling him a ruthless mercenary, and blame him for the mess. Then, the G-men were doing clean-up and being the good guys. The men in charge of those units have gotten pretty high up in their respective agencies. Anytime they have a black op that would get the public in an uproar, they blame it on 'Dorian Porter.' He's got, last time I checked, three hundred thirty-eight confirmed kills, and suspected in almost two thousand others."

"Oh, my," Selia said, staring at him in a mixture of awe and delight. "No wonder the Families fear him. Though... nah, you probably wouldn't go for it."

"Try me," he encouraged.

"Well," Selia began shyly. "You said that you'd need to choose a persona that wouldn't be wanted around the Family. I've developed a bit of a reputation for liking 'bad boys'..." She trailed off, not quite looking at him, and hoping he was following her train of thought.

Wil cocked a single eyebrow at her and started to chuckle.

"That would prove interesting," he admitted. "I can also see some options forming that aren't currently available."

She smiled shyly at him, feeling once more like the teen that was on a date with her crush for the first time. A strange feeling, certainly, but she was enjoying their unusual relationship. The elevator stopped and she looked up, quickly schooling her expression as the doors opened.

"Shall we continue this in my office, Billy?" she asked as they stepped into the lobby.

"Anything you like, Miss Selia!" he said enthusiastically.

They quickly made their way to her office, and once the door was shut, she tilted her head to the side.

"Perhaps I should have dinner with Dorian tonight. Maybe go to a good Chinese or Japanese restaurant with sushi?" She paused before asking slyly, "Think Dorian has a suit tucked away somewhere?"

"I've got the wig, cards and prosthetic stashed in a locker nearby," answered Wil. "We can stop and get a suit, if you don't want to stop by my place."

She giggled. "It might be better if you pick me up. Otherwise, we might not get out as anything other than our other alter egos."

Nodding, he replied, "Okay, I'll get to my place after taking you home."

"Sounds good to me," she replied. About to say something else, she caught the sound of the door knob turning and she moved to face the door.

Wil was at the door and armed in a heartbeat. As Bernie popped his head around, Wil, or rather Billy, pressed the barrel of his Walther PPQ against Bernie's cheek and used his freehand to pin Bernie with the half-opened door.

"Gee, Mr. Caruso, you ought to learn to knock," Wil advised with 'Billy's' hyper-cheerful voice. He released the door as he took the weapon away from Bernie's now pale face.

"What's that smell?" Alex's voice came from out in the hallway.

"Shut up!" Bernie growled at his brother. He stepped into the office, looking quite self-conscious. He smiled nervously at Wil and then Selia. "The kid certainly takes your safety seriously. I have to admire that."

"Oh, I admire that and a lot more," Selia shot back, her eyes twinkling. "I take it I don't have to introduce either of you to my current bodyguard?"

Alex popped in, looking controlled but pleasant, as always. He smiled at Wil.

"You must be Billy... hey! You used to be our doorman! Good to have you back!" Alex exclaimed, smiling broadly and putting his hand out to Wil.

Wil shook it enthusiastically and said, "Good to see you, too, Mr. Caruso!" He held his hand out to Bernie. "And you, also, Mr. Caruso! No hard feelings, I hope?"

"No, no," Bernie said as he shook Wil's hand less than enthusiastically. "Good to have you back." He cleared his throat. "Good job back there."

"What brings you two here?" Selia asked, greeting Alex with a hug. She added, almost accusingly, "I thought I was going to be seeing you two in Soren's office instead of Nicky."

"You know we can't stand that kid," Bernie grumble, seemingly glad to have a new topic. "But the reason we came is we wanted to invite you out to lunch!"

Alex squeezed Selia again. "We haven't done it in a while. Thought it was time to bring back an old favorite."

"I can definitely get behind that," Selia replied, after Alex released her. She turned to Bernie, holding her arms out. "I'll give you a hug only if you behave yourself." Her grin widened as she added, "Billy isn't the only one armed today."

Bernie chuckled and opened his arms for a hug. "I promise."

Laughing, Selia stepped forward and gave him a hug. It was good to see the brothers, and better still to be invited to lunch with them. So, there was a possibility they would be fishing for information, but she didn't care. She loved and trusted the pair.

"I'd love to go to lunch with you both," she said, as Bernie embraced her, keeping his hands in polite and proper places.

"Uh, Miss Selia..." Wil began.

"It's okay." Selia assured him. "These two have been keeping me safe ever since I arrived in the city. I trust them with my life."

'Billy' considered for a second, and then nodded.

"As long as Mr. Soren doesn't think I'm letting the side down on my job, I won't object!"

"I'll worry about Papa," Selia assured him. "He can't fault you when I'm telling you to take a break. These two can play babysitter yet again until you get back from lunch." She gave Bernie a sly look. "No teddy bears required this time, either."

"Oh, good. I'm still paying off that last one," Bernie said with a sigh.

Selia's eyes widened. Sighing, she shook her head, but she wasn't able to lose the smile. Kissing his cheek, she said, "You, dear, are hopeless." Stepping out of the embrace, she waggled a finger at Alex. "And you shouldn't have let him spend so much on me. Don't get me wrong, I appreciate the gesture, but you shouldn't be so mean to your brother."

"Well, I'm still under the opinion that he has a crush on either Nightshade or you, or both." Alex relented. "Why else would he buy one of the first available Nightshade teddy bears? The hand-stitched, made in the USA ones, instead of waiting for the inevitable cheaper China-made copies?"

"You don't know if they'll take off and there will be one on every corner and convenience store in town in less than a month!" Bernie barked. His voice eased a little as he declared, "Besides, it's about quality craftsmanship and supporting local small businesses."

"I hope whoever Nightshade is has a trademark on her image," Alex said. "And sorry, Bernie, but I can't walk two blocks in the city without seeing a girl, or occasionally a guy, sporting Nightshade's hairstyle. She's gonna be an action figure before the end of the year. Wish I knew where to buy stock in it."

"Actually, if somebody changes just a small detail here and there, and doesn't use the name 'Nightshade,' they can get away with selling dolls, bears, whatever, and make money," Wil explained in his Billy persona. "But I'm betting both Nightshade and her sidekick have somebody cashing in on the popularity."

"If they don't, they're losing out on a fortune," Selia said. She looked at Alex curiously. "I haven't been to any of the meetings with Papa lately, so I'm out of the loop on the latest gossip. Who is everyone complaining about the most these days? Nightshade or the Sandman?"

"It depends on who you ask, but the Sandman gets the most blame for things," Alex replied. "Most of the big wigs figure he brought Nightshade in to draw public attention. Personally, I think it's interesting that the pair only attack certain kinds of businesses. The kind involving stuff that really hurts people. But anyways, no one is happy about Nightshade becoming a pop culture sensation. Be it in the city or beyond."

"Score one for the girls," Selia said with a chuckle. "I can't imagine being a popular figure is going to help her in busting the bad guys."

Wil was probably going to give her a time, later, and not just for questioning the brothers about Nightshade and the Sandman. She was pretty certain of it.

"As long as she doesn't pull a 60's Batman and start running around in broad daylight, I doubt it'll impede her much," Wil suggested. "Unless she doesn't like the sound of iPhone cameras going off nearby, of course."

Yep, she was going to get scolded later. She glanced at Wil and laughed. "They do seem to like the night. Probably easier to hide. You know, more shadows and all that." Shrugging, she decided it was time to change the topic. Not to mention, she was getting hungry. "Enough about the dynamic duo, though. Billy, I'll give you a call when we're back here. I still have those letters to go through and if I don't spend at least one full day here, Papa will have my head."

# Chapter Twenty Eight

Half an hour later, Selia, Alex, and Bernie were sitting in a corner booth at the back of Bernie's favorite eatery and tavern, Jim's Place. Jim's Place served everything from fish and chips, to burgers and sandwiches. It was your typical bar-and-restaurant style eatery with dim lighting, a bar that wrapped around the center of the building and played rock music from a local station.

Selia sipped a sweet tea while Alex had a soda, and Bernie tossed back a beer from a long-neck bottle. She'd decided on a club sandwich, Alex was waiting on a loaded quarter pounder, and Bernie ordered the fish and chips to go with his beer.

Grabbing a fry and dunking it in some ketchup, she smiled at the brothers. Alex was sitting beside her, on the outside, and Bernie was across from his brother. She was effectively protected on both sides. It was good to know two of her most favorite men were also the most dangerous enforcers of the Lascari family. They were the pair that all the others in the Family strived to emulate.

Alex and Bernie said, almost in chorus, "How are you doing?"

The pair looked at each other, then to her. Selia smiled at the fact that this was one of the few times they actually acted like brothers.

"Surviving," she deadpanned. Smiling to reassure them, she continued. "I'm doing pretty good, despite everything that's happened."

"Quite a lot's happened," Alex observed.

"First kills are usually toughest," Bernie added. "You going to be okay?"

*Bloody hells*, Selia thought. She hadn't reckoned on anyone thinking, let alone questioning her, about that. It wasn't like she could tell them she'd killed before, and not just in this land or even recently. Then again, maybe she could.

"I'm not in need of a shrink or having nightmares, if that's what you're asking," she said in a soft voice. "I had a good long talk with Papa."

They weren't looking at her as though they believed what she was saying. So, she offered something of an explanation in the hopes of reassuring the brothers she was fine.

"You both know I arrived with Soren when I was sixteen. Trust me when I say it's nothing that will prey upon my conscience." Neither looked even remotely convinced, so she added in exasperation, "You're also both presuming this is my first kill."

The brothers looked at each other significantly.

"I don't think that's really a surprise for either of us," Alex finally admitted. "But let us keep our delusions of you not being a cold blooded-killing machine like us for a while longer."

Selia chuckled. "That is something I'll never become, Alex. I can assure you of that."

"It wasn't but so long ago, you promised us you wouldn't get further involved in Family business," Bernie said, a little on edge. "Now you're involved in *all* the Families, and their businesses. You're going to have to understand our skepticism."

"It wasn't my idea to get dragged further into the Family, let alone be drawn into dealing with all of them," Selia countered. Her voice grew sharp as she added, "You can place the blame for *that* on Angelo's head."

Technically, it also belonged to Lucien, but she couldn't blame Lucien for making her liaison when it really was for the greater good. She trusted the brothers, but not enough to let them know that little fact. It would open too many questions as to why Lucien wanted her involved as liaison, let alone her help with his problems.

"We'll gladly blame him," Bernie announced. "A lot of his decisions over the past year have grated Alex and me the wrong way."

"But what are you doing to protect yourself? Billy won't always be around," Alex added.

"Like the order to kill me if I hadn't been home?" Selia asked Bernie slyly. Turning to Alex, she said, "As for protection, I've been seeing someone who makes all my other boyfriends look like pansies. He'll protect me when I'm out. If he isn't around…" She trailed off with a shrug. "Guess I'll just have to step up to the plate and protect myself, won't I?"

"So it's true that you're dating Dorian Porter?" Alex almost whispered.

"It's true," Selia said with a Cheshire cat grin.

"Sweetie," Bernie began in a tone he usually reserved for newbies learning their jobs. "That Porter fellow is the kind of bad that makes guys like *us* nervous. I know you've got your charms, but if you aren't paying him, I wouldn't trust him." He paused. "And yeah, that order to kill you still doesn't sit right with either of us."

Selia laughed softly as she lowered her gaze from the pair. Yep, she was definitely going to let Wil know that

Dorian would be the perfect choice as her beau while around the Family.

Raising her gaze, she gave the brothers a warm smile. "I'm glad you two care about me so much. Don't worry about Al and his desire to see me fail. Or six-feet under. I can handle him, if the need should ever arise. My recent trip with Papa has reminded me of a lot of things, most especially of who I am." Her expression softened. "As for Dorian, I'm not paying him, but I do trust him."

"Guess we'll just have to take your trust on that, but if you need us," Alex offered, "All you have to do is call."

"I doubt Al would appreciate me pulling you away from your duties to come rescue me," Selia said dryly. "I might be able to handle him, but I doubt you two have the same choices that I do. I don't want to see either of you become his next targets."

"You worry about your back, we'll worry about ours," the brothers said in unison.

"In that case, you'll be the first I call, right after Papa," Selia assured them.

"Well, that's all we ask," Alex replied.

"So what about all these-" Bernie began.

"Selia!" An anguished cry came from not far away.

All three of them turned to the source of the outburst. A man in a suit too large for him with sunken cheekbones and eyes, wearing glasses with a mop of unruly auburn hair, half-lunged, half-tripped his way towards her. The man looked like a bookworm who had just discovered tequila.

*"Selia!"* he wailed again.

The brothers rose to their feet, hands going into their jackets.

"Tell me it isn't true!" The man nearly screamed in anguish. "Tell me that the uncouth loud-mouth from Britain didn't propose to you!"

Bernie leaned towards Selia, and stage whispered, "You want us to club him?"

"No," Selia said, drawing the word out. She wasn't certain if she wanted to laugh and applaud Wil's performance or throttle him. It was an interesting dichotomy. With a heavy sigh, she added, "Let's see what he wants."

"Pretty obvious what he wants," Bernie said with a snort.

"Yes, he did," Alex announced with a cheerful smile. "Along with two plane tickets to Paris."

The man fell to his knees as he yelled "noooo!" to the ceiling. He thrust his hands out, supplicating. "I thought we had something, Selia! Something special! Sure, only on every third weekend! Tawdry and superficial! But I thought we had a connection!"

*I'm going to kill him*, Selia thought, feeling her face burn. Okay, well, maybe not Wil, but she was going to kill someone, and soon. Oh, yes, she was.

"I, um…" Selia began, forcing a smile onto her face as she scooted to the edge of the booth and turned to face him. Through nearly-clenched teeth, she said in a too-sweet tone, "I didn't accept it, either. It was a joke… I believe."

Wil stumbled into a standing position, came over, and fell in front of the booth. "Then it's not too late?" He distinctly smelled of alcohol and Selia briefly wondered if he'd shampooed his hair with it.

"I… uh… look, Tim…" Selia managed to say.

"Seth!" he wailed. "My name is Seth! How many men do you have?" He suddenly cringed as if struck. He lay against her knee. "Forgive me, mistress! I did not mean to speak so harshly! Don't punish me! At least not here? Later, maybe?"

She was so going to hurt him later. He was going to have to make this up to her in so many ways.

"Was there something you wanted, Seth?" she asked, trying to not grit her teeth.

"Yes, yes," he said, almost pleadingly. He fumbled in his pocket for something.

*Oh, no*, she thought. *I'm going to kill him. He isn't…*

He produced a small, red jewelry box and held it out. He stuttered, "Just… just… just think about it?" He flipped open the box, revealing a simple, but beautiful diamond ring.

She glanced at it briefly before taking another, longer look. The quality and cut of the diamond, along with the no-longer used setting, made her realize the ring was an antique. At least a hundred years old.

Her eyes widened. She could only guess at the cost of the ring. She narrowed her gaze as she looked at 'Seth' who was giving her huge puppy-dog eyes, though she caught a flash of mischief and mirth for a brief moment.

"I, um… will think about it," she said, taking the box and staring at the ring. Was it an heirloom? Or had he bought it somewhere for a small fortune? She was definitely going to ask him later.

"Thank you, oh merciful one! Thank you!" Adding mock sobs and tears into his performance. He looked around, standing up, suddenly, straightened a tie that wasn't really there and said in a much more sober, and somber tone, "I believe I may have just embarrassed myself. If you will excuse me."

He hurried away from her and out the door of the restaurant, without another word.

"Not a word. Either of you," Selia commanded, snapping the box shut.

To their credit, Bernie and Alex stayed quiet for a full two seconds. Then they burst into laughter, unable to stop until tears ran down both brothers' cheeks.

"So," Alex finally said, clearing his throat. "How about I find our waiter and find out where our food is?"

"Wonderful idea," Selia said, scooting back into the corner of the booth.

Holding the box she flipped it over, looking for an idea of where the ring came from, but found nothing. For some inexplicable reason, she was tempted to open it up and look at the ring again, but she resisted by tucking it into the inside pocket of her jacket.

Alex dismissed himself presumably to look for the waiter.

"Um," Bernie said when Alex was out of sight. "That was, uh, different. You sure you're holding up okay?"

Selia raised her eyes to meet his and arched a brow. "Really? I hadn't noticed." She rolled her eyes. "I'm fine. I think someone is just trying to play an elaborate joke on me. I've never seen that man before in my life."

"Uh, sure, I believe you," Bernie said a little too quickly as he sat down. "So, how many boyfriends do you have?" He paused, thinking, his face chagrined. "I'm just wondering how many more of these we may have to worry about." His face paled, as he realized the implication of what he'd just said. "No disrespect or anything."

"I thought you were keeping a running tally on how many guys I was dating," Selia shot back, her eyes sparkling with mischief.

"Um…" Bernie stuttered. "I, uh…" He looked down at his non-existent plate. "I stopped keeping track after ten."

"That's okay, Bernie," Selia said, patting his hand gently. "If things go well, I might just stick with one."

"Have you come to a decision?" He looked disquieted. "You aren't marrying that one, are you?"

"No," she said, a little too quickly. "I'd think considering my reputation for loving the bad boys, you'd have already figured it out."

"Ah, hell, not him!" Bernie exclaimed. "Not that loud-mouthed rock guy! Marry my brother before you marry that guy, please!"

"Alex?" she drawled out the name in intrigue. "Now, why do you mention him?"

"Ah, come on, Lia. You know damn well both of us have been sweet on you since you showed up. I've come to accept that I couldn't keep up with you." He seemed about to look her in the eye but changed his mind. "But I'd much rather see you with my brother than that loud-mouthed tart."

Selia glanced away, knowing she looked guilty. "Yeah, well, Papa stepped in years ago to keep anything from growing between me and Alex," she admitted quietly. She gave her head a slight shake. "And no, my first choice wouldn't be the rocker, either. Papa would have him six-feet under after more than ten minutes around him."

Bernie smiled and said, "Well, all right." Then, something seemed to occur to him. "Holy shit, you're talking about Porter, aren't you?"

"Maybe," she replied in the guilty tone she'd used as a teen. Her face felt warm, and she could guess she was blushing, even if it was only a little bit. "I like him. He's good to me and treats me right, but I don't know how he feels about me."

"As long as he makes you happy and treats you right," Bernie relented.

"There is an added bonus to Dorian," Selia said softly. Bernie nodded his encouragement. "Al is going to hate it."

Bernie laughed. "Well, if it all turns out the way you think, you'll have my blessing. Maybe even Alex's."

"My blessing on what?" Alex asked, returning with their waiter in tow. The waiter was laden with their orders.

"Sit down, grab your food, and we'll tell you all about it," Bernie offered.

# Chapter Twenty Nine

After a great deal of apologizing from Wil, the pair showed up the next day at Soren's office at the same time. Fortunately, no one seemed to notice, or even care. In fact, word seemed to have gotten around that Billy was her bodyguard and took his job seriously. Just to torment Wil, she'd chosen a short black leather skirt and tight vest-like black and white pin-striped blouse with two-inch stiletto heels to go with her black dress jacket.

"So, what are your opinions on these charities?" Selia asked a short time later. She didn't worry about the office being bugged. Wil swept her office for such each time they entered the room. "There's about a dozen parties, three art gallery openings, and a handful of fundraisers here. I know Papa never went to all of them, but I have no clue how he picked what to attend."

"Ask him how he chose," Wil suggested.

"I'll ask him later," Selia said. "But first, are there any functions you'd like to go to?"

"Oh, anything you like. I enjoy helping people, but I hate the political formalities and faux smiles at such events," Wil said bluntly.

"Right there with you, love," Selia replied. "I was thinking maybe a couple charities and a gallery opening or two. I never did like the boring, stuffy affairs I attended with Papa. So I plan on avoiding those events."

"Are there any animal shelters on the list?" Wil asked suddenly. "I'm talking about the no-kill types. Although... if there's a standard shelter that just needs the right amount of cash to convert... that might be worth looking into."

Selia flipped through the stack and found invitations from three shelters. She leaned forward, offering the envelopes to Wil.

"These are the only ones in the stack, but I'm sure I'll be getting more once people realize I've taken over for Papa." She blushed a little. "I might be known in the social circle, since I often go to these things with him."

"Oh, you're known in many places with many faces," her lover teased. He took the envelopes, flipped through them rapidly, and put them into his inner jacket pocket. "What's the plan for the day?"

"Misbehaving with you, deciding which of these I want to go to, and playing bait," Selia replied. "I'm getting a bit tired with all these attacks, to be honest. I'm afraid things are just going to get worse with Al."

"I think you're right about Al," Wil agreed. "Still, hopefully the day will merit some good things."

Selia sighed and leaned back in her chair. "I hope so." She shook her head slowly. "It seems no matter how hard I try to move further away from the Family, the deeper I'm pulled in. I know Lucien was trying to help get me out and I can't complain because he needs me to solve his problem. But I swear I think Al knows I'm trying to leave, and he's determined to keep me tied to him and the Family business."

"That sounds like Big Al," Wil griped. "Always treating his people like property he owns."

"Uh, Selia?" Maria's voice came over the intercom. "You're needed in the lobby?"

Selia punched a button. "Um, okay. Thanks?" She looked at Wil as she stood. "Am I going to regret this?"

"I don't know what you're talking about," Wil said with a straight face.

"Of course not," she replied as he held the door open for her. Walking the short distance to the lobby, she kept her expression pleasant and schooled. As they entered the lobby, she headed to the receptionist's desk. "Hey, Cecelia, Maria said I'm needed?"

"Excuse me, miss?" a voice said from behind her. Selia turned to find a man wearing a simple royal blue polo shirt with the name of a local shelter embroidered across the breast. In his arms was something wrapped in a dark blue blanket. "Are you Selia Lascari?"

"Yes," Selia said cautiously, not looking a Wil. "How can I help you?"

The man's face brightened, and he nodded to her as he began unwrapping the now-wiggling bundle.

"This little thing is for you."

He sat the little puppy on the floor, revealing a black-and-white spotted puppy that looked to be a mix of Rottweiler and Staffordshire terrier. Not even the size of a full-grown cat, it bounced around the man's feet.

Selia's face lit up upon seeing the puppy. She knelt down, offering the puppy her hand. The man had it on a small halter, and he let the puppy bounce forward. Though not far enough for it to scratch and claw against Selia's clothing. Not worried about damaging her clothes, Selia picked the little pup up and cuddled it close, getting her face washed in the process.

"Is she seriously for me?" Selia asked, trying to not sound overly excited about it.

"Yes, ma'am," the man replied, pulling a folded sheet of paper from his back pocket. "A gentleman named 'Wil' signed the papers and said to bring her to you. If you would sign here?" He gestured to a line on the bottom of the sheet.

Despite the wiggling, squirming puppy, Selia glanced over the paper, skimming it for the details before accepting the man's pen and signing her name.

"Uh, Miss Lascari?" Cecelia cut in, her voice guarded and hesitant. "It will take a while for me to arrange a doggy bed, or puppy pads so the little girl doesn't test our stain resistant carpeting. Maybe you should tuck her into a drawer for the time being?"

"Oh, geez. Yeah, I'll have to do something." Selia eyeballed her bodyguard. "I'm surprised Wil didn't think of that. For an average-looking guy, he's usually on top of every detail."

"Gee, Miss Selia, that's a pretty little girl you've got there!" Wil said in "Billy's" voice. His smile widened as he pointed to the pup's collar. "Looks like she brought you something, too!"

Selia looked at the puppy's happy, eager face. The little pup was smiling and began trying to lick Selia's face. However, Selia could spot the twinkling of metal and gems next to the dog's id tag on its collar.

"What in the hell is this?" Soren's voice snapped through the air.

The puppy nearly jumped out of Selia's arms. Selia managed to keep a hold of the little stinker, but the puppy was now looking at Soren. It barked once and 'smiled' at Soren.

Cecelia uttered a girlish "Awwww!" before slapping a hand over her own mouth.

"I, um... was sent a puppy from Wil," Selia said, a bright smile on her face. She turned to Billy and asked, "See if you can get that off while I hold her?"

"Looks like it's another ring, Miss Selia!" Wil announced as Billy. His dexterous fingers had the ring off the collar loop in no time. He held it out to her. It was a band of titanium, with a half-carat sapphire in the center. A quarter-carat diamond sat to either side of the sapphire. Wil put his face right up to the puppy and allowed the eager girl to lick his nose. He actually giggled.

Soren looked as far from a giggle as he could get.

Selia didn't know if she wanted to laugh, scream, or jump for joy. Considering the fury on Soren's face, she opted for a different choice.

"It's gorgeous," she breathed, glancing at Wil for a brief moment before taking it with one hand. "I'll trade. You take the puppy, and I'll take the ring." Wil nodded and she was then holding the ring and smiling girlishly at it. Glancing up, she noticed the 'delivery man' had vanished.

She slipped the ring onto her right hand and wasn't the least bit surprised it fit perfectly. Looking at Soren, she smiled. "Can I keep her, Papa?"

Soren ground his teeth together so viciously that Selia and Wil could hear the molars protesting.

"Come with me... now," the elder Lascari growled.

The puppy growled in response, but her tail was wagging.

Soren glared at the pup for a moment, but finally just rolled his eyes and gestured for the three of them to follow. Selia walked behind Soren, and Wil, puppy in his arms, followed after them. He made cooing sounds and sweet talk to the canine the entire time.

Once the door was closed to his office, and everyone was inside, Soren spun on the trio as Wil let the pup down.

"Explain this damned lunacy-" Soren shouted.

The puppy barked at him, showing more than a little fang. She stood between Wil and Selia, her short fur ruffled.

Soren made the smallest of gestures towards his jacket. Wil had his gun out and pointed it to the floor so fast that Selia wondered if he had conjured it out of thin air.

"If you even think about threatening the dog," Wil said in the Sandman's voice. "I will knee-cap you right here. One shot for each knee. The dog will get to use your carpet for a toilet while the emergency services clean you up. Then, I will send Dorian Porter out to every member of your family... except Selia."

"Leave the puppy out of this, Papa," Selia said softly. "You have no one to blame but yourself, anyway." She knelt and scooped the puppy up into her arms. "Besides, if she's this protective as a puppy, think what she'll be like as an adult. Considering everything going on, are you really going to argue about me having another form of protection?"

Soren wasn't looking at Selia or the puppy. His eyes darted between Wil's eyes and the Walther PPQ in Wil's right hand.

"I apologize, but this bit with the engagement proposals has gone on far enough," Soren said, letting his body relax.

Keeping constant eye contact with Soren, Wil holstered his weapon, even as his left hand reached over and scratched the puppy behind her ears.

"Good girl," Wil said softly.

"Perhaps, Papa, you shouldn't have told a certain someone he needed to make an honest woman of me," Selia intoned quietly. "Our situation is far more unique than anyone else's. Even you have to admit that."

"You'll have to anticipate some old-fashioned expectations from me, Selia," Soren retorted. "As for you, sir. Can I request a little less smart-ass interruption in my office's business?"

"Nothing smart-ass about my proposals," Wil quipped. "She hasn't said yes. Still trying to find the approach that makes her melt and accept."

Throwing his hands up towards the ceiling, Soren breathed, "You two are impossible sometimes. No wonder I love having you around."

Selia laughed and let the puppy back down on the floor. She gave Wil a pointed look. "Well, it would help if the proposal came from someone who could be seen around here." She crossed to her father and kissed his cheek. "Love you, too, Papa."

The puppy sniffed at Soren's shoes and promptly sat down on his feet. Soren looked keenly at the small, happy animal.

"Look at the size of her paws," he observed. "She's going to be at least sixty pounds before she's done growing."

He leaned down and offered his hand. The pup sniffed and gave his fingers a long wet doggy kiss. Soren chuckled. "She's a good girl. At least she doesn't hold a grudge. Do you have a name in mind for her?"

"Luna," Selia said without thinking. It seemed oddly appropriate. "So... does this mean I get to bring her to work with me?"

"I'll check with Cecelia to make sure she gets all the needed supplies, and Luna will need to wear a rig declaring her an ambassador or something, but yes. You can bring her to work with you."

"I have a specific pet store that Cecelia can order the supplies from, and I've already enrolled Luna in the training programs needed." Wil interjected. "Also, with your permission, I'd like for Selia, you, and Luna to be photographed and used in a campaign to help raise funds and awareness for this shelter."

Wil withdrew one of the envelopes that Selia had given him earlier and held it out to Soren.

"This is from where I rescued Luna. I made a five figure donation, which is how I was able to get them to deliver her." He explained. "But I can't be their sole provider of good fortune."

Soren took the envelope, looked at the name of the shelter, and smiled. "I am agreeable to those demands. I know the owner of this shelter. He and I used to play together as kids. I'd be happy to give them a boost."

"Shall I arrange it, Papa?" Selia asked brightly. "I'll be more than happy to help the shelter this precious girl came from."

"Absolutely," Soren replied.

"I think I'll arrange that from home, if it's okay with you? I'd like to take this girl for a walk and bond with her."

"Are you taking Billy with you as well?" Soren gestured toward Wil.

"Actually, I was thinking of calling Dorian. He shouldn't be busy, and I'd like him to meet my little angel," Selia replied. "Billy, why don't you take the rest of the day off? I'll wait here with Papa until he shows up. I'm not going to need two protectors, and I doubt I can do much better than Dorian."

It took everything she had to not burst out laughing as she spoke, since Dorian and Billy were the same person.

"Alrighty," Wil said. He nodded to Soren, kissed Selia on the cheek, and kissed Luna on her head. The pup nuzzled into the smooch.

After Billy excused himself, Soren looked at Selia.

"Things are getting more complicated, sweetheart." He nodded to Luna but began rubbing the pup along her neck and jaw. "I'm not talking about the newest addition to the family, either."

Saying nothing, Selia waited for him to continue.

"Al is under the notion that Dorian is responsible for the attacks against you. He doesn't feel it has anything to do with some larger conspiracy." Soren looked levelly at her. "Even if there is one, he considers it to be Lucien's problem. So, it isn't something we need to concern ourselves with... the Family, or the liaison."

Selia blinked a few times at Soren. "You know, as liaison, my conversations shouldn't be eavesdropped upon." She thrust the puppy against Soren, giving him no choice but to take her. Stalking over to where the bug was, she removed it and tilted it in her hand as she said, "Bye bye!" Dropping the bug to the floor, Selia promptly crushed it with her foot. "Sorry, Papa, but I'm tired of worrying if someone hears or not. If Al has a problem, tell him to take it up with me. I'm the liaison and I signed that damned contract."

Shaking her head, she rolled her shoulders. "So the fact that I was attacked, as liaison no less, doesn't matter to Al. Somehow, I'm not surprised. This does mean, however, that something will have to happen so Al has no choice but to step in. If not to me, then to someone else in the Family."

"That's my girl," Soren beamed somberly. "Getting the point so I don't have to explain it further."

"Remind me again why I can't just give Al a double tap?" Selia all but pleaded. "And make it a good reason, because I really want to off him right now."

"It would leave a vacuum if there's not sufficient reason." Soren held up a hand. "You know damned well what I mean by that. If it's not a power play by one of the other Families, or the government in some form, it's seen as an act of weakness by the Family and then it's war. If he can be shown to be negligent, betraying, or not sane, then it's expected that he die. Nightshade can't just kill him because she's Nightshade. Selia cannot kill him just because he throws her to the wolves. I can't kill him because he threw my daughter to the wolves. It doesn't work that way and you know it."

She made a sour face and sighed. "Okay, those are good reasons." Scratching Luna behind her ears, she looked at her father. "Will you look after Luna while I go out tonight with Dorian? We can't make any move until we figure out who is behind all this."

Soren looked down at Luna. Luna leaned up and licked Soren's face. He smiled and looked back to Selia.

"Yeah, the two of us will be fine. Go have fun and be safe."

"I can guarantee the fun, Papa, but I can't promise I'll be safe."

# Chapter Thirty

Dorian created a bit of a stir picking her up from Soren's office, which was exactly what Selia hoped would happen. He followed her to the parking deck of her condo and together they set out to walk Luna. She hoped to stop at a pet store of Wil's choice to pick up some treats for Luna, and maybe a toy or two. Luna loved the attention and the walk. The puppy pranced along bouncing on the small piles of leaves or sniffing around at the various scents.

Selia smiled at the puppy, who trotted ahead of them. She brushed up against Dorian, smiling at him as they walked along. He kept her on the inside, away from the road and there was no question about him being alert.

After about ten minutes of walking, Selia and Dorian followed the trail into the small nearby park. Selia had always loved the parks of the city as a teen. The trees, the birds, and wildlife that thrived there. This one, the one closest to her condo, was more like a small forest with paths and playgrounds tucked within it.

They walked in companionable silence, following one of the winding trails used mainly by dog walkers. Every so often, Luna would pause and look up, sniffing the air before giving a huff and continuing on. They were alone for perhaps two minutes when Luna stopped, turned her nose to the west and growled. A moment later, Selia's own senses pick up the distinct stench of necromancy.

"Trouble," she advised Wil.

He went to one knee, as if to tie his shoe. He stood up with a small automatic in his hand, from a pocket he produced a silencer and screwed it into the barrel.

There were nine attackers. They came in groups of three. The first from the woods to the west, the second from the woods to the east, and the third from behind the trio. All were armed with melee weapons: clubs, knives, and one with a chain.

Wil wasted no time, firing precise shots into the kneecaps of the three who had come up behind them. He pivoted, facing the group who had entered from the west. Selia pulled her own weapon, the M&P .40, and cast a quick silencing spell upon it. It was difficult to do with Luna tugging viciously at her leash, wanting to defend her owners.

Selia shot the left-most western attacker in the chest, turned, and double-tapped each member of the eastern group in the center of their chests, as well. She backed up until she felt Wil's back against hers. She took a moment to check over her shoulder. Wil had dropped the final two from the western group; emptying his clip. He was now reloading.

"That was quick," Selia observed.

Luna was still growling and barking. Selia was about to tell her new ward to take it easy when she realized all nine attackers were getting to their feet, seemingly unharmed.

"The necromancer," Selia hissed. "I can smell her magic on them. So can Luna, I bet."

"Great," growled Wil. "I've been to this party before."

Selia snickered as she recalled the necromancer, Moreisa, raising every person that the Sandman and Nightshade had killed while taking out Alfi. Wil chambered the first round into his backup gun and began shooting attackers in the head.

She followed suit, taking careful aim and putting a bullet between the eyes of the three attackers from the east. They dropped once more.

"Uh, problem," Wil declared.

Selia began to look back at him when she noticed the three she had just shot in the head getting back up.

"Suggestions?" Wil almost demanded.

"I need a second," Selia replied, wondering what could be done.

Wil stuffed the silenced gun into his waistband. He drew both arms up and brought them down quickly. His steel batons, the preferred weapon used when he was the Sandman, snapped out and into his waiting hands. He charged the group that had attempted to catch them from behind. They were the closest.

It was a sight to behold. Wil moved like a professional warrior, spinning and measuring each strike to be the most effective. He did not strike to incapacitate as he usually did as the Sandman. His blows now were meant to crack skulls, break necks, and crush sternums, but mere seconds after the blows were delivered, the attackers were rising again. It wouldn't take long for these seemingly undying hench people to wear him down enough for mistakes to be made.

Selia finally recognized the spell. It wasn't actual necromancy, but Moreisa's aura of death magic tainted any spell she cast. This spell was used often by Selia's people. The best mages were called into action whenever an outside force tried to invade Temeria. The mages would cast a powerful protection spell that prevented anything man-made from causing true harm to those it was cast upon. It could not stop the force behind the attack, but the objects never truly struck. Looking to the ground around where each group had originally fallen, Selia could see the mashed bullets that had never struck home. They had been stopped by the magical protection.

Looking to the sky, Selia was grateful to see black ominous clouds overhead. She'd used the spell years ago, long before she'd come to New Campania, but she still remembered it. She trusted that her magic and skills were enough to be more precise now, than when she'd been at ten years old and learning it.

Speaking the words in Temerian, she raised her right hand, fingers splayed as she felt the energy, the magic that flowed through her blood, building until it demanded freedom from her body. Carefully she pin-pointed the targets, mentally commanding the spell to hit only her opponents. Drawing a deep breath, she let it out slowly as she spoke the words that released the magic she conjured.

White hot streaks of lightning burst from the clouds, landing dead center in the hearts of the attackers in front of her. She turned towards the others, and more streaks of lightning lashed out in pulses, killing the assailants in mere seconds.

The smell of charred flesh and burnt clothing wafted in the air. She looked at Wil, a faint smile on her face as she dispelled the remnants of the magic.

"How in the hells are we going to get this mess cleaned up?" she asked, gesturing towards the bodies. A moment later, she nearly fell, as the exhaustion of her efforts caught up with her. Wil caught her, but just barely. She let him ease her back into a standing position.

Wil then pointed to the ominous clouds overhead, where the lightning had been drawn from. "There's no way the entire city missed all that lightning coming down," he stated. "I doubt anyone saw it as nine individual bolts. It probably looked like ball lightning to anyone who happened to be looking in this direction."

He looked about pointing out charred bits of flora near the now-dead attackers.

"We gather their weapons, get away from here, and I'm betting the headline will read 'ball lightning claims group of joggers'. They'll probably even have some meteorological experts chime in on how rare this kind of thing is."

"Don't forget the bullets," Selia said, even as she started to collect everything.

"Huh?" Wil said, confused. She pointed to the misshapen bits of lead on the ground. Wil whistled. "Is *that* what happened?"

"Yup, which is why I had to pull a Thor," she replied with a grin. "The spell was basically an uber powerful shield. It was cast by Moreisa, but I don't think she's the one spear-heading Lucien's problems. Not this time, anyway."

"I think I recognized a couple of them… before they became briquettes. After the attack in the car, I familiarized myself with the latest thugs for hire that operate in the city. Some of those faces matched the ones I saw here."

Selia thought about that for a few moments as they gathered the last few items from the ground and the thugs. "That sounds like Moreisa is building her own stable of thugs for hire, and these guys were hired from her."

"Gotta figure she would be doing something to build her own power base," Wil agreed. He looked around. "I think we've got everything… wait. Where's Luna?"

Selia held up her left arm where the leash had been tethered. Calling up the magic had essentially burned the loop to ash. The charred remains hung loosely at her wrist. The two looked frantically around, trying to find the pup. Wil found her peeing on one of the corpses.

Laughing, Wil picked Luna up, saying, "I thought only boy dogs did that! Good girl!"

# Chapter Thirty One

Later that night, Selia and Wil, still in his persona of Dorian, dropped Luna off with Soren and brought him up to date on what happened. The pair then headed out for one of the many clubs owned by Vinny Scarlatti. Wil was once again driving, and Selia was wearing a long-sleeved, deep purple, tunic-style blouse, black jeans, boots, and her leather jacket. This time, she added the crystal dagger she'd had crafted on Temeria to her outfit. She'd tucked it into the inside of her left boot. She was not going to get caught unawares again. The crystal dagger would be able to break through any magical bearer. One reason the crystals were so valued and the weapons so rare.

Oddly enough, she found it amusing that she was becoming more and more armed as the days passed.

"So, where are we likely to find Vinny's boys hanging out?" Selia asked as Wil navigated the Friday night traffic.

"The Empty Room," Wil replied, turning into a parking lot near the club.

He'd changed his disguise just enough that he didn't need the prosthetic and had hidden that factor by adding thicker stubble to his face.

"Shall we see if they are once again 'honored' by my presence?" she asked, rolling her eyes. "Hopefully we won't have to deal with the annoying toad tonight."

"Absolutely," Wil replied, as they stepped from the car.

Together, they headed towards the front door of the club and, once again, they were allowed entrance ahead of everyone else. At least Vinny had the brains to inform all the clubs of her VIP position. Either that or they were afraid of angering the infamous, and incredibly dangerous, Dorian Porter.

The club was packed with people wanting to relax and enjoy a Friday night out on the town. The lights flashed and music filled the air, drowning out the conversations and the dance floor was filled with writhing and undulating bodies.

As Selia and Wil made their way to the bar, she noticed a handful of Vinny's boys amongst the crowd. The further into the club they went, the more Family she spotted, but that wasn't what caught her attention.

She touched Wil's arm lightly and flicked her eyes to their left. In the darkest corner booth, towards the back of the club, was one of Scarlatti's underbosses with four of Lucien's captains. Once she knew what to look for, she spotted the rest of Lucien's captains either dancing or tucked away in the shadows, talking in huddled groups with Scarlatti men.

Reaching the bar, she slid onto a barstool, but Dorian interrupted her from ordering her usual Shirley Temple.

"Why always with the Shirley Temples?" he asked, turning to face her.

She chuckled. "You know I don't drink anything alcoholic, Dorian. You know why, too."

"I know you can drink most men under the table. I don't understand why you don't drink sociably," he countered.

"Because it's easier to slip something into an alcoholic drink than something non-alcoholic," she argued, propping her face up with one fist, her elbow on the bar. "Unless you plan on sticking around for the long-haul, handsome, I'd rather not have to worry about getting a new drink every time I step away from a bar or table."

"Well, you're with me now. I'm not going to let anything happen to you. So live it up a little, damn it," he scolded.

"Fine," she said with a grin. "You want me to live it up, you order me a drink you think I'll like."

Wil looked at the bartender. "Make the lady a Manhattan. Don't get it wrong."

The bartender cocked an eyebrow. "Hey, I've been doing this for a while. I know what I'm doing."

"Water it down, and I'll shoot you in the face. Don't believe me? Ask your bosses," he warned the bartender.

"Be nice, Dorian," Selia teased. "I'd rather not deal with any fights tonight. I asked you out for a drink before going back to my place later, remember?"

"Dorian?" the bartender said, suspicion creeping into his voice.

"Dorian Porter," Wil acknowledged. "Your last name wouldn't be Gwin, would it?" The bartender's face paled. He nodded. "I thought so. Are you dumb like your brother? Or maybe you're now thinking about exacting revenge for your stupid, dead relative?"

The bartender said nothing as he stared wide-eyed at the infamous mercenary.

Wil leaned in, smirking. The bartender took an unconscious step back. "Well, go ahead." He challenged. "I'd like to show this lady an interesting evening."

Swallowing hard, the man said, "My brother was an idiot? Good riddance?"

Wil nodded. "Make sure there's no water in that Manhattan, or anything else that shouldn't be."

"Yes, sir, Mr. Porter," Gwin replied quickly, before turning and starting to mix the drink.

"You certainly make my life interesting," Selia murmured, shaking her head in amusement.

"Wow, the rumors are true," a male voice said from nearby. "Selia Lascari is stepping out with the infamous Dorian Porter."

Both turned to see who had addressed them. Standing behind them was one of Vinny's captains. He had medium brown hair cropped close to his head, wore a loose, black button-up casual shirt, khakis, and a designer watch. He regarded them with dark blue eyes and had a mixed drink in his right hand. Taking a sip he nodded to the pair.

"Well, the rumors have to be right eventually," Selia remarked, leaning back casually against the bar counter.

"Surprised to see you in this place," the capo said. "Would have figured you would have gone to one of Carmine's establishments. You seem to be making the rounds."

"This was my idea," Wil retorted. "Wanted to bring her someplace that might serve a decent drink."

The man smiled. "Well, they do serve great drinks here. The food's not too bad, either. Can I interest you in a private booth?"

Selia tilted her head to the side, smiling. She turned her eyes to her date. "What do you think, darlin'? Want a private booth?" She dropped a wink, as though insinuating something naughty.

"Sounds perfect," Wil allowed. He asked the capo, "What would you recommend to eat?"

"The appetizer sampler," he replied cheerily. "That way, you get a little of the best and you can discover your own personal favorite."

"Who should we place the order with?" Selia asked.

"I'll take care of it," the capo offered. "Come on, I'll show you the best private booth in the house."

Not surprisingly the 'best booth in the house' had almost no view of the floor. The better to keep the two of them from seeing anyone they weren't supposed to. Neither of them complained, however, and thanked the capo as they took their seats.

"Do you think we can trust the food here?" Selia asked.

"I believe so," Wil replied. "It wouldn't do well for you or me to get poisoned or sick from this place. After all, they don't know if you report your findings to anyone. Soren could well keep track of where you go."

"And they would also be too afraid of what you might do, as well," Selia replied, nodding. "Good point. Shall we make quick work of this place? I think we now have the answers we were looking for."

"Sounds like a good idea."

Two hours later, Selia and Wil were in Wil's basement. Instead of being snuggled in Wil's lap with his arms wrapped around her, Selia was pacing the floor in front of the sofa. She'd already had two shots of tequila and was now working on a tumbler of whiskey. It currently sat on the coffee table, which was between her and Wil.

"I can't do anything," she complained. "I certainly can't move against either Lucien's capos or any of Scarlatti's men without starting a war. Nightshade can't move against any of Lucien's men, without him having my head, starting a war, or him revealing who I am to everyone."

She paused long enough to grab the glass and toss back a third of the whiskey. Setting the tumbler back on the table, she continued her rant, and her pacing. "You can't do anything because it's too big. Soren can't do anything because Al claims it's not the Lascari Family business. Lucien can't do anything, either." She ran her hands through her hair before dropping them to her side in defeat as she looked at Wil. "What are we going to do?"

"You aren't going to like this," Wil apologized. "But we'll need to wait and see what opportunities present themselves. The only other option is to force everyone's hand."

"My love, we can't sit and wait. They came after me once using magic. Do you honestly think they won't try again? The next time, they *will* be using something more powerful than a shield. Can we really take that risk?"

"No," Wil consented. "Do you know what we'll need to do to force their hand?"

She sighed and crossed to the sofa, dropping onto it next to him. "Yeah, I do. There has to be an attack, a serious attack, against someone who isn't me." She closed her eyes. "Al thinks Dorian is the one behind my attacks and wouldn't believe anyone else is doing it, even if they left a signed, certified letter proclaiming it to be otherwise."

Wil nodded, apparently satisfied. "Do I need to explain how this is going to happen? Or have you figured it out yet?"

"Yeah, I do," she said softly. She opened her eyes and looked at him, a grim expression on her face. "There's no other choice. And it only gets better, because I also have to inform Lucien and Soren of what's going on before we move forward. They deserve to know."

At midnight, Selia, dressed as Nightshade, stepped from the shadows of the alleyway and made her way across to where two cars were parked outside a cemetery. The headlights of each car were pointed at the other and both were parked up against the stone wall that wrapped around one of the city's many cemeteries.

It was far easier to move about the city without fear of being caught, dressed as Nightshade when she was in the presence of the Sandman, who was walking beside her. As she neared the cars, she noticed that Lucien and Soren were standing at the front of their cars talking quietly to each other in Italian. Once she was within earshot, at least for her, she saw Soren stop and turn towards her and Wil. It seemed her father would always know when she was around.

"Right on time," Soren observed. "I knew I raised you right."

"I try to do you proud," Selia replied, a smile beneath her scarf. "Glad to see you came without your bodyguards, Lucien," she added.

Lucien looked back and forth between the duo, seeming at a loss for words. Finally, he opened his mouth and said, "*Christo*, when's the wedding?"

"He hasn't asked," Selia replied offhandedly.

Soren gave her a sour expression.

"She lies," the Sandman replied.

Lucien laughed. "It's good to have you on our side, this time." He smiled for a moment longer and then became serious. "Do you really think this idea of yours will work?"

"It'll have to," Selia replied somberly. "It's the only way to get rid of the traitors in your Family, and hopefully, whoever takes over won't make my life as liaison difficult." She paused. "Well, more difficult than Al is already making it."

"We can hope," Lucien agreed. "Do you think that the witch is involved? Soren explained the ball lightning in the park. Nice work, by the way. Saw it from my office window."

"Not this time," Selia answered. "The thugs were hired out by her, though, so she's obviously building a powerbase somewhere. I'm sure it won't be long before she pops back up, ready to come after me again."

"No extra pressure on you this year, eh?" Lucien said with a roll of his eyes.

"She'll manage," both the Sandman and Soren declared at the same time.

Both men looked at each other. Nightshade couldn't see the Sandman's eyes, as they were covered by the infrared sunglasses, but she could see Soren's and knew Wil's body language intimately. Each man was thinking that they should be the one to say things about Selia, not the other guy.

"You both know I'm not going to stay out of this," Selia commented, changing the topic.

"I don't think either of us is foolishly optimistic enough to believe that was even an option." Soren deadpanned.

"I'd rather you were involved, obviously." Lucien shrugged. "I did ask you to investigate."

"No, you *tossed* me into this pit of vipers," Selia countered. She waved her hand dismissively. "No, no, I can't complain or argue but so much. I did offer, after all." She sighed and shifted her weight. "Just keep me in the loop on what Al wants to do."

"Always," Soren assured her. "As long as he bothers to tell me."

She muttered a curse in Temerian. "I'll lean on Alex. I've always been able to get him to give me answers when I need them."

Something was bothering her, and it took a moment for her to figure out what it was. "Please tell me I'm not the only one who is thinking Angelo could use this mess as a chance to move against me or Papa."

"We've discussed the possibility." Lucien said somberly. "Too many actions from the old man are adding up the wrong way, or just not making sense."

Selia looked to Soren, a significant gleam in her eyes. "You know where I stand."

"Actually, you stand pretty close to where I do," was Soren's casual answer.

"We should all be aware of opportunities to change this situation for the better," cautioned Lucien. "But now is not the time. We shouldn't focus on that part, just yet."

"It's not like I have much choice," Selia said with a sigh. She gave them a tired smile. "Looks like you three were right. As much as I've tried, I can't go back to being the wallflower I once was."

"No reason for you to try," replied Soren.

"We like you better this way, anyway," the Sandman added.

"Yeah, except that I seem to be the target for every nefarious plot taking place,' Selia grumbled with a sigh.

"Welcome to my world," growled the Sandman.

"It's not that different for any of us." offered Lucien.

"No, I guess not," Selia admitted. She turned to Lucien. "Anything you need me to do until this goes down?"

"Just keep doing what you're doing." Lucien offered a smile. "Watch your back. Even if you have these fine gentlemen doing it for you."

"We'll watch each other's back," the Sandman interjected.

"I think we're done, here," Soren suggested. "We keep in touch through our already established lines. Any developments are to be brought to everyone's attention."

They all agreed and went their ways. Soren and Lucien got into their respective cars as Selia and Wil headed back the way they came. There was a lot to do, and not a lot of time to do it in.

# Chapter Thirty Two

Sunday was spent sleeping in and catching up on sensual pleasures, but when the sun set, Selia and Wil suited up as their nighttime alter-egos. Luna was left in the kitchen with a few puppy pads, water bowl, and chew toys, along with a large doggie bed which she'd flopped out on as she gnawed on a toy. The puppy didn't seem to mind the unusual costumes Selia and Wil wore, content with being in a home where she was loved and spoiled.

Wil and Selia left via the sub-basement, taking the tunnels to his electric motorcycle. From there, they crossed the city in silence, parking the 'cycle before taking to the rooftops. As usual, they wore ear buds so if they separated from each other, they could still talk to each other without difficulty.

Once again, Wil had learned of a ring that was in need of being broken. This time it was a prostitution ring and, he suspected, involved underage girls. Their destination was in the part of the city that had been the best part of the city about a century ago. Victorian houses lined the streets, along with bluestones, elegant brick manors, and townhouses. Though the era had long-ago ended, the houses were still cared for, even if the paint jobs had paled and the cobblestone walks were in dire need of repair.

The house they paused across from was a Victorian, complete with gables and elegant trim. All of it was in desperate need of a paint job, new gutters, and probably a roof. Selia glanced at Wil and tilted her head towards the house. Wil gave a single nod.

"I hope you have a plan, handsome," Selia murmured as she leaned against the fence lining the alleyway they were standing in.

"I seriously thought about pulling a bad 80's TV plot," the Sandman declared. "You know, we show up in overpriced clothing and disguises, say we are a rich couple looking for some fun that can't be had with the legal-age types. Then go mercs-for-hire and shoot our way out while freeing the kids. Cut to heart-wrenching scenes of kids being reunited with parents that suddenly give a shit. You know what I mean."

Nightshade just stared at him. "Was that a joke?"

The Sandman pulled out a stun grenade and primed it. "Only the heart-wrenching reunion stuff, but I thought we'd have better luck making a lot of noise."

"Go around back and in exactly two minutes, throw one of your 'stunners' through the nearest window," he instructed. "After they go off, give a count of thirty. Go in and make your way to the center of the house. I'll meet you there. If neither of us sees any kids, we search for underground passages. The cops will be here within minutes. I've already called them and warned them that Vice is going to think it's Christmas."

"I don't see how Vice is going to do any good. Everyone will just deny doing anything other than having a good time," Selia observed.

"Oh, I'm sure they're drooling over the web-feed I gave them. It went active about an hour ago." The Sandman smiled under his balaclava. "Also, my hacker breached the Madame of the House's firewall earlier today. He's making copies of their transaction reports. They'll be delivered anonymously, of course. Any other questions? Because now we're off the time table."

"Oh, poor man. The mean woman screwed up his attack schedule. How about I count to one hundred-eighty and then throw my grenade?" Nightshade teased.

"Whatever you say, dear," the Sandman retorted.

Nightshade made her way to the back of the building, counting off the seconds as she went. She made it to her position in plenty of time, and when her countdown concluded, she threw the stun grenade into the window nearest her. She heard glass break on the other side of the building nearly the instant that her grenade broke through. The Sandman had thrown his into the building, also.

She knelt and covered her ears.

The two grenades went off, and the chaos that proceeded was impressive. In mere seconds the back door flew open, and people began pouring out. Nightshade shouldered her way past them and into the house of ill repute. She took note that no females appeared underage, except for a pop star whose hit single was burning up the charts. She was with a woman ten years her senior. Both were dressed, at least partially, in matching leather teddies. There was also a city manager, along with a politician or three, fleeing with staff members. Most were not fully dressed either, but some had the sense to bring clothing with them. One man was wearing only his patent leather shoes.

The back door opened into what had once been a spacious kitchen. More people were fleeing the building, but in smaller amounts than the initial mob that had piled out the back. Some people were coming down a flight of stairs.

Only one person took note of Nightshade: a young man that she recognized as one of the mail delivery staff from Soren's office. He was fleeing alone, whereas those grouped together were moving and shrieking. Some were claiming it was the police, others saying it was a rival gang hit. Most were trying to cover their faces.

The young man, no more than nineteen, was named Dewayne, and he stopped short when he noticed Nightshade. He had dressed in a hurry. His usually well-tailored appearance was all wrinkles and dishevelment. Nightshade waved a finger at him and said "naughty boy" before pushing past him and into the middle hallway.

The Sandman had beaten her to the meeting point. He was in the process of disarming one of the hired muscle who bounced unruly customers. The man looked like a football linebacker. For all Nightshade knew of sports teams, he might even have been one. The hired thug also outweighed the Sandman by at least a hundred pounds, as well as being nearly a foot taller in height. The man was swinging a heavy sack, called a blackjack in past times, at the Sandman.

Ducking under the man's swing, the Sandman grappled the arm and snapped the elbow. The larger man roared in pain and disbelief. The Sandman wrenched the injured arm around to the man's back and pulled hard enough to dislocate the shoulder.

"Unless you want those well-insured knees to be broken next, Mr. Vicktor, you better tell me where the owners are taking the rest of the girls," the Sandman growled. "I'm talking about the ones who should be doing school work and playing with dolls, instead of entertaining the overpaid and over indulged." The Sandman jammed his thumb into the nerve cluster of the man's uninjured arm. The man shrieked in pain.

"Fuck you!" the man spat.

"Oh, is that what you're into? Well, I'm not against some man-on-man attention. I'm sure sports fans will learn to forgive that, too," the Sandman said casually. He pulled out a baton with his free hand and snapped it out where Mr. Vicktor would see it. "Your arms might heal, but your knees aren't going to let you run down the gridiron when I'm done with them. Not ever again. Last chance."

Mr. Vicktor grunted and nodded. "Small door under the staircase." He nodded his head at the old wooden stairs, where a cupboard-sized door was visible at the base. "That's where they keep them. They bring them up for clients."

"Thanks!" the Sandman said cheerfully. He let go of Mr. Vicktor, and then swung the baton down against the man's left knee. The man collapsed against the wall as his knee jutted outward, and the Sandman struck an even harder blow to the man's right knee. Vicktor dropped hard to the floor.

"That's for the dogs, asshole," the Sandman announced. He smashed the baton across the man's jaw, knocking him unconscious.

"Sorry. It got personal for a second," the Sandman apologized to Nightshade.

He looked around. The patrons and staff were all out of sight. The sounds of police sirens, screaming tires, and officers performing their duties began to flood in through the open doors at the back and front of the house.

"Understandable," Nightshade replied, moving towards the door and melting the lock completely off until there was nothing but a hole in the door. She glanced over her shoulder at him and said, "I would've just killed the bastard." Opening the door, she peered inside. "Do we go down or leave it for the cops?"

"There's no way of knowing if there's another exit." The Sandman sounded irritated and apologetic. "But I don't want to take the chance that these people get away with the kids. Your call. I really don't want to have to subdue cops if we end up with a dead-end down there but..."

Smiling beneath her mask, Selia pulled out a crystal pendant and tossed it to the Sandman. "I've been doing some homework. Put that on and say '*nascondere*' when you need to hide. The spell will keep you hidden from everyone around you, except me." She paused and added with a concealed grin. "Yes, it'll work even if you draw a weapon and use it."

She had chosen the Italian word for 'conceal' for obvious reasons. One being she knew he could say it, the second being Wil was still learning Temerian.

"Baby, you're the greatest," he said as he took the pendant and dropped it around his neck. He took the lead down the stairs, armed with a baton and one of his Kimber Raptor .45s.

"Show me later," she murmured, following him down the stairs, her own M&P .45 drawn. She wanted to keep one hand available should she have to throw magic instead of bullets.

The duo went down the stairs at a quick pace, weapons ready. The stairs ended in a hallway, which stretched to the west. There were four doors, two to each side of the hall, and a large door at the end some twenty yards away.

The infrared lenses showed the duo that there were no warm bodies behind the doors to either side of the hallway. The door at the end of the hallway was set in stone, and looked like it hadn't been used in decades. The images from the door were strange, and they approached the door with caution. The old fashioned lock was filled, and there was once a door knob, but not now. The Sandman took off his glasses and peered at where the door knob had once been.

"It's been recently removed, and more than once," he observed, whispering to Nightshade. "I'm betting this is removed to prevent entry. Probably opens from the other side. I'm betting we'll find someone with the door knob in their possession in the room."

"How do you propose we get in?" Nightshade asked. "Shoot the lock? I might be able to blow the door off with magic."

"Save your energy," he insisted. "I have something else in mind."

A minute later, the Sandman had retrieved a tube from his utility belt and was squirting a plastic explosive called Semtex around the entire door frame. Once that was done, he inserted a detonator and looked to Nightshade.

"We better get to this," she said. "I can hear the police moving around upstairs."

He nodded, and they retreated to the nearest hallway doors. Nightshade took the one on the right, the Sandman took the left. They opened the doors and saw only supplies, dry foods, and canned goods. The door that the Sandman had opened also revealed a number of sex toys and sex play costumes in need of repair, along with spare blankets and bed sheets. Each stepped into the room nearest them as the Sandman triggered the explosive.

There was a deep concussive sound and the foundation shook. The sound of the door at the end of the hallway falling over was the loudest sound that came next. Even as the police could be heard reacting on the ground level, the duo triggered their amulets and came out into the hallway, moving swiftly into the now opened room.

The room was obviously once used as a storage era during prohibition. Some old barrels and bottles still lined the walls. The room was now converted into a kind of barracks, with military cots from what looked like World War II, filling up most of the floor. A single wide screen TV sat in one corner, now turned off. There were video cameras posted high up on the walls, spaced apart every four feet. There were six teenagers, three boys and three girls, along with one of each gender that was certainly pre-teen. They all wore lingerie or sex play costumes.

There were four adults present, and all of them wore business attire. One, a man who looked to be the oldest, was talking frantically into a cellular phone. The other three were pointing guns at the collected kids, who were huddled on the floor near the silent TV.

Nightshade felt her anger grow and sensed the Sandman's temper growing white hot. She used that anger to fuel her spell, hissing the word for sleep in Temerian as she extended her left hand.

A light fog suddenly began to pour out from the dirt and rock floor. As soon as it touched the gathered crowd's skin, it rendered them unconscious. The whole process took less than a minute. Once the last adult, the one on the phone, had fallen asleep, Nightshade dispelled the fog with her will, and the Sandman rushed to the man and picked up the phone.

When Nightshade looked at the Sandman, his whole body seemed tense. He looked at her, with the phone pressed to his ear. He then held the phone out and pressed a button to activate the speaker phone.

"Hello?" The voice of Big Al boomed out of the phone. "What the hell is going on, Larry? Have you and the kids been located? Are the police there? Answer me, dammit! I put you in charge of that house and you'd better-"

The Sandman ended the call.

The two of them stepped to either side of the now breached doorway and waited for the police to flood in. It didn't take long. Once enough Vice, DEA, and city police had come into the room, the duo slipped out of the basement, the house, and back into the street.

They kept silent as they went to the location of the electric cycle and didn't speak on the trip back to the lair.

# Chapter Thirty Three

Monday for Selia was spent discussing the charities with Soren, requesting the past year's reports on the donations made, and creating her own filing system. She kept to her office and worked diligently, asking Wil for his opinion on several of the charities that she didn't recognize.

After informing the shelter Luna had come from about her plan, Selia then spent most of the afternoon with Luna on her lap as she discussed photographers with Wil. By the time five rolled around, she had set up the photo shoot for the campaign and informed Maria, as well as Soren.

As the pair waited for Soren to show up, Selia tossed a small ball for the puppy, who chased it happily before returning it to her or Wil, so it could be tossed again.

"The only thing I can figure is that it was a personal investment," Selia said, as Luna caught the tennis ball and gnawed on it, growling happily. "I did a little snooping on my own, and I can't find anything about the house being owned by the Family. That isn't to say I have access to everything, but I do have access to Papa's accounts. There's nothing in there about a mortgage or purchase of that estate."

"That sounds about right. I wonder how long he's been involved. Or if he actually started the place?" Wil pondered. "I think I'll check the city's real estate records, as well as zoning. Find out who owned the property. I'm certain a shell company was used, if not multiple."

Selia shrugged. "Hard to tell, but that sounds like a good place to start."

Luna brought her the ball and Selia tossed it, watching the pup bounce after it as though she were trying to catch it in her paws. "My guess would be he started it and oversaw it, but then, I'm a bit irked with him and willing to think the worst."

"I think I can keep an objective investigation going," Wil teased.

"Good to know at least one of us will," Selia said.

She was about to say more when she noticed Luna's head perk up and she took a couple steps towards the door, her tail wagging. Wil leaned over and opened the door, revealing Soren in the doorway. Luna, ball still in her mouth, padded over to Soren and dropped the ball at his feet, before dropping her front half down and yipping at Soren in an invitation to play.

Soren knelt down and picked up the drool-covered ball and rolled it across the floor. Luna bounded after it, snatched it up, and returned it to Soren, a big smile on her face. Chuckling, Soren scratched her behind the ear and tossed the ball again before standing up. Pulling a handkerchief from a pocket, he wiped his fingers on it before turning to the pair.

"You two ready?" he asked. Stepping into the office, he closed the door behind him. "You sure about this, *piccolina*?"

Selia rolled her eyes. "No, but it's not like we have much choice, now do we?" Standing, she grabbed Luna's leash, which caught the puppy's attention. Snapping it onto Luna's collar, Selia stood and heaved a sigh. "Let's go before something else happens."

Like with most businesses on Mondays and Fridays, the building had cleared out quickly, so it was just the three of them walking into the parking deck. There were a handful of cars, but there were no other humans around.

Soren turned to Wil. "I'll go make sure the guard and attendant are distracted." He turned and strode away.

Though his voice was even, Selia could tell Soren didn't like any part of the plan. It was evident in the tension of his shoulders and the set of his jaw. Barely noticeable, but she'd lived with him for a decade and had grown to recognize even the smallest changes in his body language. Wil, she knew with equal certainty, didn't like it either.

Once Soren was out of sight, Wil went to his trunk and popped it. Inside was someone who looked a lot like 'Billy'. The body had the same build, body weight, and facial structure, even though the hair was a different color. Selia's eyes widened as she stared at the corpse.

"What the hell?" she all but demanded. Her eyes narrowed as she asked in an overly cautious voice, "Where in all the Hells did you get *him*?"

"My favorite hospital: It's amazing what you can ask for when you're a prominent 'anonymous' contributor as well as the staff's favorite vigilante," Wil said with far too much pleasantness in his voice. He hefted the body out of the trunk.

"Please say hello to 'John Doe' number seven thirty-four," Wil invited. "I've had the morgue keep him in storage ever since 'Billy' came back into the Family business. He's got no ID, no family that has come forward after a month, and died from alcohol and heroin poisoning. Stuff that Vinny's family has been selling, actually."

"There are times I really don't want to know how your brain works because it gives me a headache," Selia bemoaned as Wil positioned the body behind the wheel of his car.

Though Luna had been sitting at her feet, head tilted curiously to the side, she got up and moved towards Selia's right. Selia looked over and saw Soren returning from wherever he'd vanished.

"That was quick."

Soren nodded and slowed as he neared them. "It's taken care of. No one will see or do anything I don't want them to."

Wil, or rather the living Billy, was closing the driver's door and moving around to the passenger side, where he proceeded to remove his disguise. Selia gave a wordless squawk and gaped at her beloved, more than a bit shocked at his actions. She had to look away when Wil plopped the wig he'd been wearing as Billy onto the corpse.

Staring hard at Soren, Selia did not see the rest of the transformation. When Wil stepped out of the car again, he was himself. No makeup, no wig, no prosthetics. Just the man she loved to cuddle up with, as well as everything else.

He walked up and stood between Selia and Soren.

Soren took a long look at Wil.

"So what do I call you?"

"Well, 'son,' if she'll ever say yes," Wil quipped.

The best description of Soren's expression, as far as Selia was concerned, would have been "wanting to shoot someone in the face".

"Fine." Wil sighed. "My real name is Jebediah Poindexter. Nice to meet you."

Selia turned and smacked him hard across the chest. "Then you wonder why I won't say yes! Sheesh!" She gave a heavy sigh and rolled her eyes. "One thing I ask! One little thing, and neither of you are willing to do it!" She glowered at the pair and slid the ring from her right hand. "Tell him, and I'll say yes, you jerk."

"Did you teach her to be like this?" Wil asked Soren, with real severity.

"I am not sure how much I can be blamed for her behavior, sometimes," Soren confessed.

"Oh well. Hi, Dad, I'm Wil. Wil Fredericks. Part time writer, vigilante, and full time pain in the ass."

"No wonder you two get along. You have that last bit in common," reflected Soren.

"Right, so who's going to cover Luna's ears?" Wil asked as he snatched the ring out of Selia's hand and slipped it onto her left ring finger. "Same person I'm asking to marry me, I'll bet."

"Why would I want to marry a jerk like you?" Selia retorted as she knelt next to Luna and covered her ears. Luna tried to make sense of what was happening, until Selia started rubbing. At that point, Luna was too busy enjoying it and trying to keep her back leg from thumping in pleasure.

"I'm the only one who can handle you," he challenged.

"Why the hell am I here? Aside from getting diabetes from all this sugar floating in the air?" Soren demanded.

"Oh, you're a witness," Wil explained. "Say goodbye to Billy."

Without another word, Wil held up a small device and pressed a button. The car's ignition turned over, trying to start the engine. The engine engaged, and a split-second later, the car exploded.

Soren fell back in surprise. Wil caught him with his free hand. Luna tensed at the same moment, and then started barking at the car. Clearly, she wanted to give that explosion a piece of her mind about startling her like that and being so loud in the process.

"What the fuck?" Soren yelped. He hissed at Wil, "You never said anything about blowing up a car!"

"I'm curious what you thought was going to happen here, Dad," Wil commented. "I mean, this is kinda old hat for you, isn't it?"

"Knock off the 'dad' crap, already," Soren growled through clenched teeth. "How do you think this is going to do anything but raise the property insurance rates and cost me a bundle in repairs?"

"Oh, I'll cover the repairs," Wil replied easily. "The investigation is going to show the explosive is the signature mix of the Scarlatti family. It's the same stuff they used on that bombing last year near the governor's building. As well as the rash of bombings in gang territory this past spring."

"I don't even want to know how you obtain all this knowledge." Soren eyed Wil suspiciously. "Just how much of Dorian Porter is fiction, anyways?"

Wil's smile was less than comforting.

"Jesus, I thought the Family was bad." Soren grunted. "All right, what's the next play?"

"I am going to go and change. You're going to call the cops and start spreading the news. Selia is going to be a little shook up, and you've called her darling Dorian to come and take her home."

"Finally, something that makes sense," breathed Soren.

# Chapter Thirty Four

The office was buzzing the next day with the news of the car bombing and 'Billy's' untimely demise. Somehow, Selia managed to slip past everyone without being bombarded by questions. Dorian had dropped her off at work, promising to take her to lunch and then pick her up after work. In the meantime, she promised Wil she would stay in her office. Luna, blissfully ignorant of what was going on around her, pranced along beside her, happy to be at work with Selia once again.

After her initial sweep for bugs and cameras, Selia settled behind her desk and began checking her email before starting on her work as the Director of Charities as well as Master Tradesman of Temeria.

She was thoroughly engrossed in an email from the shelter Luna had been adopted from, when she heard a knock at the door. Glancing at Luna, who was watching the door warily, Selia drew her M&P .40 and leveled it at the door.

"It's open," she called.

The door opened and Alex poked his head in. Giving an inward sigh, Selia slid her weapon back into her holster.

"Hey, Alex, come on in." To Luna, she said, "Say hello to Alex, Luna. He's a good friend for a girl to have."

Alex stepped into the office, closing the door behind her. He knelt, offering the puppy a hand. Luna sniffed him and then licked the proffered hand before hopping up, putting two large paws on his knee and trying to reach his face to lick it. Alex, thankfully, didn't complain. He merely slid a hand beneath her paws and leaned down for a wet, sloppy, puppy-kiss.

As always, he wore a business suit, this one was dark blue silk with a black dress shirt beneath the jacket. Unlike most days, he was missing a tie, so he must have decided to go for a casual look. Either that or he wasn't out on enforcer business. For some reason, he always wore a tie when he was sent out to take care of Family jobs.

Scratching the puppy behind her ear, Alex looked up at Selia. "Word has it Soren sent you home because you were 'shook up'. Pretty dedicated there, Lia, coming in the next day after such a 'shock'."

Smiling at the question and sarcasm in his voice, Selia gave a half chuckle. She shrugged. "It's not every day I see someone blown up in a car."

Giving Luna a final pat on the head, Alex stood and perched on the edge of her desk, facing her. "Girl, you aren't showing any sign of shock, or anything else. You're not even crying over poor ol' Billy who you seemed pretty damned friendly with. You don't look like someone who lost a friend. Let alone witnessed his death."

Selia tipped her head back to look up at the older Caruso brother. "How do you know I didn't do my grieving on Dorian's shoulder last night?"

"You should have been escorted in here by him," Alex snapped. "Or at the very least me and Bernie. But that doesn't change the fact that I know you. You aren't as cold as me, Bernie, or even Soren."

"No, I'm not," Selia agreed. "But I'm also not going to tell you my secrets. Not when I care so much about you." She paused, her brows furrowing. "Why isn't Bernie here with you?"

"Because he likes being kept in the dark," Alex said with a grim smile. "Me, I worry about you and care for you. I like having answers to my questions. Something you should know by now."

"And you're not going to get the answers you're looking for, either." Selia smiled up at him. "Guess that means you'll just have to trust me."

"Yeah, I've heard that one before, and nothing bad ever came from it, either," Alex grumbled.

Selia laughed softly. It brought back so many memories from her first couple years in these lands, when she had been in high school. "Come on, you enjoyed it when you had to tell Soren I'd been sent to the office. Especially when I hadn't been caught doing anything other than smacking down a bully or two using techniques *you* taught me."

Alex laughed and it was a welcome sound. Warm, lively, and it always brought a smile to her face, no matter how annoyed or dour a mood she was in.

"Do you know how many times Soren threatened to have my head?" he teased.

"Probably as many times as I was grounded," Selia shot back, grinning. "So, what brings you to brighten up my day?"

Alex was about to answer, when they heard the knob to the door turn. Selia watched in fascination as Alex slid from the desk, turning as he drew his SIG Sauer from beneath his ever-present jacket. She was even more fascinated by the fact Wil, dressed as Dorian, held a big Sandman teddy bear in his left hand and seemed to be oblivious of the gun pointed at him.

Dorian closed the door, the teddy bear prominent as he turned. He wore a black leather jacket, black jeans, and a black polo. Selia noticed his jacket moving a little before he whipped around, his right arm out holding his own SIG in his hand. It was pointed directly at Alex.

Neither man moved. Luna, the precious thing she was, had turned towards Alex and was barking, as though chastising him for pulling a gun on Wil.

"Okay, Mr. Orange and Mr. Blonde," Selia said, propping her arms up on the desk and steepling her fingers. "Would you please put the toys away?" She nodded towards Luna. "You've upset Luna. One of you is cleaning up the mess."

"Have you made a decision yet?" Dorian asked her, not turning his gaze from Alex.

Selia glanced at Alex, who was waiting with a solemn expression on his face before looking back at Wil. "Yes."

"And?" he prodded.

"Yes," she replied, adding emphasis to the word.

Wil, still in the Dorian persona, nodded once. "Aren't you going to congratulate us, Alex?"

Alex shot a glance to Selia, who was smiling warmly at Dorian, and heaved a sigh. Shrugging, he slid his weapon back into his holster. Dorian followed suit.

"Yeah, sure," Alex said. He shot Selia a significant look. "You really plan to marry him, Lia?"

"Yeah, I'm really going to marry him," Selia replied, laughter ringing in her voice. "He's good to me, he's protective of me, and I love him. Think you can get along with him?"

Turning to 'Dorian the Merc', Alex gave the other man a thoughtful look before smiling. "You sure you want to marry her? She can be a handful."

"Alex!" Selia exclaimed, her face burning. She chanced a look at Wil who was giving Alex an equally appraising look.

"I know how to handle her," Wil replied, his eyes twinkling. Not quite ignoring Alex, Wil moved closer to Selia and handed her the toy. "Since I know you have a thing for teddy bears." He paused, his lips quirking into a semblance of a smile. "Thought Nightshade should have a mate."

"I hate to interrupt this… whatever this is," Alex said, pulling Selia's attention away from Wil and the toy. Wil had never really stopped watching the Caruso brother. "If you're planning on marrying Lia, maybe you'll have a better shot at keeping her out of Family business than Bernie and me."

Selia snorted. "He's not god." Dorian's eyes narrowed as his smile grew cooler. Selia rolled her eyes as she said, "What's my dear uncle got planned?"

Alex gave Dorian a cautious look. "You're certain you want to discuss it with him here, Lia?"

"I'll tell him anyway, Alex. He has protected me, and we both know Dorian isn't who's been coming after me," Selia replied sharply. "Either you're going to trust me, or you aren't." She reached out and touched Alex's hand lightly. "Please don't make me get the information I need another way. You know I will."

Alex sighed heavily. "Girl, you're going to get yourself in so deep one day, none of us are going to be able to save your hide." He shook his head at Dorian, holding a hand up in what seemed to be supplication or defense. "I've known Selia since she was sixteen and new here. It's not a threat. Merely an observation."

Dorian gave a nod and Alex continued. "Al plans on sending us out tonight to move against Vincent Scarlatti. From what I've heard, Lucien is moving against his capos who were trying to unseat him. I don't know what Lucien is actually planning, but I do know Bernie and I are supposed to take our own teams and take out the trash."

"When?" she asked, leaning forward in her chair.

"It's not as if Al has a real sense of strategy or preparation anymore," Alex lamented. "He just gives orders and wants it done yesterday. The man didn't used to be like this, but…" He trailed off, shrugging. "It's the way things are now. The hit goes down at midnight."

"Thanks, Alex," Selia replied with a small smile.

"You're telling this because you expect her to get involved," Wil asked with a cocked eyebrow. "Or because you hope she will stay out of the action?"

"Selia *cannot* be involved, man!" exclaimed Alex. "I am informing her, so she isn't going to go snooping around and get herself into bigger trouble. There is also the fact that it would compromise her already precarious position as liaison between the Families."

"I never said I was going to tag along," Selia said sullenly. "Despite the desire to do so."

Wil narrowed his eyes at Alex. "I think there's more to Alex's thinking than that. I can assure you, Alex, that Selia Lascari will not be witnessed at your… hit, tonight. She will also be in much less danger than you will be."

"Is there more to your thinking?" Selia asked Alex softly. Alex looked uncomfortable and something flashed through his eyes too fast for her to recognize what it was.

He was saved, however, by her phone ringing. Like a dutiful employee, she hit the speaker button. "Selia Lascari, how can I help you?"

"Hey, how's my favorite girlfriend?" asked the voice of Nicky, the wonder hacker.

Selia rolled her eyes. "Not your girlfriend, Nicky," she said, dropping a wink at Dorian. "Something you need from me?"

"Yeah, an explanation." Nicky now sounded sulky. "Care to explain why I can't find this supposed fiancé of yours, one Dorian Porter, anywhere? Nothing on Google, or Twitter, or Yahoo. Hell, I thought maybe he was a dinosaur and even tried MSN, but he doesn't show up. Gonna drop the act and finally give in to a real, existing man?"

"Oh, he's a real man, all right. Complete with warm flesh and hot blood," Selia replied in the husky, sultry tone she knew Wil loved. "You aren't looking in the right place, dear." She paused, grinning devilishly at Alex and Dorian. "How good are you at hacking the CIA or FBI database?"

"Are you kidding? Those guys are still trying to figure out how I got in the last time!" Nicky boasted. Selia heard the tapping of keys and the occasional click of a mouse being used. "Okay, fine, I'm in the big ultra-secure Pentagon database. Oh, so intimidating. Now, then... let's just do a search for Porter, Dorian."

"Oh, by all means, do search for Dorian," Selia encouraged cheerfully. She mouthed the words 'this should be fun' to Wil and Alex. Alex was watching her with his usual amused smirk. She paused before asking suddenly, "How did you know he's my fiancé? I didn't give an answer until just a few minutes ago and he didn't ask until last night."

"I guess Soren is a Jedi knight, or one of those psychic people or whatever, then," Nicky said tartly. "He's the one who called Mr. 'Classified Information Only' Porter, your *fiancé* to me. Gimme a second while I bypass these outdated security measures."

She giggled. "More like he figured Dorian would ask and I'd say yes, considering how often I've mentioned him in the past couple days."

"Yeah, yeah, how sweet." Nicky grumbled. There was a clanging alarm coming from Nicky's side of the connection.

"Oh, come on! How much security is around this guy? Are you marrying a spook?" Nicky sighed, and rapid typing could be heard. "Yeah, yeah, yeah, you're gonna hunt me down. Eat my tracer buster, fed-rats. I swear, I'm thinking you're trying to get me arrested, Selia. Not a very nice thing to do for the guy who.... oh..."

There was a pronounced silence from Nicky. Selia wondered if he was even breathing. Finally, Nicky spoke again, and his voice was quite reserved, and almost business-like. "It seems I may be going away for a while, Future Mrs. Porter." His voice grew softer as he spoke. "I sincerely hope you and Mr. Porter have a wonderful life together. May I give my respects the next time I see you?"

"Certainly. I almost feel guilty about that," Selia replied. "It would probably be better than informing Soren and Dorian that you're stalking me, though."

"He's there with you, isn't he?" Nicky said in a whisper that was nearly panicked.

"He's not the only one here, either," Alex offered.

"Aha. I see." Nicky replied, and every one of them could hear him swallow. "That's nice. So, about the stalking thing..."

"Yes, Nicky?" Selia asked, sweetly.

"I am not stalking you, ma'am. I am admiring you from afar. I shall be doing so a great deal more quietly and probably from a lot further afar, from now on. I believe I hear sirens. I need to go." Nicky's voice sounded sincere and then the connection ended abruptly.

"I kinda do feel guilty for that," Selia said, tilting her head to the side. "Think you can help the kid out? After he's good and thoroughly scared witless, of course."

"I have no idea what I could do to help the boy... except end his pain," Dorian replied, arching an eyebrow at Selia.

"I'd rather he not die," Selia said with a sigh. "He is, after all, helpful to the Family, even if he doesn't know when to give up."

"Hopefully something will appeal to the G-men to not lean too heavily on the boy, then," Dorian said dismissively.

"Uh huh," Selia replied, rolling her eyes. "You wanna tell Papa our wonder boy just got busted and why, Alex? Or did you want me to call Lucien for details on the hit tonight?"

"It would be my pleasure to tell Soren," Alex said, and excused himself, taking a moment to pet Luna before leaving.

"You're going to help him, right?" Selia asked the moment the door closed behind Alex. "And yes, I'm pretty sure Alex suspects, at least about me."

"It seems pretty obvious." Wil agreed. "Yes, I will call my contacts at Langley and DC to appeal to their gentle mercies on behalf of the foolish hacker who tried too hard."

Selia snickered. "Thanks. I'm not surprised about Alex, though. He has probably been suspicious since that first picture." She shrugged. "Of anyone, aside from Papa, Alex has always been the closest to me. You already know I crushed heavily on him when I was a teen." She laughed a little. "I guess the only thing surprising is the fact that it's taken him this long to piece it together."

"He may have pieced it together a while back, and just not brought it to your attention before now," Wil commented.

"Very true," Selia admitted. "I also highly doubt he'll say anything to me until he has no other choice." She turned the Sandman teddy bear towards her and snuggled it. Over the toy's head, she asked, "How about we take Luna for a walk, grab some lunch, and call it a day until we depart to follow Alex and Bernie to the party?"

Wil smiled. "Sounds perfect to me."

# Chapter Thirty Five

As with all major cities, businesses opened and closed at a suicidal rate in New Campania. There were buildings that seemed to be cursed: no business could stay open in them for more than a year. So the buildings had "for lease" signs up more often than "new management," "coming soon," or, for that matter, "Open".

What may not be true of all cities is that those buildings were sometimes owned by people who preferred the buildings to be in a constant state of flux, so they could use them for their own means. Turning a profit is always nice, but a place where you can throw whatever kind of party you want is priceless to those with the means and appetites.

The building Alex and Bernie were leading a group of four men into, and that Nightshade and the Sandman were planning to enter right after, was such a place. The last business there hadn't had enough money to remove the five-figure sign they'd had made for it, and although dark and lifeless, the sign still proudly proclaimed it as "The Fire Tavern".

It had a neon structure that, when lit, showed a large stone pit with a spitted pig, and colors used to imitate a roaring fire stood between the pit and the pig. Stick figure patrons danced around the fire.

They had specialized in an *avante garde* style of eatery- primitive open flames and blowtorches cooking up meats and vegetables, the occasional roasted pineapple, with walls designed to look like cave stone. There were primitive style drawings on the walls. But the tables, chairs, and bar were top-shelf steel and wood. It could have been sold as functional art. The business had closed down a month before, and the property was owned by Vinny and his Family.

Rather than use the front entrance, guests were entering via the service entrance. The alleyway dock where supplies and food products had been delivered was now the front door. People were still entering and leaving, all of them dressed in a variety of costumes.

There were banana costumes, the expected number of vampires and ghouls, gangster costumes, flappers, and a large selection from the "sexy" brands of Halloween outfits. Two large men in black trousers and turtlenecks worked as doormen, guards, and probably were hoping to help the inevitable gang of bouncers and made-men with anyone who got rowdy inside the establishment.

The Sandman nudged Nightshade on their vantage point across from the entrance and pointed. It only took Nightshade a moment to notice what he was pointing at and silently laughing about: Many of the women, especially those wearing the skimpier style of costumes, were sporting hairdos identical to her own wig.

Blonde hair with green tips could be seen floating in the crowd, both entering and leaving. There were even a few women dressed in cheap versions of Nightshade's outfit. There was a pair of Sandman wannabes going in, but the Nightshade outfits outnumbered them by at least five-to-one. That was just what could be seen from the outside.

"Little Miss Popular," the Sandman sang quietly.

Nightshade made a rude gesture towards him, which only provoked more silent laughter. She waved dismissively at him and pointed to the east end of the alleyway.

Alex and Bernie were leading their group towards the entrance. None of them had visible firearms, and they were all dressed in well-tailored suits. They were, however, all wearing latex Halloween masks that covered their entire heads. The masks were all of popular horror monsters.

Alex wore a Creature from the Black Lagoon mask. Bernie was Frankenstein's Monster. The other men were from more modern film classics, and Nightshade wondered if the one fellow's chainsaw was a working model or just a prop.

The Sandman motioned, and the duo moved over to the next roof, preparing to descend to the ground level. Nightshade would have enjoyed keeping their perch to see how well her friends got into the party but made no objections. They could see what was transpiring well enough.

Alex, Bernie, and the fellows with them approached the doormen without causing a scene. They even mingled with the people outside for a bit. Someone obviously made a compliment about the Lascari boys' choice of costumes, because several of them, including Alex, nodded and gave a thumbs-up to someone in the crowd. When Alex was facing the doorman to the left, he was talking in a relaxed manner. Nightshade saw him palm a small wad of money into the doorman's hand under the pretense of a handshake. The doorman nodded to the other guy, and the Lascari group joined the party without confrontation.

"You didn't bring your wallet with you, by any chance?" Nightshade asked the Sandman. "Or perhaps your money clip?"

"Actually, I brought the money clip. Never leave home without it, or Liam's Visa black card," the Sandman assured her.

As the two of them came into the lighted part of the alleyway's street, the Sandman lurched over and put his arm around Nightshade's waist. He then began to stumble along as if drunk. Nightshade put an arm around him and pretended to be steadying him, or perhaps supporting her partner. They wandered that way until passing by a passed-out party goer. The Sandman fell out of Nightshade's grasp and appeared to trip over the inert body of the unconscious party hound.

"Omigod are you okay?" the Sandman asked the unconscious "musketeer" even as he deftly picked up the man's half-empty rum bottle out of sight of the crowd and doormen.

The fellow did not respond, although Nightshade could see the man was breathing.

"Aw, shit! I killed Cap'n Morgan!" the Sandman continued loudly in the reedy, drunken voice he was using. The crowd laughed appreciably.

Shuffling over to Nightshade, the Sandman brought the rum bottle to his covered mouth. He didn't actually swallow through his balaclava, but he did spill enough rum to make an appreciable odor.

*Yeesh*, she thought. *I'll need to stay down-wind from him the rest of the evening. I hope alcohol comes out of Kevlar.*

The duo made their way through the crowd, getting more than a few sour glances from those wearing imitation Nightshade and Sandman costumes. Facing the doorman to the left, the Sandman started up the rest of his performance.

"Hey!" He breathed heavily into the doorman's face. The doorman wrinkled his nose but kept a steady eye and a fixed smirk on the "drunkard" before him. The Sandman hoisted up the rum bottle and saluted the doorman with it.

"My baby told me this was *the* party to be at!" the Sandman slurred. "Guess she was right! Although..." He looked around, swaying a bit as he did so. "Some a' these people shoulda spent more money on their costumes, my man. Maybe you should've had a price requirement to get in!"

The Sandman drunkenly laughed at his own jest and mimicked almost falling on his ass. The doorman glanced over Nightshade's form-fitting costume with appreciation but said nothing to the Sandman. Nightshade bore the examination and added a girlish giggle to soften the doorman.

"Time to pay the Ferrymen!" The Sandman announced loudly.

He brought up the rum bottle, shook his head, and then used his empty hand to dig into the voluminous side pocket of his trench coat. He did so without opening the coat and exposing his weapons. The doorman tensed slightly, waiting to see if there was going to be trouble, but relaxed when the Sandman produced a gold money clip that was fat with one hundred dollar bills.

"Alrighty," the Sandman said, clumsily pulling out bills with two fingers while retaining a hold onto the rum bottle. He placed two of the bills in the doorman's hand. "We've paid the toll. Hey, be a pal and clean up the Cap'n back there, will ya?" the Sandman put another hundred in the doorman's hand.

"I'm gonna need help to do that." the doorman said, taking the bills out of his right palm with his left hand and putting them in his trouser pocket. The right hand stayed out, waiting.

The Sandman leaned over and looked at the open hand, then drunkenly to the other doorman, before straightening up.

"Oh, yeah! Of course!" The Sandman slowly fished out another bill and put it in the open, waiting palm. He then put the clip away. "There you are, my good man. May we pass?"

The doorman considered for a moment, wondering if he could fleece this sheep a bit more, but then smiled broadly.

"Have a good time. Make sure to send your lady friend out if she gets too lonely."

The Sandman laughed drunkenly and the two of them moved past the doormen, and into the party.

Walking into the party was an assault on the ears, nose, and eyes. There was a dull drumming sound once the duo got into the loading area. People were laid out, dancing to no particular rhythm, drinking, smoking everything possible, and engaging in all manners of fornication. Opening the back door increased the drumming sound ten-fold, and the amount of smoke increased at the same level. Lights were flashing, and for a moment, Nightshade thought she and the Sandman had stepped back into the Rave the two of them had interrupted a few months back.

But this party was blasting 70's disco, not techno or dubstep. There was an actual disco ball suspended from the ceiling. The colored lights were reflecting against it, spraying the walls, floor, and people with dancing lights. The costumes were more varied, but Nightshade noted with private amusement, the number of people wearing cheap copies of her outfit and the Sandman's had quadrupled.

The two of them blended in easily.

The Sandman, the real one, continued to mimic the drunken stumble, although she could feel his body tensing in the right places so he could leap into action whenever called upon.

"I feel like I should be charging these women for using your hairstyle," the Sandman quipped.

It looked like one out of every three women at the party was sporting, if not the identical style, then a similar style that could not be dismissed as a coincidence.

Nightshade shrugged at her partner. "Who can say where trends will come from?"

"Speaking of trends." He nodded toward the middle of the dance floor. "Looks like the brothers are about twenty years behind. Their tactics are also outdated by at least thirty years and they're about to get pinched."

He gestured minutely to the left and right.

The brothers and their four men were wandering through the crowd, in the center. Vinny, his underbosses, and all but two of his *capos* were dancing there in the company of at least twenty beautiful women. To the left and right of the crowd, however, groups of three men each were coming in slightly behind the Lascari group. These men were not being tactful or sly. They were drawing pump shotguns and large automatic handguns as they walked up to either side of the Lascari men.

Nightshade was about to move forward, to take out the threat of the six men that were positioned to ambush her friends. The Sandman grabbed her by the arm and stopped her. She was about to object, to make him let go, but at that moment the people in the crowd shifted and someone Nightshade hadn't noticed before became visible.

"Son of a bitch," she hissed and looked at Sandman. "What the hell is Ignacio Vaschetti doing here?"

She ignored any concern about drawing attention to herself and pointed at the former underboss to and cousin of Lucien Vaschetti. He was laughing and toasting Vinny, ignorant of the growing tension and probable violence around them.

Ignacio had been in charge of the data that Selia had stolen earlier in the year. She had been confronted by two of Lucien's men, and the Sandman had intervened. Selia had never discovered who the men had planned to take her to or why they had been there. All she had found out was that Ignacio had been disgraced by the theft of the data and reduced in rank to a captain.

"That certainly finishes a puzzle or two," the Sandman observed. "He must have been available to the highest bidder for a while now. Probably got an offer after the necromancer's plans fell through and Alfi was recognized as very dead. Vinny wants a rat. Seems Ignacio is looking for the biggest piece of cheese he can get, no matter where it comes from."

"Not to mention the added benefit of revenge against Lucien," Selia growled.

"Some people just can't handle getting caught." The Sandman sighed. "But I think your boys are going to be okay for the moment."

She looked over to see the two Lascari men in the back of the group turn and drop to one knee. They pulled submachine guns from their expensive jackets and opened fire. They cut the knees out from the approaching men, and only a few civilians seemed to take any hits. Those that did, received minor scrapes and flesh wounds.

"I recognized the two in the back from the way they carried themselves," the Sandman said into Nightshade's ear. "They're former Army Rangers, named Trivole and Gum. Best soldiers Soren ever put on the payroll."

Selia looked at him curiously. The names were familiar. There were maybe a dozen enforcers she'd met, but she couldn't put a face to either name. That, she decided, was going to change.

"How long have they been working for him?" she asked. "The names sound familiar."

"They were hired on as a response to me," the Sandman said with a shrug. "Before Soren figured out that I only went out after the illegal business, he thought all of you were in danger of me. He hired them as the highest level of protection. Alex understood it. Bernie just got miffed."

"Oh." Selia laughed softly. Shaking her head, she raised her eyes to the pair. There was a lot of yelling that had followed the initial gunfire, and the two of them had talked over it. But the sudden silence made them turn back to the business at hand.

The Lascari men were all armed now. Each of them carrying a sawed-off shotgun or a compact submachine gun. Bernie and Alex both had shotguns, their barrels were fixed on Vinny. The Scarlatti men were all armed, although a few of them looked to be more likely to shoot the crowd than their adversaries. The barrels of some were shaking pretty badly, and the men behind them looked as if they were ready to pass out. Too much partying had made them less than effective in this situation. Nightshade figured they should get taken out first, to minimize the risk to innocent civilians.

"What's this? Someone crashing my party?" Vinny said, his voice booming and arrogant. "Hey, you boys should know better. There's no way you're getting out of this alive, unless you put down the heat and walk out of here slowly."

"Family business," Bernie announced. "You don't attack the other Families and get away with it."

"That sounds like a Vaschetti accent to me." Vinny spat on the ground near Bernie. "After we take you apart, I'm gonna personally carve your boss's heart out and take a nice squat in his office."

Nightshade heard the Sandman arm a pair of his personal flash grenades. She glanced over and saw that he wasn't throwing them yet. He was letting the timers run down.

"Guess we'll find out who gets torn apart." Alex challenged Vinny.

"Yeah, looks like we-" Vinny began, just as one stun grenade sailed past Nightshade, at the level of her waist, followed by the second, which was arching high and headed between Alex, Bernie, and Vinny.

Nightshade turned away quickly. She barely got her eyes away before the two grenades went off.

The concussive thump of the grenades hit against the protective earplugs she wore, the ones that doubled as Bluetooth communication devices between her and the Sandman. She spun around, drawing her two M&P .45s. She took out the men who had been barely holding on to their weapons. That is, the ones who hadn't just passed out from the visual and auditory overload provided by the grenades.

`Trivole and Gum had been caught unaware by the exploding grenade that the Sandman had thrown between them at a height level with their shoulders. They were still crouched, shaking their heads to try and clear them while still holding onto their weapons. The Sandman had thrown the grenades when there had only been a second or two left before detonation, giving no time for anyone to grab cover.

The rest of the men, from all three of the Families represented at the party, were all in states of disorientation or unconsciousness from the brunt of the blast.

The Sandman leaped forward, his batons extended. He struck both of the ex-military men near their necks, rendering them unconscious but more or less unharmed. He moved past them, striking down the rest of the Caruso brother's team and then Bernie. Alex turned to look at the Sandman. Nightshade swore she saw Alex nod at the Sandman just before the vigilante dealt Alex a blow to the neck that knocked Alex out.

As Alex crumbled to the floor, Vinny came into view. He was waving his handgun, a large revolver, in wide arcs. His eyes were wide open and dazed. The Sandman threw his left-hand baton, and it struck Vinny's gun hand. The large gun dropped out of Vinny's damaged fingers, and he gave a short bark of pain. Even as the gun and baton fell to the floor, the Sandman drew out the .45 Raptor from the left-hip holster and aimed it at Vinny.

A shot rang out from another gun and the Sandman stumbled back. Even as the Sandman raised his left hand, still holding the Raptor .45, to press against the left side of his neck, Nightshade's eyes fixed on the shooter. The Vaschetti traitor, Ignacio, was holding out his 9mm

Beretta, and the barrel still had wisps of smoke escaping from it. He was looking to get another shot, clearly wanting to shoot the Sandman in the head again.

He never got the chance. Roaring in an inarticulate combination of war cry and rage, Nightshade emptied both of her guns into Ignacio Vaschetti. Ten rounds hammered into his torso and face within a matter of seconds. His body didn't twitch as it fell.

Not bothering to reload the empty firearms, Nightshade holstered both .45s and unsheathed her swords. The two short, curved Japanese swords were crisscrossed in sheaths across her back, but she had both blades out in a heartbeat. She began cutting down the still breathing Scarlatti family members, and when more rushed down the stairs in response to the slaughter, Nightshade laughed and went after them. She noticed at the edge of her peripheral vision that the Sandman was charging towards the front of the building. Figuring he either had a bead on Vinny or something of equal importance, she never wavered in her approach to the fresh outpouring of gun men. A dozen men fell before her swords in less than a minute.

Some of her rage had ebbed at the sight of her beloved running, whole and intact, towards a target, but her battle lust had not decreased. The men got off shots, and some small part of her worried that people who had no real connection to the Families, or hired help for the party, would get injured or worse. But the largest part of her was humming with savage energy, measuring strikes and taking down her opponents before they could cause her harm. Every fallen foe was a cold triumph in her heart. When no more came forward to attack or challenge her, she nearly screamed in impotent frustration.

She managed to keep enough control to stay quiet and look around. The only people still inside were dead or unconscious. Save a pair of college age girls who were still snapping pictures or video with their smartphones. They were dressed in costumes that Nightshade figured had to be from some Japanese television program. They looked up, wide eyed and open mouthed, when they realized that Nightshade was staring right at them.

"Girls, do you mind? We're trying to work here," she said, altering her voice to sound deeper than usual.

"Looks to us like you took down the house!" One of the girls, dressed in some odd version of a sailor's outfit, all but squealed excitedly.

"We are, like, *huge* fans!" gushed the other. She was dressed in a skin-tight black mini skirt, leather halter top, and thigh-high boots. Her hair had been styled to match Nightshade's, except the tips were a royal blue. The smartphone in her hand was trembling.

"Um... thanks," Nightshade said. "You better get out of here before the cops show up."

"Right!" they both squeaked and gave her a smart military salute before running off, or rather shuffling off on their five-inch heels.

Nightshade shook her head and headed for the front of the building.

The Sandman came into view a moment later. He didn't come through the front door but entered from the left. Nightshade peered down the direction he came from and saw a still warm body lying in the alcove.

"Is he alive?" she asked.

"Not unless he's a super villain that can regenerate from a .45 bullet in the heart and the back of the skull," he replied, turning her away and urging her to the stairs. "We need to get out of here."

As they ascended the stairs, she asked, "Are you okay?"

"It was a grazing shot across the side of my neck," he assured her. "My balaclava is made of Kevlar. The bullet didn't get past it. But the impact is a little hard to ignore. I'm going to have one hell of a bruise and stiff neck in the morning."

She breathed slowly as they reached the top of the stairs. The Sandman kicked open the fire escape door leading to the roof. The alarm went off as they dashed through the door.

Fortunately, no police had decided to occupy the roof. The duo made their way over the connected buildings without incident or being seen. The first cop cars sped to the front of the closed business as they ducked down the nearest street, activating their pendants to ensure no one saw them. Five minutes later, they were on the cycles and heading back to the lair.

# Chapter Thirty Six

Selia slept in the next morning, waking to find Wil missing, as usual, from the bed. It seemed the man rarely slept past nine, no matter how late they were up. Even Luna, who they had brought back from Wil's townhouse, had apparently decided to get up early. Crawling from the bed, she took a quick shower, letting the steaming hot water wake her up.

Wrapping a fluffy terry cloth robe around her, she padded to the living room, following the smell of bacon and coffee. Luna, apparently, had beaten her to the bacon and was curled up on a large dog pillow, staring at Wil as though she were waiting to be tossed another piece.

Wil was leaning against the bar that divided the kitchen from her living room, watching their sixty-two inch television. Taking a few minutes to admire his bare chest and sculpted muscles, she finally followed his gaze to the television.

He had left the sound down and turned on closed captioning, but when he noticed her standing in the living room, he turned the sound up, letting the news reporter's voice fill the room.

"Last night, police responded to a feud between two of the city's most notorious Families, in what was a deadly shootout," the lady was saying. "Witnesses state seeing the vigilantes, the Sandman and Nightshade, attacking two groups from opposing Families, before killing members of the Scarlatti syndicate. Vincent Scarlatti was amongst the dead, as was Ignacio Vaschetti, a suspected underboss to Lucien Vaschetti."

Selia walked over and hit the mute button. She didn't need to hear more. About to say something, her phone rang, and she picked it up off the bar, giving Wil an accusing look, since she typically kept it on the nightstand in the bedroom. He smiled and turned back to the skillet.

Unlocking the phone, she turned back to watch the TV as she said, "Good morning, Papa."

Her eyes widened as the scene flipped to a small house in one of the suburbs on the outside of the city. Police had cordoned off the house with their yellow tape and were milling about in the yard. A stretcher was being taken out of the house, a black bag zipped up on top of it. Selia didn't need to read the caption to know what had happened.

"Selia?" Soren's voice pulled her back to the phone. "Sweetheart?"

"Uh, Papa? Did you have anything to do with Vincent being killed? The one on the news at the moment?" Selia asked as the camera panned around to show the crowd of people. One woman was crying on the shoulder of a young boy who looked to be in his late teens or early twenties. His face was fixed in an expression of fury and grief.

"Ah, that murder out in Hedgeview," Soren said, a smug tone to his voice. "Did you think I wouldn't make it known what happens when someone betrays my family and puts my daughter in danger?"

"Yeah, that would be the one," Selia said, almost dismissively. "Guess he deserved it, then." She shrugged and turned away from the television. "Obviously you didn't call me to tell me good morning or to find out if I'm home." Soren chuckled and Selia smiled. "What's up, Papa?"

"No, I don't need to worry about my daughter playing with the enemy," Soren teased. His voice grew serious as he continued. "Don't go into the office today. Take the day off. I'm not going in today, either. Come over when you can and bring your fiancé with you. Alex and Bernie will be showing up at some point, so let Wil know."

"Papa wants us to come over," Selia said as Wil glanced over his shoulder at her. "Alex and Bernie are supposed to arrive at some time, too."

His eyes sparkled with mischief as a sly smile pulled at his lips. "Tell 'dad' to have some good sushi for dinner and I'll be nice."

Selia rolled her eyes as she muttered, "Remind me to never leave you two alone in a room."

"What was that?" Soren asked as Wil laughed. "Do I even want to know?"

"Probably not, Papa," Selia replied sweetly. "Can we go somewhere with good sushi for dinner?"

"I think that can be arranged," Soren agreed amiably. "Be safe, Selia. Things are pretty tense right now, and not just between the Families."

"I'll be fine, Papa," Selia assured him. "We'll see you in a couple hours."

The line went dead and Selia sat the phone on the counter.

"Right, so, time with dear ol' dad with sushi for dinner," Wil stated, sliding a plate of pancakes coated in real maple syrup and powdered sugar, slices of bacon, and a steaming cup of tea to Selia. "Should I take a suit?"

"Might not be a bad idea," Selia said with a laugh. Luna whined and pawed at her foot, before looking up at her with wide, sad brown eyes. "Okay, Luna, but only one piece."

Selia broke off a piece of her bacon and handed it to Luna, who took it daintily before sitting and practically gulping it down.

"You're spoiling her," Wil chided lightly.

"So do you," Selia retorted.

Wil laughed, nodded, and turned back to the stove. Putting dishes in the dishwasher and returning items back to their proper place, Selia watched in companionable silence as she ate her breakfast. It was, she thought, a good life.

Nearly an hour later, Luna bounded from her car and raced up the steps to Soren's house, where she pawed lightly at the door. It opened and the puppy began bouncing happily around Soren's feet and legs, clearly delighted to see Selia's father.

"Down, girl," Selia heard Soren say and Luna sat immediately, looking up at him expectantly. Soren dropped something and Luna snapped it out of the air before smiling at him, her tongue lolling out the side of her mouth.

"I see I'm not the only one who's spoiling her," Selia remarked as she neared the pair.

Soren raised a brow, a smirk on her face. "How else do you train one, if not with positive reinforcement?"

"I don't know," Selia quipped. "Did you ever manage to train me?"

Wil snickered as Soren laughed heartily and pulled her into a tight hug and kissed her cheek.

"If I had trained you properly, girl, you'd never have gone out to steal from Ignacio," Soren teased her. "Come on, we'll talk in my office."

Selia had always loved the decadence and charm of Soren's manor. The foyer was about the size of a small room that led into the wide, expansive living room. There were small hallways on either side of the large staircase in the center of the room. A fireplace sat directly opposite the stairs, with a mantel that Selia had often perched on as a teen, much to Soren's amusement. A long, plush sofa sat opposite the fireplace with chairs circling around. Near the windows, along the same wall as the fireplace, were bookcases and two windows on each side. Small loveseats, perfect for curling up on to read a book or to take a nap, sat in front of the windows. Paintings adorned the walls, and there were several plants dotting the room, giving it life.

There was a single door to the left and right. The door nearest the foyer opened into a small den, while the one to the right held Soren's office. The kitchen was tucked further back into the manor, as were several more rooms. The basement held a 'game room' of sorts, complete with full-size pool table, full bar, big-screen TV, the latest gaming console Selia loved, Blu-ray player, sofas, and even a dartboard. The second floor held the bedrooms, including Selia's old bedroom she still used on occasion.

Soren led them into his office, opening the door for them to go in ahead of him. A green light shone on the black security box to the right of the door. Selia knew her father kept his office secured by not only a thumb pad but also a retina scanner. Thumb pads, she knew, could be tricked, but a retina scanner was far more difficult. Aside from Soren, she was also the only other person who had been programmed into the security device.

Soren's office was lined with deep red cherry paneling and had thick, plush black carpet. Against the far wall was a second fireplace, smaller than the one in the living room, with several plush chairs curved around it. A small end table sat to the side of each chair. A rich red rug lay on the floor in front of the chairs. There was a single bookcase filled with classics and a handful of newer novels. The rest of the walls held paintings of Italy, and surprisingly, Temeria. There was a sofa against one wall with an antique coffee table in front of it.

Nestled against the wall opposite the fireplace, to the left of the door, was a large, antique desk. Behind it were shelves built into the wall. Photographs of Soren with Selia sat on one shelf, while books and various other items lined the rest. On the top shelf was a sword sitting on a display stand.

Luna, she noticed with amusement, crossed the room and hopped up on the plush sofa and plopped down, head on paws.

Soren closed the door before settling down behind his desk. Selia, without thinking, kicked her shoes off to the side and wiggled her toes in the carpet before crossing to one of the chairs and curling up in it.

This office had always been a favorite of hers, and Soren had always known it. She couldn't remember how many times she had snuck into his office, curled up on the rug in front of the fireplace, and read a book or did her homework. On more than one occasion she had fallen asleep watching the fire burn during that first year she'd spent beneath Soren's roof.

"I'm guessing you want to know what happened," Selia said, breaking the silence. Soren gave a single nod and she snuggled into the chair, glancing at Wil who had settled in the chair next to hers. "Well, we snuck in, your Rangers took out a couple of Vinny's men before Wil lobbed a pair of stun grenades and we took out everyone else." She turned her head to Wil. "Just what did you say to Alex before clubbing him?"

"I said 'sorry'. When he looked at me, it wasn't in surprise or anger," Wil offered. "It was more an expression of 'about time you got here', if that makes any sense. I just felt the need to apologize before clouting him. But he just nodded, slightly, as if it was okay."

"That's interesting. Do you think Alex has figured out some part of your dual identities?" asked Soren.

"We're pretty sure he knows who I am," Selia admitted. "You know Alex, Papa. He's never happy until he has every little piece of the puzzle, and it makes absolute sense. I'm surprised he hasn't said anything sooner, to be honest."

"He's also a cautious man," Soren reminded her. "Accusing someone of being a known vigilante, especially if the wrong people overhear it, is not something one does lightly."

Selia nodded. "He won't say anything. Not as long as Al is alive. Even then, it would depend on who steps into Al's position." She chuckled. "He would, however, have a fit if he was aware Lucien knew who I was."

Both men chuckled.

"I think Alex would have a great many fits, over a great many things, if he knew all the details," Soren rejoined.

Selia blushed. "Well, what he doesn't know won't hurt him." She bit her lip and changed the topic. "How much trouble are we going to have to deal with due to the hit?"

"We are, no cliché intended, still waiting for the smoke to clear," Soren replied solemnly. "There will be a meeting of the existing dons, and soon, if I know how the Families work. A replacement for Vinny will need to be announced soon to prevent a power vacuum or allow for further violence."

"What kind of worse-case scenario are we looking at?" interjected Wil.

"The Families, or at least Vinny's successor, declaring war on you two," Soren mused. "Or another family. Hell, he could declare war on everyone and although it isn't justified, there isn't much recourse. Just gearing up and waiting for the body count to start."

"That's delightful news," Selia said dryly. About to add something more, her phone rang, and she pulled it from her purse. She recognized Lucien's number and put it on speaker. "Hello, Lucien. What brings about this delightful honor?"

Leaning forward, she sat the phone on Soren's desk, so they could all hear the conversation.

"Good day to you, *belladonna*. No doubt you have heard of last night's activities. Quite a mess to be sorted out. I am calling for a meeting of the dons tonight. You will need to be there."

"Obviously I know of last night," Selia replied. She looked at Soren and shook her head in amusement. "Where is the meeting taking place?"

"I think I will invite all the dons to eat at my refurnished Italian eatery on the West Side of the city- the Palazzo Pisa. We're having a grand re-opening this weekend, but the place is ready to open, and the cooking staff is second-to-none. I find that some cooking that is truly reminiscent of our home land puts us all at a better place for intelligent conversation."

Soren looked thoughtful and a little surprised at that statement but nodded in appreciation and acceptance. He nodded again at Selia.

"I'll be there," she said slowly, "but it will be my fiancé who drops me off." She shot Wil a glance, curious as to what Lucien's reply would be to that statement. "I am also curious as to why it is you arranging this, and not Angelo, since it was the Lascari family who moved against Vinny."

"Oh, my dear, the rumors are much more interesting than any truth we can attach to them." Lucien laughed. "Accusations against everyone from your delightfully clad alter-ego and her BFF, to aliens and government conspiracies are flying around the city. Did that idiot Vinny actually declare someone from Soren's group as 'sounding like' one of mine?"

Selia and Wil exchanged amused grins. Soren wore a dour expression. They all remained silent.

Lucien continued, the mirth in his voice clear. "Regardless, there are no reliable witnesses to the event. Even the arguably 'best' footage is blurry and worse than a 90's action film. Two high school seniors who crashed the party- probably by blowing the doormen- caught something looking like Nightshade shooting up my former underboss, but the camera jumps and shakes constantly. Not to mention the fact that there are about a dozen other

'Nightshades' running around, screaming like girls. I'm also sure that at least one of them was a guy in drag, considering he was interviewed by the local news and swore it was his ex-boyfriend shooting a guy that was flirting with him."

"That is all rather interesting," Selia admitted. "And yes, I was the one who took out Ignacio." She paused before adding, "But I'm not apologizing. I presume it is due to Vinny's incorrect belief that it was your men making the hit, that you're calling this meeting?"

"No, this meeting is being called because a don is dead. As for why I am calling the meeting, it's because Al hasn't bothered to yet."

"I'm certain this is pretty close to treason, but I am appreciating your methods far more than that of Al." Selia turned her gaze to Soren. Her lips quirked upwards into a smile as she added, "I presume you'll take steps to ensure there won't be problems with Dorian being at the restaurant, as well."

"I will make everything as hospitable as possible for all concerned," Lucien replied.

"What time do we need to be there?" Selia asked, propping her elbow on the desk before resting her cheek on her fist.

"Six o'clock. Dress is formal. Any other questions?" Lucien asked.

"None that I can think of," Selia replied. "I look forward to seeing you again."

The call ended.

"I wonder how long it will take for him to call me," Soren asked sarcastically.

"You certainly seem to be his favorite, Selia," Wil observed.

Selia shrugged, shifting in the chair until she could plunge her toes in the thick carpeting. "He just likes pretty ladies who he can claim he influenced."

"Uh huh," both men said simultaneously.

Soren's phone rang and he answered it. "Hello, Lucien, what's on your mind?"

# Chapter Thirty Seven

Wil, in his Dorian persona, sat beside Selia in the limo he had rented for the night. Selia wasn't surprised, considering he obviously wanted to make sure she cut a formidable appearance, which was easier to do stepping from a limo than a full-size luxury SUV. They arrived with a good fifteen minutes to spare. The chauffeur opened the door, and they stepped out. Not surprising, it was one of Lucien's bodyguards who opened the eatery's door and gestured for them to enter before vanishing into the restaurant, probably in search of Lucien.

Selia glanced at Wil and smiled, taking a moment to admire him. He wore a tailored tuxedo, complete with white shirt and black bow tie to go with her beaded chiffon gown. While his tuxedo gave him a very Bond-like appearance, her gown would have done justice to any of Bond's famed women. The dress hugged her from bodice to thighs before flowing free, giving her the appearance of a mermaid out of the water. The tiny black beads that ran in diagonal lines from right to left glittered in the dim lighting of the restaurant.

Though the outside of the restaurant was bland and simple, with a black eave to help keep customers dry in the rainy weather, the inside was far more elegant with an almost rustic charm.

A stone wall, complete with twin stone arches, separated the foyer from the dining area. The walls of the restaurant were also brick with stones wrapping around the top two-feet of the wall. The ceiling had been done in some sort of stone-like stucco, giving it a breathtaking beauty. There were black tables with white linens and matching ebony chairs.

Small lanterns and vases that would be filled with flowers sat scattered about on the tables, giving it a whimsical, romantic feeling. The most modern part of the restaurant was the bar along the back wall and the desk tucked away in the far left corner, where customers would pay for their meal. Two large racks of wine sat on each end of the bar, silently waiting to be used.

Selia and Wil were apparently the first to arrive, which was exactly what Wil had planned. Lucien stood near the back talking with a couple of the staff, who wore white dress shirts, black bow ties, and black dress pants.

The Vaschetti don paused in his discussion as the guard spoke quickly and quietly to Lucien. Lucien dismissed the staff and turned to Selia and Wil, a frown marring his features before swiftly changing into a welcoming grin.

"Good to see you both!" Lucien exclaimed. "Since you're the first to arrive, you get to pick your seats."

Smiling impishly, Selia draped an arm around Wil's waist and led him forward towards Lucien and the large table that had been set up for the dons and their bodyguards. There were a total of eighteen chairs, Selia was pleased to note.

"I don't believe you've been formally introduced to my fiancé," Selia said warmly once they were within arm's reach of the don. "Lucien Vaschetti, please meet Dorian Porter. Dorian, this is Lucien."

Lucien's pallor became a little gray. "Dorian Porter, you say." Lucien carefully examined her fiancé. "Yes, that certainly would explain a great deal."

"People keep saying that," Dorian muttered. "I should decide whether or not I'm mildly offended by it."

The don's color did not improve.

"No, no," he said quickly. "No offense is meant. It's simply a matter of Selia's coming out of her wallflower phase. It seems she's developed a taste for dangerous partners." He paused, looking uncomfortable. "Charming, but dangerous partners."

"Ah, yes, well, it keeps me on my toes," Selia murmured. She tilted her head to the side and couldn't resist needling Lucien just a bit. "I thought you had already heard the rumors about us, Lucien."

"I tend to ignore rumors and wait for confirmed facts," Lucien said, focusing on Selia and looking slightly more comfortable. "Rumor is so prone to being more fantasy than fact."

"And how do you know I'm not just a fantasy?" Dorian inquired.

Lucien paled once more. "Well, I've seen the portrait of you on file, of course." He stopped suddenly as if he'd said the wrong thing. "Not that the picture does you justice, but your file certainly makes for an interesting read."

"And which file have you read?" Dorian said with an inhumanly calm voice.

"The one from Interpol, actually," Lucien answered. He smiled hesitantly.

"Why Interpol and not one of the United States services?" asked Dorian.

"I have better sources in the Italian government than I do State-side."

"Ah," Dorian replied. "Interesting."

Selia bit back a laugh as she asked innocently, "It's not going to be a problem having Dorian here, is it? There is a reason he's endeared himself to me, after all." She giggled. "Well, other than his charming demeanor and talented hands."

Lucien let out a bark of a laugh before collecting himself. "Have any of the other dons met Mr. Porter? Socially, of course."

"Tony and Carmine have," Selia replied, impish grin fixed on her features. "Al, however, has not."

"Vinny no longer has a vote," joked Lucien. "And even if his replacement were inclined to object, I'm betting the majority vote would be to allow Mr. Porter to remain. That's certainly how my vote would be. Did Tony or Carmine have any problems with you having Mr. Porter along, when they met him?"

Selia shook her head. "None, though they were a bit shocked. I can't imagine why that would have been." Shifting her weight, she looked Lucien dead in the eyes and asked, "Who *is* Vinny's replacement? Or has no one stepped up yet?"

"Chuck, although he hasn't formally accepted, yet. That should happen tonight, unless someone else presents themselves or a reasonable cause to dismiss his appointment."

Selia laughed softly. "Oh, now that should be as interesting as Al discovering I'm engaged to Dorian."

"He doesn't know?" Lucien asked with a snort. Selia just shook her head smiling. "My god, the man is slipping."

"It's not as though he's been paying any attention to me," Selia countered. "So far, only three people know: You, Soren, and Alex." She didn't count Nicky, since he was still being held by the government. "Should be interesting to see his reaction, shouldn't it?"

Lucien laughed and shook his head. "I would say you like to play dangerous games." He remarked, looking at Dorian. "But it's rather obvious."

"You have no idea," Dorian countered.

"There's a saying in my country, Lucien," Selia said softly, her voice low. "Find your opponent's weakest point, and push until they snap. I believe it's the same here. I won't go out of my way to destroy, but that doesn't mean I won't give a nudge where it's needed."

The don nodded in appreciation, but Selia held up a hand, turning towards the door that was opening behind them. She felt Wil tense for a moment before relaxing as Carmine Pavanello strode through the archway, a bodyguard to each side of him.

Carmine smiled warmly at the sight before him. "Selia, looking as lovely as ever! How are you?"

"Doing well, Carmine, and yourself?" Selia returned his smile with one of her own.

"Splendid, my dear; simply splendid." He looked at her partner. "Mr. Porter, good of you to join us. Planning on making an honest woman out of Ms. Lascari soon?"

"No, actually," Dorian replied with a smile. "But I will be marrying her."

Carmine and Lucien both laughed heartily and genuinely at Dorian's remark.

"Am I late for the joke?" came the voice of Tony Carenzo.

"You're always late for the joke, for dinner, for your wife's waning desire to have you in the bedroom," Carmine retorted.

"Just because you want my wife, Carmine, doesn't mean she wants to be rid of me," Tony replied.

"Nah, of course not," Carmine said with a sly grin. "She needs a break from a real man after I'm done with her. That's where you come in."

Lucien stepped between the two men. "What kind of impression do you think you're making on our young liaison with all that shit?" he scolded.

"I've already been subjected to their sense of humor, Lucien," Selia said, trying to not laugh. The man really was endearing in a rather fatherly way. A frightening thought, if she took time to consider it. "Thank you for the consideration, though."

"Ah, Mary Mother of God, you mean she already knows there's no hope for any of us?" replied a new voice.

Selia leaned to the side and peered around the three men in front of her to see Chuck and his two bodyguards entering the dining area. "Hello, Chuck. A pleasure to see you again. Come to join the festivities or to watch the two clowns?"

"Both, of course," Chuck replied enthusiastically. "One of the benefits of having a better sense of humor and self-worth than my *cafone* predecessor.

"To answer Mr. Carenzo's question," interjected Dorian. "I was just informing Mr. Pavanello that I do intend to marry Selia soon, but I fail to see how that will make her an honest woman."

Tony and Chuck laughed appreciatively.

Chuck held his hands towards Selia. "That is wonderful news! Congratulations to you both!" He began to offer his hand to Dorian, smirked, and then held his hands up in deference. He shrugged. "Ah, but of course, we are both armed and make no pretense of not being willing to shoot each other. Do we, Dorian?"

Dorian smiled and held out his hand. "I'll accept a handshake as a symbol of congratulations."

Chuck laughed, nodded, and shook Dorian's hand. "Damn," Chuck said, once they released each other's hands. "Is that the hand you strangled the Albanian prince with? What a grip!"

Dorian's smile didn't fade. "No, it was my left. I leave the right hand for the heavy work."

The room filled with raucous laughter. Lucien snapped his fingers and a waiter appeared moments later, carrying an opened bottle of *Fumaio* chardonnay. Two waiters came behind, carrying empty wine glasses, which they distributed.

When the wine waiter was serving Selia, Carmine objected. "I didn't think you drank."

Smiling, Selia gave a nod to the waiter before replying. "Typically, I don't drink in a social setting," she explained. "I'm not a very trusting person. I'm certain you can understand why. But with Dorian here with me, and it being a special occasion, I see no harm in imbibing in a glass or two with all of you." She dropped a wink as she added, "I may even start drinking in a social setting now that I have Dorian by my side."

"Meaning she figures Lucien won't poison all of us," Tony observed.

"Well, I wouldn't go that far," Carmine offered. "I wouldn't put it past the sly fox to roofie all of us just to have something to laugh about at our next gathering."

"If you're this charitable when I'm in the room, I hate to think what you say behind my back," Lucien chided, with a smile.

Selia laughed. She gave Lucien a knowing look before taking a sip of her wine.

The sound of the door opening nearly slipped past her, but she looked around in time to see Al standing beneath the curve of one archway, his dark eyes fixated on her and the wine in her hand. Her smile faltered slightly, and she lifted her chin a fraction in a silent challenge. Bernie and one other guard Selia didn't recognize stood to each side of Al. Bernie didn't look too pleased, despite his stoic expression.

"We don't wait for everyone to show up anymore?" Al demanded. "Is there some reason you feel a need to insult me, Vaschetti?"

"You're late," Lucien fired back. "And I wasn't assured that you'd even come."

Soren entered a moment later. "My apologies for our tardiness. My driver didn't know the best route here from Al's office."

Lucien nodded. "Apology accepted." He snapped his fingers and the wine waiter hurried along with one of his assistants to get glasses of wine poured for the final arrivals.

When his glass had been filled, Al nearly glared at Selia as he said, "I thought you didn't drink."

Selia glanced at Soren, who gave a slight nod. "Things change," She paused before giving Angelo a slow, wicked smile. "Besides, he asked nicely."

"Al, good to see you," Carmine interrupted, turning towards the Lascari don. "Quit giving the lady a hard time and relax."

Al looked at Carmine. "Good to see you as well, Carmine." He nodded to the other dons while ignoring the rest of Carmine's statement.

Taking another sip of her wine, Selia leaned against Dorian. "Al, I'd like you to meet someone very near and dear to me: Dorian Porter." She turned towards Dorian, keeping Al in her peripheral vision. "Dorian, darling, this is Angelo Lascari, Papa's cousin."

"And head of the Lascari Family," Dorian amended, his voice holding no discernible emotion. He didn't offer to shake. "Your reputation as a businessman precedes you, sir."

"And you are the notorious Dorian Porter, mercenary extraordinaire," Al said, his tone close to impudent. "Your reputation as a businessman precedes you, as well. Is there any contract you won't take?"

"Not unless it's boring," Dorian countered. "For killing senile old men, for example, I'll charge double for wasting my time. I find such contracts unnecessary as those kinds of targets tend to do themselves in if people wait long enough."

Al looked hard at Dorian, seeming to weigh his possible responses. "How have you managed to be a part of this meeting?" he finally demanded of Dorian.

Selia angled her hand slightly until the light of the room caught on the diamonds on her ring, causing it to sparkle as she held the glass. "Can't you guess?"

The Lascari don looked at Selia coolly, but it was obvious when he finally noticed the ring. He stiffened minutely, trying to keep his expression neutral.

After several beats, he said, "Ah, congratulations." He sounded anything but happy.

"It's so gratifying to know we have your blessing," Dorian commented through a too-wide smile. He waited to see if Al would take up the challenge. Al did not.

"Now that all of the pleasantries have been tended to," Lucien said in a playful tone. "Shall we get down to business?"

There was a general murmur of agreement and people took their seats.

"The first order of business is the replacement of the recently deceased don," Lucien announced. "Do we have any objections to Chuck, the most successful underboss in that family, being raised to the title of don?"

There was no immediate response in the negative, just the dons looking around at each other, the bodyguards looking at everyone and the room. No one spoke. Lucien nodded.

"Chuck, you are now the don. I trust you have met our newly appointed liaison, Selia?" Lucien continued.

Smiling, Chuck nodded. "Yes, I have, and I am confident in her ability to perform her duties without biased emotions. I thank you all for the confidence in my appointment as don. I will work for the betterment of my Family, without working against the other Families. I so swear."

A murmur of agreement went through the rest of the room, with one exception.

"Do you know why your predecessor thought it wise to act against the other Families?" Al demanded.

"Vinny was an arrogant ass, which was, I'm sure, known to all of you." Chuck said easily. "He became convinced that the reason our family has been the least successful of the five was because some of the syndicates, specifically the most financially successful, were working against us. I don't know what idiocy influenced him to form this opinion, but I do not share it. While you-" he nodded to Al, "-and Lucien have seen the most profits and own real estate and other holdings that could only be taken by force or corporate take down, that does not mean there are no other assets to be had in this city. Nor are they the only way to accumulate wealth and power. New technologies and communication systems now allow for fresh methods, and I intend to bring that to my Family."

"Ah, hell... the new guy is gonna bring us out of the Stone Age," said Tony with a playful wink and smirk.

Chuck smiled appreciatively. "None of us is quite that ass-backwards, even if popular TV and fiction still portray us that way. But our Family has, under Vinny's influence, ignored opportunities in favor of what worked forty years ago. Some of those business methods are still viable, but many are not. It's time to put the useless to rest and move on with what is available and useful."

"Well enough said," Al grumbled, but he didn't add anything more.

"Next on the agenda is the business of peace," Lucien continued, trying to keep an optimistic mood. "Is anyone prepared to come forward and claim responsibility for the assault against Vinny? Or does anyone want to file a grievance?"

"I claim responsibility for the initial assault," Al declared boldly. "I sent six men to take out Vinny for his actions against my Family. I cannot account for the claims that the two vigilantes became involved. I was not there, and my men were taken out before they could identify their assailants."

Against Billy, that is, Selia thought in disgust. She glanced to Soren before turning her gaze to the rest of the men at the table as she slid her hand over Dorian's.

"I am concerned about the amount of time it took you to assemble an assault, then," interjected Carmine. His playful and relaxed manner had vanished, and he almost seemed to be another person. "I believe I am accurate in remembering that your assault team went after the former don only after one of your minor underlings was blown up. But that was the third or fourth attack against your Family, was it not?"

Selia squeezed Dorian's hand, but she kept silent, her gaze aimed towards the glass in front of her on the table. She wanted to speak up but knew it wouldn't be wise. Not when she was supposed to stay neutral to these proceedings.

"I am a little behind, it seems," Chuck interjected cautiously. "I knew of the plots against Lucien's family and at least two against Al's. Including the car assault against Selia. But you're saying there were more? Are you including the plot to blow up Soren's office?"

A hushed silence filled the room, and all eyes went to Chuck. Chuck sat back in his chair and frowned.

"I take it no one knew about that last one. Well, I'm here to improve communications with everyone else, so, what the hell. Yes, the plan was to plant a bomb in Soren's office and trigger it when the maximum number of people would be inside the building." Chuck elucidated. "Somehow the bomb got removed from the office, and conveniently wound up getting stuffed down the throat of one of Vinny's men. The one staking out the building to trigger the explosion, no less."

Selia didn't dare look at her mate but couldn't completely suppress the smile on her face. She'd have to ask him about that one later.

"What I am surprised by the most, however," continued Chuck. "Is that Lucien, who really was the primary focus of Vinny's plans, didn't act against him as well."

"I was waiting for verification that it was Vinny," Lucien explained. "I knew I had several traitors in my organization. It turns out it was all but one of my captains, for starters, but I did not want to act against a don until I had proof."

"Yes, that's why I didn't act sooner as well!" Al added a little too quickly and enthusiastically. "I didn't want to start a war with anyone except the person responsible. We didn't have a clear picture on who was responsible until Billy was blown up. The explosive used was the kind Vinny... I mean, Chuck's Family, has been known to use."

"I hope that was one of the guys killed at the club," Chuck commented. "I've been trying to discover who was involved in that, and so far, no real leads. But I will keep looking. There was no excuse for Vinny's behavior, and I won't tolerate that kind of thinking in my organization."

Tony nodded. "It's good to have another level-headed man at the helm." He held a hand up to Selia. "No offense, dear lady."

Selia shook her head and smiled. "None taken, dear sir."

Lucien was still eyeing Al with something that looked like bitter contempt. Al was not looking at Lucien. He continued to stare at Chuck.

"Regardless, I hope we have had the last vile bit of treachery among the Families. At least for a while," Lucien added.

The other dons nodded.

"Do we want to declare war against the two vigilantes?" Al abruptly suggested.

Tony and Carmine looked at Al with curious expressions. Lucien's scowl deepened, while Soren maintained a neutral expression. Selia hoped her tension wasn't visible, but she calmed when Dorian squeezed her hand.

"I'd like to thank them, personally," Chuck stated casually. "If they hadn't intervened, it would have been a complete bloodbath instead of just the elimination of Vinny and the fools that followed his idea."

"Yeah, you wound up with no casualties, isn't that right, Al?" Carmine demanded, glaring at Al. "Exactly why is it you want to put a hit on them? Afraid we're going to think they're on your payroll?"

"I wouldn't give a shit about them at all, especially when they do stuff that benefits us, like last night," Tony rejoined. "As it is, they only hit our business when it's the drugs or skin trade. If they stopped on that, hell, I'd consider making them an offer. Could use some solid fighters, even if they do wear funny pajamas."

"While we're all speaking out, I'd also like to point out that I owe the Sandman. As do you, Al, albeit in a round-about manner." She paused long enough for her words to settle. "In August, after I left Cerestes with the data I was tricked into stealing by Alfi, he rescued me from two of Lucien's thugs." She turned her gaze to Lucien. "No offense meant, Lucien." Lucien nodded and she continued, her gaze returning to Al. "He took out the pair of men and let me go, without harm."

"I suppose we should also thank Nightshade, since she was there," Soren amended with some sarcasm. "She was, what, in the alley below, keeping an eye out for more trouble?"

Selia gave a shrug. "I don't know, Papa. I didn't even see the Sandman until he appeared in front of me, since the street light had been shot out. We had a short exchange, I thanked him for the rescue, and by the time I got to the ground, I was alone." She gave a slight smile as she added, "Nor did I stick around to search for either of them."

"Regardless, they have been less of a problem and more of a help. At least in some cases," Lucien rejoined. "I don't condone wasting time and money, and probably our men, trying to get them."

"Are you sure?" Dorian spoke up. "They could be taken care of."

All the dons looked at Dorian, with surprised expressions. Selia realized she was doing the same and willed her eyes to not be so wide open.

"Are you saying you could be hired for the job?" Al asked with real curiosity in his voice. The other dons remained quiet and attentive.

"It wouldn't be a boring job." Dorian answered with a chilling smile. "It wouldn't be cheap, either. But I'm looking to take someone on a very expensive vacation. Maybe even retire."

"But you're saying you could do it... if the price is right?" Al pressed.

A wide smile burst across Selia's face, and she felt her face flush. Ducking her head, she lowered her lashes to hide her amusement.

"I can guarantee they would... disappear. Permanently," Dorian replied.

There was a long, considering silence at the table.

"Well, that certainly is something to consider." Carmine spoke up. "But I agree with Lucien: I do not see the need to go after them. They aren't costing us enough money against the benefit they've created so far. Hell, most of the public still considers them a myth."

"We don't even know if it's just two people," Tony added. "There were a lot of people in those costumes at the party. How do any of us know they weren't intentional decoys? How do we know there aren't a group of them taking turns?"

"Alex told me that there were several people who looked the part at that party," Soren commented. "There might be something to that theory, Tony."

Selia took a sip of her wine. "So there is a count of four against declaring war on the vigilantes and one for it." She swept the table with her gaze. "Majority rules which means no war will be declared at this time, yes?"

"I didn't say I was for it." Al corrected her. "I was simply asking if we wanted to consider it. We at least know there is a possibility if it's decided for. If not now, then if the question arises later." He nodded to Dorian.

"Correction noted," Selia replied smoothly, not believing a word that dripped from his tongue.

"Unless the two of them- whether it's a group of people posing as the pair or not, I don't care- start causing some real damage to our overall business? Or personally threatens us, you won't get a vote of 'aye' from me," Chuck informed the room.

"I like how this guy thinks, and I agree with that," Tony agreed. Carmine was nodding.

The table remained silent for a few moments and Selia took the opportunity to voice her own objective for the night.

"If I might, I have something I'd like to say." The men turned towards her and remained silent, a few nodding. "I'm quite aware that I've just been granted the position of liaison, but considering all that has happened?" She shot a sharp glance towards Al before continuing. "I plan on taking a couple weeks off. All things considered, I think I've earned at least two weeks of relaxation."

"We are getting off topic." Lucien cut in. "I personally think you have earned a vacation, but you should wait until we have this clutter cleaned up and Chuck is well-established. It shouldn't take a week, though. Think you two can wait that long?"

"The first time someone shoots at me, I'm leaving for Jamaica," Selia countered, a smile on her face.

"Sounds fair!" exclaimed Chuck.

The room burst into laughter again. This time, even Al joined in.

"Our last piece of business," Lucien continued, "is the position of liaison. This might be a foregone conclusion, but the formalities must be done. Everyone is familiar with Selia Lascari. The proposed liaison for all five Families?"

All of the dons agreed, and when Tony and Carmine toasted her with their almost empty wine glasses, the rest did the same.

"Well enough," Lucien said with a smile. "Are there any objections to the appointment of Selia Lascari to the position of liaison between all Families of the New Campania territory?"

No one spoke up. Lucien smiled, nodded, and clapped his hands together twice, rapidly.

"Business is concluded!" he declared as the room began to fill with servers and trays of food, bottles of wine.

There were several slices of *bruschetta*, salami and *capicollo*, along with a mound of *mozzarelline fritte*, and of course, olives. Large steaming bowls of minestrone and *pasta e faioli* were placed on the tables next to loaves of *Michetta, Ciriola* and a stack of pitas.

"Dorian," Lucien called out. "I have some risotto with clam sauce on hand, just for you, but if you prefer, I did send somebody out to get some fresh sushi. It's tuna and salmon."

Dorian picked up a *mozzarelline fritte* and smiled. "I think I can manage some good Italian food today. I'll pay you for the sushi and take it for a midnight snack."

Lucien smiled and raised his now-filled wine glass. "*Salute.*"

# Chapter Thirty-Eight

Selia was getting a little tired of waking up to a ringing phone. Yet again it was Al calling, demanding yet another meeting in his office. This time, however, she had been expecting the call and the demanded meeting. That didn't mean she enjoyed it.

When the elevator doors open to reveal Al's outer office, Selia was a bit surprised to see Soren waiting for them. Wil, or rather 'Dorian', gave Soren a nod as Selia gave her beloved father a hug.

Sandy, curiosity shining on her face, interrupted the family bonding time, though. "Al's waiting for you two."

Selia turned away from Soren and pulled Dorian into a hug, kissing his lips lightly. "Don't get into too much trouble, okay? At least not without me."

Dorian smirked and nodded. "Then don't take too long."

Giggling, Selia turned and followed Soren into Al's office. Her smile faded as she noticed the fury glittering in Angelo's eyes. Though she kept silent, she crossed the room until she stood in front of Soren.

Soren may have been her father, as well as her employer for the past decade, but this argument was to do with her personal choices and her duties as liaison. There was no need to involve Soren, but Al had done just that. His choices were growing more erratic, and her choices were becoming more dangerous, at least in Al's eyes.

Selia knew it was a dangerous game she played, but Al had crossed her one too many times. She hadn't grown up in a land where monarchies were overthrown by subtle, and sometimes not so subtle, coups without learning the intricacies of how it was done. Often it took years, sometimes decades, but she had the time and patience to push, needle, and pry until it happened.

"You wished to see us?" Selia asked. Her voice was calm and cool.

"I want you to explain a great many things," Al demanded without preamble or pleasantries. "Feel free to have a seat."

Selia glanced at Soren as she took a chair to the left. "What is it you wish for us to explain?"

Al walked over to his desk and opened a drawer. From it he produced a bottle of old single-malt scotch and a clean glass. He poured two fingers worth and put the bottle away. There was no offer of a drink to either Soren or Selia.

"You seem very friendly to Lucien, Selia." Al said without looking at her. He took a deep drink from the glass. "The other dons also seem quite taken with you. Yet you seem determined to treat me as an inferior."

Once again, it was time for her to take a stand, Selia decided. She didn't look to Soren as she replied, "Papa, you know I love you, but I need the room."

Her adopted father didn't respond with words or ask Al for his permission. Soren simply left the room. Al looked over when the door shut, and then glared at Selia.

"I'm liaison for the Families, Uncle Al," Selia replied, meeting his gaze evenly. "A position you placed on me after Lucien *forced* it upon me. It benefits all the Families for me to be friendly to the dons."

"That explains, to a small extent, the charm you put to those dons. But what of the don that gave you a place after you were banished from your homeland? When you were marked for death? Yes, Soren brought you, but I could have sent you back- a show of good relations with Temeria. Is there no respect for the man who has made it possible for all that has come to you since arriving in the city?"

Al took another drink and waited for her answer.

"My respect lies with the ones who are concerned about my welfare," Selia countered. "Or do I need to remind you of the order you gave my former babysitters when you absurdly believed that I could be the pajama-clad vigilante, Nightshade?"

Al grunted. "I have to work for the survival and benefit of everyone in my family. If anyone turns traitor and becomes a threat, is it not the duty of the clan's leader, especially in your homeland, to make sure the threat is eliminated? If you cannot respect the hard decisions that a don is bound to make, then there is no question why you would never be a leader, or why a woman is not a don."

"Is that also why you didn't do anything despite all the attacks against me?" Selia asked softly. "Or why instead of giving me protection, as you did just a few months ago, you made me bait? Needless to say, I'm very thankful for Dorian, and the subsequent result of his help."

"It seems you cannot respect the hard decisions I have to make. There is the greater good, Selia." Al's voice was heavy with disappointment. "No one wants to be the one dangling, but everyone takes a turn. I cannot put a single person, not even myself, before the benefit of everyone else."

"Oh, no, I can certainly respect the decision to eliminate a threat. More than once I witnessed a traitor executed by my people on Temeria," Selia replied coolly. "The problem is, Angelo, despite the fact I proved to you that I wasn't, nor could I possibly be Nightshade, you still have shown little regard to my welfare. Both then and now." She shook her head slowly. "I received more protection from a freelance mercenary than I have from my own family."

"So, you feel that I have less concern for your wellbeing than I do for others?" Al replied. "That would certainly explain your behavior. Some time you will have to talk with Soren about the many times he has been in harm's way. Or the number of times I have been the target. I hope we can put aside this misunderstanding and work together in a mutually beneficial way."

*Just one problem with that*, Selia thought coldly, *I don't forgive and forget.*

"I have absolutely no problems with that proposition," Selia replied, settling into her chair comfortably. "What else do you wish to discuss?"

"Why was I the last one to learn of your engagement?" Al quickly retorted.

"Because you were the last one to arrive at the meeting," she replied simply.

Al seemed a bit stumped by that explanation, but only for a moment. "Very well, but you couldn't have waited to tell everyone? I expected you would tell Soren, and then I would be informed by either of you." Al put his glass on top of his gleaming desk. "Of course, I also expected when that day came, it would be Alex you were engaged to."

"Oh, Uncle. Have you ever known a woman to keep exciting news to herself?" Selia said, playing on Al's old fashioned mind-set. "Especially that kind of news? Don't we run around the instant after accepting a ring, trying to get everyone to acknowledge it?"

Chuckling, Al nodded. "All right, you have me there. But why a mercenary? Why Dorian Porter? The man would kill you if the price were right."

"Didn't you send Alex to do the very same thing?" Selia asked pleasantly. "You didn't even offer him a bonus, I bet. So he'd have done it for the same pay he gets for picking up your dry cleaning or driving your car."

Wincing, Al admitted, "Okay, you have a valid point there, as well. I think two strikes is enough. I'm not going for a third round. I will only instruct you to be very careful. There is a great deal of danger around you, and you cannot avoid it if you push blindly forward."

"That is some of the best advice I could ask for," Selia replied cheerfully. She stood up and kissed Al on the cheek. "Do you need me to send in Papa?"

"Yes, I need to have a few words with him, I suppose," Al said, kissing her on the cheek. "I expect to get the first wedding invitation, though."

"Of course!" she declared dutifully and went to the door.

"Papa, Uncle Al would like to speak with you," Selia said after opening the door and stepping out.

Soren noticed her demeanor and chuckled quietly, shaking his head. He kissed her before going into Al's office and whispered, "I will see my way home. We'll talk later."

She nodded and watched Soren go into the office. When the door closed, she zeroed in on Wil. In true Dorian mode, he stood military straight in the hallway watching nothing and everything.

Selia walked up and slipped her arm through his. "Let's go, handsome."

Wil nodded and they started down the hallway to the elevators.

"Are we waiting for Soren?" Wil asked.

"No, we are going to a nice brunch," Selia said. "While there, we are going to make wedding plans, including the very short guest list... which won't include Al."

# Epilogue

Two weeks later, Selia smiled at her reflection in the mirror of the cabin's main bedroom. Soren had suggested Dogwood Lodges, a small business owned by an old friend, as well as the small historic church near the luxury cabins for her and Wil's very small and private wedding.

Dogwood Lodges, as well as the church, were located in the mountains of Love, Virginia. The cabins were nestled in the center of nearly twenty acres of wooded property in the Blue Ridge mountains. Dogwood trees were everywhere around the cabins and Selia could only imagine what they looked like in full bloom during the spring months. Her father swore that while there, Wil wouldn't have to worry about being anyone but himself because Soren had rented all twelve cabins to ensure complete privacy.

Anything for his little girl, Selia thought happily.

Wil's mother stood behind Selia, hands clasped together at her waist with a smile on her lovely face. For a moment, Selia felt a sharp pang, knowing that she would age slower than her soon-to-be husband. That in all likelihood, Wil would die before her. A sad, sobering thought that fortunately didn't last very long. It was hard to think of depressing things when one was about to marry their true love. Their life mate.

The silver trim along the bodice and waist of Selia's white chiffon gown sparkled and glittered in the bright light. Her brown hair had been curled with half of it pulled up into an elaborate and elegant design while the rest drifted around her shoulders.

Selia stared at her reflection, almost mesmerized by the simple elegance. Wil's mother vanished suddenly, before reappearing in seconds, a camera in hand. She began snapping picture after picture from nearly every angle, causing Selia to giggle. No one had ever done such before and she found it almost overwhelming.

Luna, her precarious little puppy, was lying on the bed watching with what could have been called a bored look. The pup wore a white lace bow. Two other bows lay under her paws in tatters, having discovered a method to pull them off before promptly shredding them.

Thankfully, Selia had several more lengths of lace in a duffle, ready to be pulled out and tied into yet another bow.

There was a knock on the door and Wil's mom froze. Selia, however, turned and smiled, recognizing her father's distinctive cologne.

"Come on in, Papa," she called.

Wil's mother, she noticed in amusement, relaxed visibly as the door opened and Soren stepped in. Even more amusing was the fact that Mother Fredericks wasn't fazed by Soren's charm or dashing appearance. She was, however, very happy to see Selia's father and greeted him with a click of the camera and a mischievous smile that reminded Selia a great deal of Wil.

Soren crossed to Selia, his eyes filled with love, and perhaps, a touch of sadness. Gently, he held her shoulders and kissed her cheeks. "You, my dear, look amazing."

He released her and took a single step back. Pulling a slender box from his inner jacket pocket, he held it out to her. Selia looked up at him in surprise, receiving only a smile.

"Thank you, Papa," she said, removing the lid.

Inside sat an exquisite necklace that dripped diamonds. Selia gasped and Soren chuckled softly as she nearly dropped the box.

"Oh, my," she somehow managed to breathe. "It's gorgeous."

Chuckling softly as he removed the necklace, Soren stepped behind her, fastening it around her neck. In a distant part of her mind, Selia realized Wil's mother was snapping away on her camera, capturing this special moment between father and daughter.

Soren turned her gently until she was staring in the mirror again. Hesitantly, she touched the necklace glittering around her throat.

"Thank you, Papa," she whispered, tears stinging her eyes. Selia didn't understand why she wanted to cry, yet she did. Looking up at him, she smiled softly.

Her father merely kissed her forehead. Both ignored the continued click of the camera.

"Oh! I almost forgot," Wil's mother finally said, snapping her fingers. She dashed to a dresser on the other side of the room, the camera hanging around her neck. "A nice gentleman had this delivered to our hotel room in New Campania just before we left for here."

Selia and Soren glanced at each other warily. Wil's parents, who lived two hours outside New Campania's city limits, had arrived in the city a week before they'd all departed for their vacation. Not surprising, both mother and father understood why Wil had adopted the persona of a famed mercenary after being introduced to Selia and

Soren. Emma and Philip Fredericks had quickly accepted Selia into the family and had warmed up to Soren by their third day in the city.

Emma pulled out a rather large square box that was wrapped in very expensive wrapping paper and a bow that had probably been hand-tied. She offered it to Selia. A small card had been tucked beneath the ribbon.

Uncertainly, Selia slid the ribbon off and handed the card to Soren as she removed the lid of the box. Her eyes widened as she stared at the contents. Inside was a very delicate tiara made from silver, or perhaps platinum, that glittered with diamonds and crystals.

Wil's mother gasped in awe, forgetting about the camera as she almost reverently pulled the tiara from the box.

"It's something a queen would wear," Emma murmured softly. "Fit for royalty. Though I don't believe I've ever seen one that's so exquisite!" She turned to Selia. "Rather appropriate for my son's bride, I think."

Selia smiled hesitantly. She had no foolish beliefs about being a queen or princess. Not even for a day. Wil knew she wasn't nobility. He knew her heritage. In fact, a person couldn't get further from nobility than her. She was the daughter of a peasant from a land ruled by nobility. Nobility who took a strong opposition to anyone pretending to be royalty of any caliber.

Though most women desired to be a queen or princess for a day, Selia had no such aspirations. She hadn't been raised in a land where it was allowed. Having been reminded of where she came from, she had an even greater wariness about wearing the tiara. Especially since she recognized the tiara's design as being Temerian.

She didn't have to look at the card to know who had sent the gift. There was only one person, aside from her father, who could have sent such a gift.

"Lucien," Selia and Soren said together.

Soren pulled the card out and inside was a simple card with the words 'best wishes' written in the Vaschetti don's writing. There was also a Visa gift card. The kind that came from a bank. On the back was a five-digit number. A small note fell to the floor and Selia knelt down, picking it up. She unfolded the slip of paper and chuckled.

"Consider this a payment for services rendered, *belladonna*," she said.

"What does that mean?" Emma asked. "Stand up and turn around so I can position this correctly."

Selia did as she was told, allowing Emma to place the tiara on her head. Soren, meanwhile, tucked the card into an inner pocket of his jacket while placing the box on the dresser.

"You really don't want to know, Emma. Let's just say this is Lucien's way of one-upping Al."

"You can send him a thank you note, then," Emma stated in her typical matter-of-fact tone. "There! Now, you two stand together so I can get a couple pictures of the beautiful bride with her father."

Giggling, Selia wrapped an arm around Soren's waist and did as she was instructed. There was no mistaking the amusement in Soren's eyes, as he held his daughter close.

Twenty minutes later, Selia stood in the vestibule of the small nearby church. It was an old, historical building and she doubted more than thirty people could possibly fit inside. Not that it mattered, since it was just her, Soren, Wil, and Wil's parents, along with the priest and his wife, who played the organ.

The music began and together, she and Soren entered the chapel. Her eyes didn't move away from Wil, who had eyes only for her. Soren gave her a kiss before handing her to Wil and moving to stand opposite Emma and Philip.

The priest smiled at her and Wil, an ancient-looking bible resting in the palm of his hands. Selia slipped her hand into Wil's as the priest began the ceremony.

No matter what the future brought, Selia knew they would face it together.

We hope that you enjoyed this title and look forward to many more to come. Please, leave us a review! Reviews matter to all of our authors.

Take a look at some of our other award-winning series at https://threeravenspublishing.com/series-universes/

Visit us at https://www.threeravenspublishing.com and sign up for our newsletter for the latest and greatest news on upcoming titles and events.

Other series and titles you might enjoy.

AVAILABLE ON
AMAZON
JOINT TASK FORCE
13
HOLDING THE LINE
BETWEEN HEAVEN AND HELL
13

DECLAN FINN
DECLAN FINN
DECLAN FINN
DECLAN FINN
Demons Forever
Honor at STAKE
Live & Let Bite
Good to the Last Drop
The Dragon Award Nominated Series
FREE on Kindle Unlimited!

MYSTERY,
MAGIC &
MAYHEM
WITH A TWIST
OF ROMANCE
J.F. POSTHUMUS
ON AMAZON
FIND ME

B.E.N.T.
BIOLOGIC     ENHANCED     NASCENT     TALENT

THE RAVEN
AND
THE CROW
MICHAEL K. FALCIANI
FIND ME
ON AMAZON

STARFLIGHT

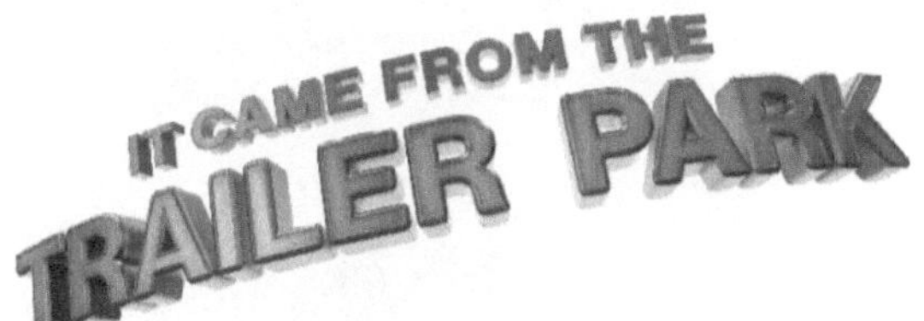
IT CAME FROM THE
TRAILER PARK

You can also keep up to date with our latest release announcements on Scifi.radio and get some of the best fandom programing on the planet.

**Scifi for your Wifi**

And don't forget to check out our other Sponsors and Affiliates

A southern Appalachian jewel for craft beer lovers, Buck Bald Brewing offers something for everyone. With delicious, locally brewed beverages from across the spectrum, Buck Bald Brewing offers craft brews that are consistently amazing.

From the dark and smooth Shesquatch Scottish ale, to the intense hops of Hippibilly IPA, to the puckering sour of the blackberry and cinnamon in Berry My Heart at the Trailer Park, and more than 60+ rotating brews, you'll find what you're looking for and more.

With smiling faces behind the bar ready to help you find your next favorite brew, a constantly rotating selection of delicious craft beverages, toe-tapping tunes always playing, and the biggest games on TV, you can kick your feet up in either Copperhill, Tennessee or Murphy, North Carolina and immerse yourself in the Buck Bald Brewing experience. So, come out, fill a pint, fill a growler, and fill your mind at your new favorite family-owned craft brewery.

To discover more visit us at buckbaldbrewing.com or follow us on Facebook @buckbaldbrewing and @buckbaldbrewingmurphy.

Vesper Wren's
TRAILER PARK
PIXIE
PUNCH
· A PEACH STRAWBERRY SELTZER ·
BUCK BALD BREWING

And don't forget to check out the latest edition of *Car Wars*

http://www.sjgames.com/car-wars/

Or the other amazing titles from
Steve Jackson Games

http://www.sjgames.com

…or the latest in the Car Warriors: Autoduel Chronicle fiction series.
https://threeravenspublishing.com/car-warriors-autoduel-chronicles/

Comprised of active or retired servicemen and civilian volunteers, Shepherd's Men enthusiastically raises awareness and funds for the SHARE Military Initiative (SHARE) at Shepherd Center in Atlanta, GA.

This nationally renowned program focuses on assessment and treatment for American military veterans who have sustained mild to moderate Traumatic Brain Injury (TBI) and Post-Traumatic Stress Disorder (PTSD) during post-9/11 service.

Find out more at: https://www.shepherdsmen.com/

www.ingramcontent.com/pod-product-compliance
Lightning Source LLC
Chambersburg PA
CBHW032009310726
48972CB00002B/335